The will was forty-ei... instructions, all couc.............. ~~~~~~ ~~~~~~ ~~~~ bewildering than Sanskrit. Nearly an hour passed before he turned the last page and, with a deep sigh of contentment, looked up.

It was foolproof—his masterpiece.

Lucas Brokaw had defied the laws of man and nature. All he possessed, his personal fortune and the corporate empire, was bequeathed to the man who had built it. The man who would one day live again to claim his own legacy . . . Lucas Brokaw reincarnated.

Lucas Brokaw was going to "take it with him" . . . And heaven help anyone who tried to take it from him!

THE
SECOND
COMING OF
LUCAS BROKAW

MATTHEW BRAUN

A DELL/BERNARD GEIS ASSOCIATES BOOK

To My Folks
Who lighted the path

I change, but I cannot die. . . .
I silently laugh at my own cenotaph,
And out of the caverns of rain,
Like a child from the womb, like a ghost from the
tomb
I arise and unbuild it again.

—Shelley

A Dell/Bernard Geis Associates Book

Published by
Dell Publishing Co., Inc.
1 Dag Hammarskjold Plaza
New York, New York 10017

Dell ® TM 681510, Dell Publishing Co., Inc.

ISBN: 0-440-18091-0

Printed in the United States of America
First printing—November 1977

AUTHOR'S NOTE

Can you believe that a man as wealthy as Howard Hughes or J. Paul Getty would go quietly to his grave without at least *trying* to cling to his fortune? The super-rich—men of power and a sense of their own immortality, men who have amassed fabulous wealth despite taxes and government and wily competitors—would not go gentle into the dark, meekly accepting the axiom "You can't take it with you."

No. They would search for still another loophole or legal maneuver to escape the inevitable. In fact, I do not believe that such men ever truly resign themselves to the finality of death. Nor are they easily parted from all they cherished throughout life. I am supported in this belief by the experience of a man who *did* succeed in taking it with him. His name was Lucas Brokaw, and this book is his story.

Matthew Braun

PROLOGUE

June 25, 1947

His horse faltered and broke stride.

All around him the battle raged, punctuated by shrill war cries and the garbled sounds of death. Dust rose thicker above the hill, mixed with the billowy dinge of powder smoke, blotting out the sun. Under the haze, flashes of gunfire blinked like golden fireflies. Arrows slithered past, swift and angry, whispering on the wind. A wayward slug whumped into flesh, splattering blood across the saddle. His horse suddenly went down, tumbling headlong beneath him, and he leaped clear of the stirrups. Clutching his carbine, he hit the ground in a rolling dive that left him stunned and gasping for breath.

As he scrambled to his feet, he saw Custer, roaring commands and gesturing like a madman, urging what was left of the battalion toward the top of the hill. Fewer than fifty men were still alive, and Sioux warriors were pressing them from the rear and on both flanks. There was only one way to go. Uphill. And fast. Take the high ground and hold it until the regiment came to their support. The general apparently meant to do just that. Rally the men back to back and make a stand. Buy themselves some time, and with it, their only hope of salvation.

An icy terror suddenly swept over the sergeant. He was afoot and alone, the last of the rear guard, cut off from the general by a long stone's throw. With more goddamned Indians at his heels than he'd ever seen. Or believed imaginable. And he already knew what hostiles did to live captives. Especially the Sioux. Unnerved, all thought shunted aside, he simply reverted to instinct.

Hugging the ground, he sprinted forward, leaping across the bodies of men and horses. Custer had everyone dismounted now, fanned out in a rough crescent around the guidon. Yet there was no sense of panic. The troopers were loading and firing like seasoned veterans, pouring volley after volley into the crazed horde below them. Miraculously unscathed, the sergeant quickly closed the gap, dodging and twisting under a hail of covering fire. Then, just as he reached the line, too late for anyone to react, the trap was sprung. A wave of mounted Sioux came boiling over the crest of the hill.

Their leader, astride a bay gelding, was brandishing a rifle and blowing shrill blasts on an eagle-bone whistle. Behind him, a hundred warriors charged down the slope, followed by another hundred and then a hundred more. The air came alive with the whine of bullets and the feathery hiss of arrows. At last, struck from behind, surrounded on all sides, the troopers broke and ran. Yet, to the sergeant, these were swift and fleeting images, distinctly etched but somehow apart. His eyes were fastened on the general, and he froze in numbed disbelief.

Amidst the slaughter and swirling carnage, he saw Custer stagger, grievously wounded. Then the general steadied himself, legs stiffly braced, and coolly, quite deliberately, placed a pistol to his head. There was a puff of smoke, and Custer's skull exploded in a burst of crimson mist. A moment later he vanished beneath the hooves of the onrushing war ponies.

The sergeant was aghast, unable to credit his own eyes. It simply wasn't possible. Not what he'd seen. Not the general! It was a coward's death, lacking either glory or pride. An act unbefitting any fighting man. Unforgivable if the man's name was Custer.

Abruptly jolted from his funk, he saw a howling Sioux bearing down on him, war club upraised. His jaws tightened, his teeth clenched, but he made no ef-

fort to escape the blow. He merely stood there, staring calmly at the warrior, waiting with a sense of utter resignation. A moment ago it had all ceased to matter.

He simply didn't give a damn. Not now.

The dream was always the same. Never quite ending. Like a single frame in a newsreel, suspended forever in space and motion. The war club upraised and the cavalry sergeant calmly resigned to the last. Yet it bothered Lucas Brokaw not at all. Nor was he left to ponder the meaning of this grisly cliff-hanger. He knew what happened and why and to whom. And these days, curiously enough, the dream revitalized him. He felt young again, full of piss and vinegar, as if each new dawn was a rare and tantalizing challenge created especially for his benefit. Which in a very real sense was precisely the case.

Alert and rested, fully restored by his afternoon nap, he rolled out of bed, favoring his right leg, and padded barefoot to the bathroom. It occurred to him that he would never have need of pajamas again, and he casually tossed them in the direction of the dirty clothes hamper. Then he stepped into the shower stall and spun the cold water tap. An instant later the icy blast hit him, and he whooped, gasping and shivering as he filled his lungs with a great draught of air. After a quick, vigorous scrubbing, he shut off the water and stepped onto the bath mat. His skin tingled and stung, a welter of goose bumps. Seldom in his life had he felt so alive or quite so invigorated, so eager at last for the night ahead. And what lay beyond.

As he toweled dry, Brokaw studied himself in a full-length mirror. The image reflected there was a monolithic figure whose square jaw and craggy features, capped by a thatch of white hair, seemed hewn from a slab of granite. Tall and lean and hard. Scarcely the body of a man turned seventy-one. Or for that matter, the body of a man ravaged by cancer. Yet as he looked closer there was something more, not so much a new dimension as a burnished reflection of the old. The man staring back at him appeared smug and somewhat cocky, perhaps even arrogant.

But what the hell—why not?

He'd pulled it off, and there were damn few men who could have conceived such an undertaking, much less transformed it into a reality. All things considered, he had timed it perfectly. And if it was the last day, it was nonetheless the appropriate day. His birthday.

He dressed with meticulous care, limping slightly now as he made several trips between bureau and closet. Out of a wardrobe containing some fifty suits, he finally selected his favorite, a conservative double-breasted flannel in charcoal gray. To complement the suit and add a dash of color, he chose a powder-blue oxford shirt, a maroon necktie, and a matching pocket handkerchief. Monogrammed cuff links and a gold signet ring lent a final air of elegance to his ensemble. The ring had been a gift from his wife, and while he'd always thought it pretentious, it seemed suitable to the occasion. Tonight he must look his best. A bravura performance!

Aside from this token gesture to vanity, however, he had little need of outward pomp. In the rarefied strata of California society few men had climbed so far so fast. And there were none who had climbed higher. Lucas Brokaw was an industrial colossus, the sole stockholder of a diversified empire that embraced shipyards, airplane factories, and several lesser manufacturing concerns. Universally acknowledged as an engineering genius, he had parlayed modest wealth into one of America's great fortunes by virtue of a world war and a highly pragmatic approach to power politics. In his time, he had supped with presidents and ambassadors, contributing heavily to the campaigns of all the right people, and his largesse had been repaid a hundred times over by defense contracts worth billions.

Though he was a widower, having lost his wife

shortly after MacArthur returned to the Philippines, he hadn't allowed personal misfortune to interfere with ambition. He was without children or other family, and not unlike an aging czar, he still commanded his corporate empire with an iron fist. Since he was blunt and outspoken, almost joyously abrasive in his candor, he reveled in the image of a tough, vindictive adversary.

Apart from business and political alliances, Brokaw gave little thought to the opinion of others. He'd never been a social butterfly anyway; it was his estimate of himself that counted. At heart he remained an irascible old pragmatist who considered expediency the first law of nature. Unless there were some advantage to be gained, he seldom stepped out of character, and while his detractors often vilified him, none would deny his extraordinary powers.

Nearly a year prior to VJ Day (before the atom had yet become a bomb), he had predicted a swift end to the war, and with it, a consumer-oriented age. Consequently, while his competitors were still haunting the Pentagon, Brokaw had been busy converting his factories to the production of washing machines, clothes dryers, and micro-relay systems. By the time the troopships returned home, he had established himself as the foremost industrialist of the postwar era, a visionary without rival in a period of unsurpassed opportunity.

Thinking about it as he finished dressing, Brokaw was reminded that it had been a joke all along. A monumental joke, and one he'd played on himself. As a visionary he had proved decidedly myopic. Though he had correctly forecast the state of the world, he had overlooked that most common of denominators, the mortality of man.

And a slight case of cancer.

Still, for all his shortsightedness, things had worked out in a rather satisfactory manner. Considering the alternative, very satisfactory indeed. Tonight he would sign his last will and testament, and while some people might find it bizarre, the will he had devised was a legal instrument of uncanny originality. For Lucas Brokaw had bequeathed his entire fortune—the industrial empire plus $184,000,000 in stocks and bonds—to himself.

The very thought of it set him to chuckling. It was bold and innovative, brazenly audacious, a trait he prized above all others. Yet there was nothing whimsical in what he'd done, none of the blathering nonsense commonly attributed to doddering old skinflints. Nor was it an exercise in fantasy, some improbable pipe dream concocted in a moment of psychic vertigo. Instead, it was a genuine reflection, however unorthodox, of his innermost belief: an unshakable conviction that he would come back, and by returning, accomplish what no man had ever done. Not just to live again, but to collect in the hereafter all he had accumulated in the here and now.

In high good humor, Brokaw checked himself one last time in the mirror, adjusting the knot in his tie with a deft tug. Then, satisfied that he was as spry and dapper as ever, he left the bedroom and walked along the hall toward a sweeping staircase.

By now, his limp had grown more prounounced, as it always did when he'd been on his feet any length of time. But he chose to ignore it. Compromise was foreign to his nature—cancer or no cancer—and he'd be damned if he would submit to a bunch of cells run amok. There were important things yet to be done, and to his way of thinking a gimpy leg was just a minor distraction. So he put it from his mind, descending the stairs at a fast if somewhat hobbled clip, and hurried across the foyer as an old grandfather clock began to chime.

Dinner had been ordered precisely at six, and he felt confident the servants would have arranged some little surprise in honor of the occasion. Not that it really mattered one way or the other. It was to be a solitary celebration, with the guest of honor toasting himself. Since he found his own company eminently pleasant, he was assured of both a congenial atmosphere and a festive spirit. That it was to be his last birthday merely heightened the moment.

As he moved through the drawing room, Brokaw paused for a moment to stare at the art collection that adorned the walls. The paintings and tapestries hung there would have done credit to the most prestigious museum, and looking at them now brought a wistful twinge of remembrance. Aside from business, the one passion he had allowed himself in an otherwise single-minded existence was his wife, and he had indulged her love of art with boundless generosity. In time, he'd become something of a devotee himself, and after her death the objets d'art she had left behind were all the more cherished. This affection extended as well to the mansion they had shared for nearly fifty years and to the grounds of a vast, baronial estate located north of San Francisco, overlooking a coastline of rugged cliffs and rocky beaches. It was a site he had selected himself in 1901, shortly after making his first million in the timber business.

Those were days he remembered with fondness. When they were young and vital, building their mansion and scouring the world for rare works of art. Yet the excitement had never dimmed. Nor had their love. Not even in those final years together, when Stephanie was frail and constantly plagued by illness. Although his sorrow was undiminished by time, the thing he recalled most was her exquisite serenity in the face of death. Tonight that memory gave him courage and a buoyant certainty about what lay ahead.

Much as he'd expected, the house staff surprised him with a lavish meal. Not ordinarily a heavy eater, tonight he polished off a dozen escargots, followed by a brace of squab with honeyed wild rice and nearly half a bottle of superb Château Mârgaux '39. The pièce d'occasion

13

was his favorite dessert, a creamy cheescake with a single candle tactfully planted in the center.

Surfeited, but thoroughly impenitent that he'd made a glutton of himself, he thanked James, the butler, for a delightful meal and sent his compliments to the chef. Then he proceeded to the solarium, where he let himself out by a rear door, suddenly intent on a stroll through the gardens.

The rest of the evening demanded a clear head, particularly the hour or so after he'd signed the will, and a breath of fresh air seemed very much in order. Briskly, his stride purposeful if a bit lame, he walked off down the path toward the cliffs, where an orange ball of fire was slowly settling into the ocean. Dusk had always been his favorite time, yet this evening he was struck by the symbolism of things so commonly taken for granted—like a birthday candle and a sunset eternally quenched by distant waters.

Shortly before seven, Brokaw returned to the house and entered the study. It was an imposing room, like the man himself, large and substantial, paneled in dark walnut with a black marble fireplace and rows of morocco-bound classics lining the bookshelves. A massive desk dominated the room, and grouped before it were several wing chairs and a couch upholstered in lush chocolate-colored leather. The credenza behind the desk was flanked by Remington sculptures, and on the wall directly opposite hung an enormous Bierstadt wilderness scene. At the west end of the room, which projected slightly over the cliffs, the upper half of the wall was a solid pane of glass, affording a spectacular view of the ocean and the rugged coastline.

The study was Brokaw's inner sanctum where he found solitude and privacy. It was a room seldom opened to visitors, and those who had been allowed inside always went away meeker for the experience, as though, having once entered his lair, they understood at

14

last that he really was invincible. An iron man, never to be crossed except at great peril.

At the moment, though, Brokaw felt anything but invincible. He was reminded instead of his own mortality, and despite the iron man image, he was none too steady on his feet. The fresh air had cleared his head, but his pain medication had worn thin and the long walk had overtaxed his strength. All up and down his spine there was a fiery sensation, as if dozens of white-hot ice picks were being plunged into every vertebra along his backbone. The pain ebbed and flowed, allowing him brief respite. Already there was an acute numbness in his right leg, another warning sign, and one not to be dismissed so lightly as he'd done earlier in the evening.

These days, particularly over the past week, he was able to judge the time he had left by the intensity of the pain. Tonight's attack was an unmistakable message. The terminal stage had begun.

Upon entering the study, he moved directly to a liquor cabinet, dragging his leg along behind him in a crablike shuffle. As he opened the cabinet door, another spasm racked his body and he clawed at a vial of Dilaudid on the top shelf. His hands were trembling and beads of sweat popped out on his forehead, but he steadied himself and took a small medicinal beaker from the cabinet. The beaker was distinctly marked, graduated in milligram levels. After uncapping the vial, he carefully poured off a one-centigram measure.

His doctor had admonished him, after he'd refused to be hospitalized, that Dilaudid was lethal in as little as half-gram doses. However severe his pain, he was to exercise restraint in its use. One centigram every eight hours was the limit, and under no circumstances was he to exceed the dosage. Wary as he was of hospitals, Brokaw's threshold of pain was abnormally high; he had restricted himself to two doses a day. The vial was something more than half full.

But here tonight, face to face at last with true agony,

15

he quaffed the dose in a single gulp. Though the drug was tasteless, its reaction was almost instantaneous. A sudden warmth kindled deep in his bowels, radiating outward with astonishing speed, and within seconds a euphoric glow spread throughout his entire body. As he returned the vial and the beaker to the cabinet, a slow smile tugged at the corners of his mouth and it occurred to him that all was right with the world. His timing was flawless.

Before he could pursue the thought further, there was a discreet rap at the door, and he turned, somewhat annoyed at the interruption. Edgar Pollard, his attorney, hesitated in the doorway a moment, noting the frown, then nodded, smiling unctuously, and entered the study.

"Good evening, Lucas. Hope I'm not disturbing anything?"

"You're late." Brokaw waved him to a chair with a brusque gesture. "And why the hell didn't James announce you?"

"Well, it really wasn't . . . that is to say, I'm not exactly a stranger here. I just told him I could find my own way."

"You never did have any class, Eddie. A butler is supposed to butle. Or didn't they teach you that at Harvard?"

"That's an unkind remark, Lucas. And for your information," Pollard consulted his watch, "I'm not late. To be precise, I'm three minutes early."

"Humph! Don't get your bowels in an uproar." Brokaw scowled, limping around behind the desk. "And stop squinting at me like some goddamned banty rooster. Have you got the papers with you?"

"Right here." The attorney patted his briefcase. "Everything in order down to the dotted *i*—and as you requested, I've already had my secretary notarize them."

"Well, at least you can follow instructions. Go on, sit down, for Christ's sake! Take a load off your feet."

Pollard obediently took a chair, not at all surprised

by the churlish reception. He was a wizened gnome of a man, diminutive and bald, somewhat taller than a dwarf by virtue of his elevator shoes, but a skilled lawyer and a shrewd judge of character. Although his client seemed hard and cynical, Pollard had always considered the circumstances highly extenuating. Since the death of his wife, Lucas Brokaw had undergone a radical transformation in character. His behavior had become erratic, almost schizoid, and he was given to sudden bursts of temper in which his voice took on a peculiar staccato bark. In the old days he had welcomed argument, and on rare occasions, had even been known to accept advice.

But now he brooked neither interference nor dissent from anyone. It was Pollard's opinion that the old man had lately exhibited symptoms of acute paranoia concerning not only his financial affairs but some mysterious construction project taking place beneath the mansion. Pollard himself hadn't been allowed near the project. From the little Brokaw had told him, he understood a separate contractor had been engaged for each stage of the project. Like some cloak-and-dagger intrigue, the construction had proceeded strictly on a need-to-know basis. The only man who possessed all the pieces and knew how the jigsaw fit together was Lucas Brokaw.

After seating himself, Pollard unsnapped his briefcase and extracted six copies of the will, each bound separately in a blue portfolio. He handed the documents across the desk, aware that any attempt at small talk would draw a stinging rebuff. Then he lit a Chesterfield and sat back to await the verdict. Brokaw placed the original in front of him, shoving the carbons aside, and began pouring over it in an earnest, word-by-word scrutiny.

The will was forty-eight pages long, devoted mainly to a convoluted maze of instructions, all couched in legalese hardly less bewildering than Sanskrit. To connect

17

the interlocking directives required total concentration, and Brokaw became oblivious to everything about him. The only sound in the study was the slow riffling of paper, interspersed with an occasional grunt.

Nearly an hour passed before he turned the last page. A lopsided grin spread across his face, and Pollard quickly stubbed out his ninth cigarette, waiting expectantly. But Brokaw sat there several minutes longer, clearly gloating over his masterpiece. Then, with a deep sigh of contentment, he finally looked up.

"I guess you think I'm nutty as a fruitcake, don't you, Eddie?"

"It's your money, Lucas." The lawyer pursed his mouth, thoughtful a moment, then shrugged. "Of course, anyone who leaves his fortune to himself might be thought . . . well, to say the least . . . a bit balmy."

"If you mean senile, you're all wet." Brokaw tapped the will with his finger. "Anybody who could hatch that scheme still has all his marbles. And besides, since I don't have any heirs, there's no one to contest it anyway, is there?"

"No, I suppose not. Although we have to presume the tax boys are going to take a long, hard look at this foundation arrangement. I mean, you'll have to admit, it has some rather unorthodox features."

"In a pig's eye! You told me this thing was ironclad. Now, none of your fancy double-talk, Eddie. Is it or isn't it?"

"In my opinion, it is," Pollard assured him. "Which is not to say the government won't try. Good God, Lucas, we're talking about upward of a quarter billion dollars!"

Brokaw's fist slammed into the desk. "Quit waltzing me around and just answer the question. Can they break it? And make goddamned sure you're right, Eddie. This isn't a dry run—we're playing for keeps."

There was a long silence of weighing and calculating.

Brokaw waited, glowering at him, and at last Pollard dismissed it with an elaborate little wave. "Nothing to worry about, Lucas. We've anticipated every possible contingency. It's airtight, absolutely foolproof."

Brokaw nodded, apparently satisfied with the answer, but his gaze drifted back to the will. Unhurried, quite methodical in his examination, he subjected it to the acid test. One final review, with all the cold objectivity he could muster.

Unlike Rockefeller and Ford, who had merely sheltered their wealth by creating foundations, Brokaw had added a personal touch to this loophole of the rich. While all revenues from his foundation would go to Stanford University—which made the foundation itself immune to tax laws—it was stipulated that at some future time he would return to collect his millions, in effect defying the laws of both man and nature.

All he possessed, his personal fortune and the corporate empire, was bequeathed to the man who had built it and therefore the man who deserved it. The man who would one day live again to claim his own legacy.

Lucas Brokaw *reincarnated*.

That the scheme was susceptible to hoax bothered him not at all. It was inevitable that false claimants would come forth, but he had anticipated this eventuality. While Eddie Pollard wasn't aware of it, there were several surprises awaiting anyone who tried to pass himself off as the real Lucas Brokaw—surprises of such a nature that the lawyer's promise of a moment ago was in sum and substance a very literal truth. Even if the will failed, the plan remained foolproof.

After considerable deliberation, having assured himself that nothing had been overlooked, Brokaw set the will aside. There was a peculiar glint in his eye when he glanced up at Pollard, who by now had reduced to ashes nearly an entire pack of Chesterfields.

"Well, I guess that does it. But you better be damn sure this thing doesn't develop any leaks while I'm gone.

Otherwise I'll drop around to see you when I get back. And believe me, Eddie, you wouldn't enjoy the reunion. Not even a little bit."

Pollard lifted an inquiring eyebrow. "I wish I had your faith, Lucas. It must be a great comfort, although it beats me how you can be so certain."

Brokaw's mouth quirked in a mirthless smile. When he spoke it was with a sort of sepulchral exultation, and the very intensity of his words gave the statement a ring of prophecy.

"Take my word for it, Eddie, I'll come back. I have proof. As you lawyers are so fond of spouting— incontrovertible proof!"

Before Pollard could reply, he wagged his head with a condescending air. "Don't even ask. Like we used to say when we were kids, that's for me to know and you to find out. Now, suppose you go round up James and a couple of the servants, and we'll let them witness my signature." He sank back in his chair, the glitter suddenly gone from his eyes, and sighed heavily. "Time grows short, Eddie, and I've still got things to do. So let's get with it. Chop, chop!"

Edgar Pollard scooted from his chair without a word and dutifully hurried off in search of the servants. But as he went through the door, he happened to glance back, and it occurred to him that Brokaw had the look of an elderly lion—an old and venerable monarch, wearied by the chase, in need of a peaceful snooze to regain his strength.

Sometime later, after Pollard had gone and the servants had been dismissed for the night, Brokaw again found himself alone. All the fuss over the will, compounded by the grim manner of everyone involved, had left him bone tired. His pain was merely an aggravating throb, but he felt sapped and depleted, and he dearly needed a bracer. For as he'd told Pollard, there was still work to be done. One last step.

The key to all that lay ahead.

Rising, Brokaw went directly to the liquor cabinet and poured himself a liberal dose of cognac. Then he walked to the window and halted, gazing out across the coastline. A livid moon flooded the cliffs in a spectral light, and far below he could hear waves crashing against the rocky shore. As he sipped the brandy, relishing its crisp bite, he reflected briefly on the curious chain of events that had led to this moment.

It had started the day his doctor confirmed the diagnosis and gave him six months to live. And the damnable irony of it! Now, with the war ended, and his industrial empire already geared to peacetime production; in an age of scientific marvels—the atom bomb and jet aircraft—*his* brain tumor remained inoperable. It was almost diabolical. As though the gods, after all, toyed with a man's life for mere sport.

That night he'd had the dream for the first time. And afterward it was always the same dream. At first, before he understood, he thought it related in some way to the cancer, and he'd feared for his sanity. The shadow of pain had been with him constantly at the outset, and he knew its cumulative effect would be the horror of anticipation, a dread that might well undermine his will to endure. It was the very thing he'd feared most, the psychic terror, and through it, the slow rending of his spirit. Yet all that had passed once he grasped the meaning of the dream—the night he'd accepted not just who he was *but who he had been*.

Sergeant John Hughes. C Company, Seventh Cavalry. Killed at the Battle of the Little Big Horn on June 25, 1876, at four o'clock in the afternoon. Precisely one hour and twelve minutes before Elizabeth Brokaw gave birth to a son in a Denver charity ward.

All indications were that his reincarnation would follow the same pattern, that he would be reborn on the day of his death. But he meant to hedge his bet, to ensure that everything went off according to schedule.

Nothing would be left to chance, for in his view the gods were inept as well as whimsical and could use a helping hand. Particularly from someone crafty enough to have arranged a way to take his fortune with him.

Now, restored by the cognac, Brokaw was alert and unafraid. Just as the dream was a window into the past, so it was a reflection of the future, a glimpse beyond the veil. To die was nothing, a minor inconvenience, for he was possessed of complete and utter faith that he would live again. This very night.

After draining his brandy glass, Brokaw left the study and walked to a staircase at the far end of the foyer. The steps were hewn from natural stone, as was the cavernous passageway, and descended by slow spirals into the bowels of the cliff. Although lighted, the descent was steep and long, ending some 200 feet beneath the mansion and slightly below sea level. There was an eerie, netherworld quality about the winding corridor; Brokaw felt his pulse quicken as the echo of his footsteps bounced back from the depths of the earth. Whenever he came here, it was as though he had stepped through a time warp, erasing whole centuries, and was moving inexorably downward into some dank, medieval dungeon. Which was precisely the illusion he'd hoped to achieve the night he drafted the master plan.

At the bottom of the stairs was a short landing which led to the entranceway of a subterranean crypt. The crypt was comprised of two rooms, an outer chamber and an inner vault, both of which had been excavated from the rocky substrata of the cliff. The walls were solid stone, as was the floor and the ceiling. The entranceway leading into the crypt was not a door but merely a large, rectangular opening in the stone.

Brokaw stood for a moment surveying the crypt. It was an undertaking of such complexity that he considered it the masterwork of his life. The outer chamber was spacious, roughly ten by twenty feet in dimension, but it was completely bare except for a table in the center of the room that supported a curious machine similar in appearance to a typewriter. The device was actually a cryptography machine of the sort normally used in enciphering government communiqués into secret code. Beyond the machine, centered along the far wall, was the entrance to the inner vault. A massive steel door, an exact duplicate of those found in banks, guarded the vault, which was square and substantial, approximately ten by ten, and solid as a fortress.

Satisfied that all was in order, Brokaw walked to the table and quickly checked various adjustments on the cryptography machine. Then he programmed a sentence into the machine, ripped the enciphered printout from the carriage, and spent several minutes memorizing the oddly juxtaposed characters. Finally, certain that the coded sentence was indelibly etched in his mind, he pulled out a Zippo lighter and burned the printout, grinding the ashes underfoot.

Intent now on the next step, he shoved the steel door ajar, entered the vault, and proceeded directly to two large wall safes at the back of the room. The safes were recessed into the stone wall, and on the inside of each safe door there was a projecting flange, unusual in design and obviously custom-built. Sophisticated explosive charges cased in the olive drab of military demolitions were visible on the bottom shelves of both safes. Working swiftly, his movements skillful and precise, he wired the explosives to a small mechanism inside each safe, and in turn, wired these mechanisms to the irregular-shaped door flanges. With the booby traps properly rigged, he extracted two sealed envelopes from his coat pocket, inspected them carefully, and placed one envelope on the upper shelf of each safe. Then he set the combination locks, paused briefly to run over his mental checklist, and firmly closed the safe doors.

Finished, he turned and walked from the vault into the outer chamber. With the utmost care, gingerly avoiding any contact with the door handle, he swung the steel door closed, waiting until he heard the muffled thud of the lock rods. Then he twirled the combination knob and halted it on zero. Symbolic yet ambiguous, another little riddle to be unraveled by anyone foolish enough to try.

A faint smile crossed his face, giving him a curiously beatific appearance, as he crossed the outer chamber and passed through the entranceway. Without a backward glance, almost jubilant, he mounted the stairs and hurried toward his appointment in the world above.

Shortly before the hall clock tolled nine, Lucas Brokaw reentered his study. Three hours was cutting it close, but he had every confidence that the time remaining was adequate to the task. Limping noticeably now, wearied by the long climb upstairs, he moved directly to the liquor cabinet. His hand steady, thoroughly at peace with himself, he took the vial of Dilaudid from the top shelf and emptied its contents into the medicinal beaker. After capping the vial and returning it to the cabinet, he held the beaker to the light. Squinting, he studied the level with a critical eye, then nodded and chuckled softly to himself. It stood well above the half-gram mark.

Walking to the window, his limp all but forgotten, he looked down upon a world shrouded in moonglow. Somewhere out there a new life awaited the transmigration of his soul. In that other life—young again—he would return to claim his own legacy. And in the meantime, his crypt was impregnable, as safe from desecration as a Pharaoh's tomb. It was a moment to be savored. Not so much an end as a beginning. A journey to immortality.

At last, eager to be on his way, he lifted the beaker to his lips and drained it.

I

Stanford University
October 3, 1977

The tower carillon began to peal as he stepped from his car.

On a still day the chimes could be heard all across campus, thundering pleasant variations on a battery of nearly three dozen bells. Tanner had often envisioned a squad of Swiss monks hammering and pounding in a stone-deaf frenzy as they scurried about the tower. But that was in his undergraduate days. Later, after he'd discovered the world was no laughing matter, his sense of imagery had undergone a pronounced change.

The thought bothered him, as did his presence here today. It was nothing he could articulate, but all the way down from San Francisco he'd been badgered by it, searching for a reasonable explanation. Hearing the bells again merely aggravated his uncertainty, except that he wasn't quite sure where the chance left off and choice began.

And the hell of it was he didn't need a job!

Squinting, head canted back, he stared up at the tower. It rose majestically above the Hoover Institute, framed against a gauzy autumn sky. He had always found it an impressive sight, never more so than when the chimes rumbled to life. Yet this was the first time in almost five years that he'd visited the campus. Since law school, he had felt no desire whatever to see the tower or hear the chimes or look again upon the old sandstone quadrangles.

Until yesterday.

Which left him not just perplexed but thoroughly mystified. However vagrant, it was one of those spur-of-the-moment things that had drawn him here to seek a position about which he knew little or nothing, that he hadn't even known existed until he'd seen the advertisement in the *Law Enforcement Quarterly* less than twenty-four hours ago.

Perhaps that was what bothered him. The impulse. Upon reflection, it seemed too quick, too frivolous. Not just enticing but damn near irresistible.

So he'd called in sick that morning and driven down to Palo Alto. Yet he hadn't the foggiest notion of why he was here! Granted, he was bored and overworked and underpaid, but that was all part of the drill. An occupational hazard of working for the bureau. And he'd long ago reconciled himself to the fact that playing gangbusters was nine parts drudgery and one part bravado.

Or had he?

As he started up the walkway, it occurred to him that perhaps this trip wasn't a lark after all. If a man really was content, completely satisfied with his lot in life, then why would he . . . the question hung there, unanswered, just as it had since yesterday.

Why, indeed?

A few minutes later, Tanner entered a suite of offices on the second floor of the institute. The plaque on the door bore a simple inscription—Brokaw Foundation—but the waiting room was hardly what he'd expected.

Several of the office staff were gathered near the coffee bar, while a girl at the reception desk struggled to maintain her composure. Opposite her, waving a bird cage over the desk, was an elderly woman who appeared on the verge of tears. She wore a nondescript raincoat, wedgie shoes, and perched atop her head was a hat that vaguely resembled a fruit salad. While she talked, thrusting the cage in the girl's face, a huge green parrot vented his outrage with a stream of raucous, ear-splitting squawks.

"You're not fooling me. Not for a minute! Oooh no, dearie, not me. I've got rights just like everybody else, and I won't stand for it, d'you hear? I won't stand for it!"

"Of course you have rights, Mrs. Zackowski." The girl managed a look of genuine concern. "All I'm saying is that there are procedures to be followed. Your case will be taken under advisement, and the director himself will personally review it. And he'll give it every consideration, Mrs. Zackowski. I assure you he will."

"Then I want to see the director, right now. I demand to see the director! And don't try to soft-soap me. I won't budge from his spot till he hears what Tommy has to say with his very own ears."

"I'm sorry, Mrs. Zackowski, but that's quite impossible. The director is a very busy man, and his calendar is filled for the rest of the week. If you care to call me, perhaps we could arrange something for a later date."

"But why won't you believe me? Tommy is *him*, I tell you!" The old lady rattled the cage and a blast from the parrot momentarily drowned out her words. "Just give him a chance. Listen to him. He'll convince you himself if you'll only let him speak his piece."

Tanner remained just inside the door, amused but inscrutable, observing the exchange with professional curiosity. The old woman was quickly catalogued—a harmless crank—and dismissed. The girl, on the other hand, held his attention. There was something about her . . . a wisp of recollection he couldn't quite identify. She was small and compact, with a kind of bustling vitality, and she had extraordinary eyes. Dark sable hair cascaded over her shoulders, accentuating her high cheekbones, and he caught a hint of something puckish beneath her expression, minxlike and slyly impudent. Yet to all outward appearances she was cool and crisp, quite obviously in control of both herself and the situation—which included Tommy and his keeper.

Then he listened more closely, zeroing in on her voice, and it came to him. She was no receptionist. This was the girl he'd spoken with yesterday to arrange the appointment. The director's executive assistant, which implied something more than a secretary. Though he had forgotten her name, he remembered the voice, soft and sibilant, yet surprisingly forceful for a woman. An altogether rare combination that immediately stoked his interest. Brains and beauty seldom came in the same package.

At the desk the seriocomic debate suddenly ended. The girl's manner was guileless but firm; with perfect aplomb, she maneuvered the old lady toward the door, all the while assuring Mrs. Zackowski that it was merely a matter of time. Tommy would definitely have his chance! Just as soon as it could be fitted into the director's schedule. An instant later, smiling earnestly, she waved good-bye to the parrot and his mistress and closed the door with a small sigh of relief.

Nothing if not resilient, she collected herself and turned to meet his gaze. "You must be Warren Tanner."

"That's correct. And as I recall, you're Mr. Knox's assistant."

"Executive assistant." The distinction noted, she stuck out her hand. "I'm Stacey Cameron."

Her grip was firm and her appraisal deliberate. She looked him up and down, scrupulously impersonal, as though the assessment was *de rigueur* to any interview. What she saw was a tall man, lithe and muscular, built along deceptive lines. Bronzed by the sun, his hair burned a lively chestnut, probably an outdoorsman. Not a handsome man, although certain women would be fascinated by the squared jaw and chiseled features and whatever lay hidden behind that sardonic gaze. But a determined man, quietly arrogant.

Tanner wasn't in the least uncomfortable under her scrutiny. But it led him to a quick-felt insight of his own. While she was friendly enough, there was an aloof quality about her, something very unyielding and businesslike. Clearly a woman whose approval and confidence must be won, and the place to start was within her own orbit. Not on the personal level but within the job, where she lived.

"If you don't mind my saying so"—his expression was deadpan, one pro to another—"I thought you handled Mrs. Zackowski very tactfully."

"All in a day's work, Mr. Tanner." She gave him an odd look, intrigued but skeptical, and then stepped back, indicating a hallway. "Shall we join the director? I believe he's expecting you."

"By all means. But first, let me ask you a question." He cocked one eyebrow and jerked his thumb toward the door. "Call it morbid curiosity, but I was wondering about the old woman. Was it a con, or do you think she was really serious?"

"Oh, yes indeed." A tinge of mockery crept into her voice. "Mrs. Zackowski was very serious."

"Evidently I asked something amusing. Is it a private joke, or can anybody play?"

Stacey Cameron laughed a droll little laugh. "Mr. Tanner, the one certainty in a very uncertain world is that Lucas Brokaw would never come back as a parrot."

II

"Allow me to say that your credentials are impeccable, Mr. Tanner. Most impressive."

Tanner was seated across the desk from Hamilton Knox, director of the Brokaw Foundation. At the moment Knox was scanning a telex report, nodding to himself as if immersed in some lofty abstraction. Stacey Cameron had taken a chair at the end of the desk, a strategic gambit that wasn't lost on Tanner. Hers was the role of observer, and she was positioned to catch the slightest nuance of reaction during the interview. It was a transparent device, one he considered rather amateurish, but the report in Knox's hand was an altogether different matter. That aroused his interest.

Feigning indifference, Tanner lit a cigarette. "Don't believe everything you read, Mr. Knox. The credit bureau is notorious for supplying inaccurate information."

"You underestimate our resources, my boy," Knox admonished him with a sly look. "This report came from a bureau well enough, but it's from a bureau based in Washington."

"And you managed to get it overnight?"

"As a matter of fact, that's precisely what we managed to do." Adjusting his glasses, Knox peered intently at the report. "Now as to accuracy, let's see what it has to say. Warren Tanner. Age thirty. Unmarried. Parents deceased. Graduate of Stanford and Stanford Law—incidentally, that's a point in your favor—and immediately thereafter joined the FBI. Spent two years in Tulsa, followed by two years in Denver, and last year was assigned to the regional office in San Francisco. Rated a top-notch investigator. Has a particular gift for undercover work. Currently in line for promotion."

Knox paused, eyes darting over the telex sheet, then he shrugged and glanced up. "Well, I daresay that's enough. Suppose you judge for yourself. Accurate or not?"

Tanner conceded the point. "Apparently somebody up there likes me."

"Apparently so. Which brings us to the pertinent question." Knox frowned over the top of his glasses. "With a record such as this, what prompts your sudden decision to leave the FBI?"

It was the very question Tanner had been asking himself. Yet even now, confronted with it openly, he had no ready answer. A leaden silence settled over the room, and he was aware of Stacey watching him intently. At last, unwilling to fabricate some flimsy pretext, he stubbed out his cigarette and simply told them the truth.

"To be perfectly frank about it, I don't know. Since yesterday, I've been mulling it over, and as yet I haven't come up with an explanation. All I can tell you is that I saw your ad and ten minutes later I was on the phone. Perhaps it was subliminal. I can't really say."

"That's it?" Knox demanded skeptically. "Some sort of irresistible impulse?"

"Curious as it sounds, that same phrase occurred to me."

"You're not disillusioned with the government? All those disclosures about the FBI being involved in dirty tricks? The political corruption?"

"Perhaps. But no more than anyone else. I'm hardly an idealist."

"Could it be the opportunity?" Knox persisted. "Perhaps you're more ambitious than you realized. I daresay every man views the future with a different perspective once he turns thirty."

"I've thought of that. And I can't wholly discount it. But again, I'm not sure it's what prompted me to pick up the telephone yesterday."

"So we're back to your subliminal stimulus. The irresistible impulse?"

"At the risk of repeating myself, I don't know." Tanner glanced at Stacey, who appeared a bit bemused, and then looked back at the director. "I'm here, and I presume I wouldn't be if I was altogether satisfied with my job. But right now that's the best I can offer you." Tanner leaned forward as if to stand. "If it isn't good enough, then just say so and I'll be on my way."

Hamilton Knox gave him a sharp, appraising look and gestured for him to take his seat again. The director had no particular skill in unraveling the tangled skein of human emotions. His insights were extremely analytical; seldom in his life had he experienced a quick, intuitive perception. Invariably dressed in tweeds, with glasses fixed low on the bridge of his nose, he resembled a kindly baffled owl. Yet he was a member of one of California's oldest families, and his heritage, along with a lifetime of exposure to campus intelligentsia, gave him a patrician manner that required little affectation. He was properly indulgent, moderately tolerant, and while his own life was as neatly mounted as a butterfly collection, he nonetheless made allowance for the flaws and frailties of those who inhabited what he considered to be a highly imperfect world.

As director of the foundation, ever vigilant to the avarice of that outside world, he had devoted nearly thirty years to preserving Brokaw's millions. Administering the foundation, however, was a monumental task. All the more so since Knox had shrewdly unloaded the Brokaw industrial empire during the boom economy of the 1960s.

Lucas Brokaw's fortune was now calculated in excess of $512,000,000.

To Knox's everlasting grief, the burden of his stewardship was compounded by a steady parade of claimants. Scarcely a day passed without one or more persons—each claiming to be Lucas Brokaw reincarnated—appearing in the foundation offices. Stacey Cameron had become his indispensable surrogate, a buffer of sorts, and he relied on her to contend with the worrisome details of day-to-day operations. But he was in need of an investigator, a replacement for his old and trusted friend Harry Atkins, who was retiring at the end of the month. Acting as watchdog over the Brokaw millions was no small chore in itself, for it entailed guarding what was perhaps the world's most vulnerable fortune.

The job called for a man of experience and resourcefulness, with that blend of congenital skepticism peculiar to all first-rate detectives. Of equal significance, it required a dedicated man, someone whose sense of pride and self-esteem were so compelling that the mere suggestion of defeat was anathema to his nature.

Now, despite certain qualms, the director was forced to the conclusion that he'd found his man. The record spoke for itself. Warren Tanner was a skilled investigator, unmatched by anyone he'd interviewed yet. Perhaps his motives were a trifle cloudy, but of course personal aspirations weren't the point at issue. What was at issue were his qualifications, and on the basis of past performance, logic dictated that Tanner was the man for the job.

The decision made, Knox steepled his fingers and peered thoughtfully across the desk. "Since you're a Stanford man, I presume you have more than a passing acquaintance with the foundation and its rather unique background."

"That's an understatement," Tanner replied. "Introduction to the ghost of Lucas Brokaw is considered part of the freshman initiation rite."

"Quite so. Nevertheless, suppose I give you a thumbnail sketch of the foundation and how it operates. With that as a focal point, assuming our interests are mutual, we might then proceed to a discussion of the job itself."

"Yes, I'd like that very much. To tell you the truth,

I've always wondered where fact left off and fiction began."

"In the case of Lucas Brokaw I believe you'll find they're inseparable. If you're a student of mythology, by any chance, then the reason will become self-evident."

"You're not suggesting they're the same . . . the man and the myth?"

"Exactly. All the world loves a good fable, and in this case, time simply blurred reality somewhat faster than normal. Usually it takes centuries to create a myth. Lucas Brokaw did it in thirty years."

"Pardon me, but I get the feeling . . . that's not altogether speculation, is it?"

"Hardly. It's based on personal knowledge."

"You actually knew Brokaw?"

"Oh, yes, quite well. He and my father worked rather closely together, mainly in politics. So I was around him a good deal in those days, and I must say, we got along famously."

"Then you liked him?"

"Nooo. I suspect no one ever really *liked* Lucas Brokaw. But he was a man of great vigor, very dynamic. It was impossible not to admire him, and in all honesty, I learned more from him than I did from my own father. You see, he had no children, so he always considered me as something of a protégé."

"Of course, and that explains . . . or maybe I'm jumping to conclusions. Are you saying Brokaw himself appointed you to the foundation?"

"Not exactly, although he did make his wishes known. But that's a mere anecdote, quite apart from our discussion here today. Suppose we concentrate on the foundation . . . there's the real story."

Hamilton Knox leaned back in his chair, collecting his thoughts, like an old and wrinkled thespian contemplating some cherished soliloquy.

Then he began to talk.

III

By the terms of his will, Lucas Brokaw had directed that all revenues from the foundation would go to Stanford University. This arrangement was to remain in effect until the day his future incarnation appeared to claim the fortune.

Hamilton Knox had been selected by a board of trustees to administer the foundation and, further, was charged with the responsibility of protecting the fortune from false claimants. It was also stipulated that certain funds would be used to publicize the terms of the will on a regular basis. Presumably this was meant to alert Brokaw's reincarnated self, so that he would eventually come forward and demonstrate valid claim to his legacy. The test to determine that validity was, if anything, more bizarre than the will itself.

One of Brokaw's firms was a company that had pioneered the development of cryptography machines. In utter secrecy, working with a select staff of engineers, he had constructed the ultimate cryptography device. It was one of a kind, and Brokaw had personally destroyed the blueprints. After devising a code known only to himself, he had programmed a single sentence into the machine and burned the cipher.

The properly encoded sentence, when fed into the cryptography machine, would produce a plaintext message: THIS IS THE REAL LUCAS BROKAW. However, the machine was merely a hurdle, intended to weed out cranks and con artists. Its primary function, as indicated quite clearly in the will, was to serve as the first step in a series of tests to determine the validity of claimants.

The second step was somewhat more hazardous.

Brokaw had built a subterranean vault beneath his mansion, and within this vault were two wall safes. He had placed a list of questions in one safe and the corresponding answers in the second safe; afterward he wired the safes with explosives that would detonate if an incorrect combination was used. The safe containing the list of answers had also been rigged to explode if it was opened first. Brokaw had then committed to memory the combinations to the vault door and the safes and, as he had stressed repeatedly in the will, only Lucas Brokaw reincarnated could negotiate this perilous maze without triggering the booby traps. Anyone else would blow himself to Kingdom Come.

In the event a claimant should pass the cryptography test and gain entry to the vault, he was to be escorted inside by the director. After the first wall safe was opened, the claimant would be required to answer the questions. Only then was the second safe to be opened, so that the director could check his answers against the answer list. If he passed all these tests—cryptography, explosive safes, and secret questions—he would have proven himself to be Lucas Brokaw reincarnated. And at that point, by the terms of the will, the entire fortune automatically passed from the foundation into his hands. This in itself was yet another safeguard, for Brokaw knew that the foundation, at the risk of losing vast revenues, would jealously guard his estate against false claimants.

To bolster that effort, the will contained several additional clauses.

The foremost condition was one directed specifically at con artists and charlatans. In the event *anyone* successfully claimed the fortune there was a $10,000,000 reward for the person who proved the claimant to be an imposter. A calculated hedge, it indicated Lucas Brokaw had forseen the possibility of fraud and was willing to pay handsomely to expose anyone who passed himself off as the legitimate heir. Also, he had directed that the mansion was to be preserved exactly as he'd left it on the eve of his death, and the foundation was to maintain a security force to guard the estate night and day. While the reason for this was never actually stated, it was clear that Brokaw had been afflicted with extreme paranoia concerning his underground crypt.

There was one final stipulation in the will, not only curiously vague, but couched in veiled terms. Stripped of legalese it stated that "should disaster occur" while a claimant was attempting to pass the tests, there was an unrevealed test—a secret known only to Brokaw—and whoever later uncovered this secret would be acknowledged as Lucas Brokaw reincarnated.

The terms of the will were publicized regularly, as Brokaw had directed, and with time, this extraordinary arrangement had become something of a legend. Over the years, thousands of men and women from every corner of the earth had come forward to take a shot at the prize. But to date no one had been able to outwit the cryptography machine. In the three decades since Brokaw's death, not one person had made it inside the vault itself.

The foundation's success in thwarting fraud, of course, was no mere happenstance. It was the result of constant vigilance and an elaborate screening process. Through trial and error, the director had slowly evolved a technique of interrogation that seldom failed to separate weirdos and thieves from seemingly legitimate claimants. As a further precaution, the foundation investigator conducted an extensive probe into the background of anyone who survived this initial grilling. The upshot was that fewer than one out of a hundred claimants ever reached the stage of challenging the cryptography machine. Nor had the Brokaw estate been slighted. In addition to a caretaker and housekeeper, there was an around-the-clock security force of watchmen and guard dogs. The mansion itself was virtually sealed off from the outside world, and as a practical matter, the subterranean crypt was no less impregnable than Fort Knox.

The director concluded his monologue with a modest disclaimer, crediting Stacey with several innovations that had improved the internal operation. Yet the remark was almost an afterthought, and in his mind, hardly germane to the discussion. The issue here today was security, and he meant to drive that point home as if spiking a tenpenny nail.

"Stated bluntly, Mr. Tanner, my personal goal is to discredit every claimant who walks into this office. Thus far, that's precisely what I've done . . . and the man I hire as investigator would be expected to adopt a similar attitude."

"I understand," Tanner replied. "It's an enviable record and you mean to keep it that way."

"To be more precise, it's an unblemished record. And that, Mr. Tanner, is the very marrow of this foundation!"

Knox leaned forward, gesturing with quick, choppy motions. "We live with the guillotine forever poised overhead. Why? Because our first mistake would be our last. Fatal, Mr. Tanner. Fatal! A single penetration of our security system—just one—and the foundation simply ceases to exist."

"I assume you're speaking of a fraudulent penetration?"

"Of course. Is there another kind?"

"How about Lucas Brokaw?"

Knox gave him a bland stare, silent a moment, then chuckled appreciatively. "Very clever, Mr. Tanner. Very clever indeed. However, as Miss Cameron will confirm," swiveling around in his chair, he smiled at Stacey, "my views on reincarnation are my own. And hardly relevant to the job. Isn't that so, my dear?"

"Totally irrelevant," Stacey acknowledged. "You see, Mr. Tanner, we aren't concerned with a man's beliefs, metaphysical or otherwise. Our obligation is to the foundation—nothing more. All we require of a staff member is that his list of priorities be adjusted accordingly."

"Duty before self. Zeal and commitment. Unstinting loyalty to the cause. Is that about the right order?"

Stacey held his gaze, not at all amused by the wry tone. "I might have phrased it differently, but . . . yes, as a matter of fact! That's exactly what I mean."

Tanner had an instinct for the truth, an uncanny gift for touching the sore spot. Just as he knew that the director was scornful of anything outside the realm of logic—particularly spiritual matters—so he understood that Stacey Cameron was dedicated not to the foundation but to herself. Or, rather, to an image of herself. An intelligent, highly talented woman who had found her niche in life: the executive suite. That she was fulfilled, immensely content with career and status, he never doubted for an instant. Whether or not she was happy was an altogether different matter, one he fully intended to explore at the first opportunity.

After a moment's reflection, he merely smiled at her and swung back to the director. "I've had considerable experience with Miss Cameron's philosophy. If the bureau has a credo, it would be duty before self."

Knox eyed him with a long, speculative look. "Correct me if I'm wrong, Mr. Tanner, but I seem to detect a note of discontent."

"Let's just say the rewards were never quite commensurate with the sacrifice."

"Ah, yes, filthy lucre! The root of all evil."

"Or deliverance, depending on your outlook."

"And what is your outlook . . . may I call you Warren? Excellent. Now, please speak freely. I do believe we've come at last to common meeting ground."

"Perhaps we have." Tanner covered his surprise by lighting a cigarette. Oddly enough, the idea had been there all the time, and he was mildly astonished it hadn't occurred to him before. He examined it quickly, satisfied with the rationale, and clicked his lighter shut. "Reduced to fundamentals, I suppose it sounds a bit mercenary. But you asked for candor, so . . . five years with the bureau merely entitles me to another thirty before retirement. That's a long way off, and damn little to show for it when I'm through."

The director was no longer in doubt. Any lingering reservations had been erased by the younger man's thinly disguised note of bitterness. Far from a spontaneous impulse it was hunger—a quest for independence—that had brought Warren Tanner here today. And a taste for money was the one motive, not to say the one god, that Hamilton Knox accepted with blind faith.

"Warren, if I were to offer you these things"—Knox ticked off the points on his fingers—"an initial salary double what you're now earning, plus fringe benefits far exceeding what the government provides"—the third finger lifted with tantalizing slowness—"and $10,000,000 in the event you were to expose a successful imposter" —behind the glasses, his eyes grew wide and owlish— "what would be your response?"

Tanner blinked, dumbstruck. A moment passed, and then, as if an echo formed the words, he heard himself speak. "I'll need a month. To resign and obtain clearance from Washington."

The director rose to his feet. His mouth creased in a benign smile, and he extended his hand across the desk.

"Permit me to welcome you to the Brokaw Foundation."

IV

Nothing about the day seemed quite real.

A nave of redwoods crowning the road suddenly opened onto the estate. Beyond the stark symmetry of the cliffs, bathed in a brassy haze, the mansion loomed majestically against a honeycomb of forested hills. The air was drenched with the smell of the sea, and a long driveway swept onward across spacious lawns and verdant, rolling fields.

The overall effect, absorbed in a single glance, was breathtaking—far grander than anything Tanner had imagined. Unwittingly, he felt his pulse quicken.

At the front gate a uniformed guard armed with a service revolver and a suspicious scowl stopped the car. Stacey leaned out the window, identifying herself, and introduced Tanner as the new investigator. When she explained that it was his first day on the job and she'd been elected to give him the grand tour, the guard's manner thawed slightly. He returned to a small gatehouse, and a moment later the gates were electronically activated. As the car pulled away, Tanner glanced back and saw him speaking into a walkie-talkie. Someone else was being alerted to their presence, and it prompted him to inquire about the security setup.

Stacey briefed him in a crisp, businesslike fashion. Her tone was pleasant if somewhat neutral, as it had been all morning.

The entire estate, except for the steep cliffs along the coast, was bounded by a ten-foot electric fence. Not only would the fence shock an intruder insensible, but if touched it triggered an alarm system that could be heard miles away. Inside the fence the perimeter was patrolled night and day by two armed guards accompanied by attack dogs. The gatehouse served as a command post, and the guard there coordinated the overall operation. By pressing a single button he could automatically seal every door and window in the mansion, and at the same time alert the state police.

To date, however, that hadn't proved necessary.

Several raccoons and stray dogs had been stunned senseless by the fence, but there was no evidence that an intruder had ever attempted to penetrate the estate. A high voltage fence, backed by a paramilitary security force, apparently acted as deterrent enough.

Tanner was impressed. Certain refinements occurred to him, but all in all, security was tighter than he'd expected. He began a remark, then suddenly broke off, his attention diverted as Stacey swung the car into a circular driveway. Before them, towering ominously in a glare of sunlight, was the mansion. He squinted and looked closer, unprepared for what he saw and left speechless by the very sight of it.

Viewed from the front, the mansion presented a dizzying array of pinnacles and turrets, climaxed by a three-story entrance pavilion that supported an immense pierced-stone parapet. Gables and flying buttresses shot off in all directions, and along the far end of the east wing there was a spectacular porte cochere leading to a courtyard beyond. It was as though parts had been selected at random from an assortment of jigsaw puzzles and flung together. The result was a structure that overwhelmed the mind even as it assaulted the eye.

"Grotesque, isn't it?"

Stacey's comment snapped him out of his daze, and he realized the car had halted before the entrance. He grunted and shook his head. "It looks deformed . . . only worse! Like a hunchback with warts."

She smiled. "I've always thought Brokaw must have done the outside and left the interior to his wife. At least I hope that's how it happened." She opened the door and slid out of the car. "Come on, I think you'll be surprised."

Tanner was indeed surprised and even a bit awed. In the next hour, Stacey led him through room after room, all with an aura of some bygone age. A world apart, with the elegance and graciousness of a less hectic way of life.

The furnishings were eclectic, a mélange of ornately upholstered Victorian, mixed with Norman medieval and Spanish leather, yet harmoniously composed. Timbered ceilings lofted gracefully over stained-glass windows, and intricately parqueted floors were awash with thick Oriental rugs. Bronzes and porcelains were scattered about in profusion, and on one wall of the drawing room hung a group of Flemish tapestries that Stacey identified as once having belonged to Henry VIII. On surrounding walls hung a gallery that included Renoir and Titian, Vermeer and Goya, Raphael, Whistler, Sargent, Degas and Monet, and so many others that Tanner simply lost track as the tour progressed.

At last, his head buzzing with regal splendor of all he'd seen, Stacey led him to the solarium. The room looked out across a garden filled with marble statuary, shrubs, and a huge fountain of Italian tile. In a golden ring, dancing naked around the fountain, fat little cherubs gushed water as they offered one another bunches of grapes. It was a frivolous display, suitably dissimilar to the rest of the house, and for a moment he almost forgot the magnitude of what he'd gazed upon in the past hour.

Then a flicker of movement caught his eye, where the garden sloped upward to a cathedral of redwoods. Alert, suddenly watchful, he saw a man in uniform ghosting through the trees. Slung over the guard's shoulder was a pump shotgun, and pacing along at his side was a German shepherd only slightly smaller than a

45

timber wolf. An instant later, as if never there, man and dog simply melted into the woods and vanished from sight.

Tanner forgot about the fountain and the cherubs. His thoughts drifted instead to the mansion, and he was reminded that he'd seen nothing of the servants during their tour. It had struck him as unusual at the time, and now, his curiosity aroused, he turned back to Stacey. She was staring at the spot where the guard had disappeared, and it crossed his mind that she was a very quick lady. Probably hell on a chess board and sudden death at backgammon.

"I was wondering"—she seemed reluctant to leave the window, but he waited, and finally she looked around—"about the housekeeper and caretaker. Aren't they here today?"

"Oh, I'm sure they are. But we haven't rung, so they're probably down in the kitchen waiting for us to leave. As you may have noticed, everyone around here is very, very discreet. Like the guard . . . the one in the woods."

"What I've noticed is that they're very well trained." Tanner paused, thoughtful a moment, then glanced back along the hallway. "I meant to ask before. That art collection—have you any idea what it's worth?"

Stacey smiled. "We could both retire on the insurance premiums alone. It's been appraised at $18,300,000."

There was a sudden spontaneity about her, a look he hadn't seen before, vivacious and not so businesslike. "You know, that's funny. In spite of what you said, I get the impression you like this house."

"Not the house so much, but you're right. I love beautiful things, being surrounded by . . . well, what it represents. I suppose luxury would be the proper word. Whenever I come here, I fantasize a lot. Do you find that strange?"

"Not at all. Everyone does a bit of stargazing now

and then." His smile was genuine, without guile. "It sounds like your thing just happens to be art."

"Yes, it is. Art, and of course antiques."

"And perhaps music?"

"All kinds. But how did you know that?"

"And I suspect you're a theater buff, too."

"And I have a strong suspicion you're a mind reader. Or else I'm a good deal more obvious than I thought."

Her expression was piquant, and for a moment he felt mesmerized by her eyes. They were the color of wild honey, dark brown and flecked with gold. The look jolted him. There was an air about her, the way she tilted her head, a certain poise. She had an unusual beauty, exotic, almost doll-like, but darkly luscious, with high jutting breasts and magnificent legs. It required an effort of will to look away, yet he was conscious of her very acute stare. Finally, collecting his wits, he shrugged it off with a laugh.

"You're hardly transparent. Quite the contrary, in fact. I've been trying to figure you out all day, and I still haven't moved off square one."

"I'm not sure I understand." Her gaze became insistent. "Why the sudden interest in me?"

"Nothing sudden about it, not really. It just occurred to me I might pick up a couple of theater tickets and we could have dinner one evening . . . or maybe a late supper."

A change came over her. "Mr. Tanner, I don't—"

"Please . . . call me Warren."

"Yes, of course. But as I started to say, Warren, I don't want to sound rude or . . . oh, damn! That's exactly how I sound."

She faltered, searching for words, then her face turned very earnest. "Look, what I'm trying to say is that I never mix business with pleasure. I know it's the world's oldest cliché, but we'll be working closely together and . . . well, things like that have a way of getting sticky. Believe me, it has nothing to do with you, so please don't take it personally."

"Not at all. As you said, we'll be seeing a lot of each other, and who knows . . . once we're better acquainted you might change your mind."

"No, really, I won't. It's one rule I never break."

Tanner smiled. "Never is a long time."

They stood there a moment, sparring without words, each imagining the thoughts of the other. At last, flushed and unable to hold his gaze, Stacey turned away.

"Shall we have a look at the crypt? It's a long drive back, and I've got several appointments this afternoon."

Tanner became aware of it slowly. An impression at first, vague and disjointed, but gradually taking shape. A pattern of illusion.

The mansion of Lucas Brokaw was a place where paradox dwelled. Nothing was as it appeared on the surface. As in a mirage or the distorted image in a funhouse mirror, everything had about it a refracted quality—as though the eye had been misdirected, and having seen only the illusion, was lulled into accepting it as reality.

A less observant man would have detected none of this, but observation alone might easily have led him astray. Tanner had been trained to look beyond the obvious, and there was yet a higher level of awareness he trusted even more implicitly. It dealt in abstraction rather than substance, and because it had never failed him, he'd always believed in his hunches.

The crypt reinforced Tanner's hunch.

Perhaps that was what bothered him the most as they descended the stairs. It was too subterranean, too deep. An excavation feat of such magnitude that it overshadowed its supposed purpose. It was so far beneath the earth, in fact, that it became something of another world, eerie and apart, almost as though Lucas Brokaw had very deliberately constructed a set that was meant to upstage the play and spellbind the players.

Tanner's reaction to the crypt was totally visceral. A sense of foreboding and menace struck him the moment he stepped through the entranceway. It was palpable, almost a presence, some nameless thing that . . . waited.

Deep down in his guts he felt a cold knot of disquiet, and he knew it was there. Unseen, nothing he could articulate or identify, but nonetheless real. A part of this place. Infinitely patient and watchful, lurking just beyond ken or touch or reason. Somehow there . . . alert . . . on guard. A netherworld sentinel of Lucas Brokaw's crypt.

Yet he felt no personal sense of threat. Nor was he apprehensive for Stacey. Despite his gut reaction—the feeling that they weren't alone—there was a curious lack of fear. Oddly enough, he felt welcome. Suddenly . . . somehow . . . but that was crazy! There for a moment . . . unless his mind was playing tricks on him. . . .

It was as though he'd been expected.

Crazy or not, the thought persisted. Baffled by it, but thoroughly intrigued now, Tanner spent several minutes prowling around the outer chamber. Stacey watched, standing just inside the entranceway, while he methodically inspected the cryptography machine, the vault door, and all four walls. She thought his interest a bit excessive, but she was herself again, poised and businesslike, and as he poked about she filled him in on the controversy surrounding Lucas Brokaw's death.

A servant had discovered the old man's body on the night of his birthday, seated in a chair beside the study window. Everyone knew he was dying of cancer, and over the years speculation had persisted that he might have committed suicide. Yet there was no hard evidence that he'd taken his own life—or at least none had been made public—and the coroner had ruled it death by natural causes. In fact, the affair had been treated with considerable dispatch, with a quick inquest and an even quicker burial. In accordance with his wishes, Brokaw had been laid to rest beside his wife in the family plot, a small gravesite overlooking the cliffs.

Nor was any connection ever established between Brokaw's birthdate and the time of his death, all of which coincided rather neatly with certain remarks in his will, never stated openly, but expressed in muted terms, that he would be reborn on the very day he died. Since Brokaw had left no explanation behind, choosing to take his secret to the grave, it remained a mystery, perhaps the most unfathomable of all the riddles surrounding his death.

"I suppose most people consider the whole thing a little spooky. But if you stop and think about it, Brokaw's idea was really quite sane."

Stacey had the feeling she was talking to herself, and she was growing weary of the conversation. She hesitated, watching Tanner inspect the vault for the third time, and finally went on. "Well, anyway, my point was, he had everything to gain and nothing to lose, so why not try? Or don't you agree?"

Tanner merely nodded, offering no comment. He kept pacing around the crypt, studying it from various angles, clearly preoccupied. At last, he halted behind the cryptography machine, directly opposite the entranceway, frowning thoughtfully to himself. A moment passed, then he patted the machine with his hand and gave her a quizzical look.

"Doesn't it seem odd to you that Brokaw left this in such an exposed position?"

"Exposed? I'm afraid I don't follow you."

"Think about it a minute. Unless I missed something, there's no alarm system of any kind leading into this room—not even an electronic eye. Nothing along the stairs. Nothing in the entranceway where you're standing. Nothing at all, right?"

50

"Yes, that's correct. But I still don't—"

"And yet this machine was just left sitting here, totally unprotected, in a room that doesn't even have a door. Now, wouldn't you say that's a little strange, almost *too* casual? Especially when breaking the code to this thing"—he tapped the machine with his finger—"is what qualifies a man for a shot at the vault."

"Not really." Stacey sounded a bit defensive. "Aren't you forgetting the guards and the fence, not to mention the dogs? I'm no expert, but it seems to me it's an exaggeration to say the machine is totally unprotected."

"I *am* an expert," Tanner informed her. "So take my word for it. There's never been a security system invented that couldn't be penetrated. All it requires is know-how and determination, and the world's full of men who have both."

"If that's true, then I've missed the point." Stacey searched his face, suddenly very intent. "Or is there a point? What is it you're trying to say?"

"The point is quite simple." Tanner's gaze sharpened perceptibly, and he glanced down at the machine. "A genius doesn't make stupid mistakes."

"Yes, but really! Don't you see, that would mean—"

"Exactly. Brokaw left it here on purpose. Went out of his way, as a matter of fact, to make it seem vulnerable."

Stacey caught her breath, darting a look at the machine, and in the stillness of the crypt her words were barely audible. "Why? What could he hope to accomplish?"

"Good question. And just to be truthful . . . I don't know." Tanner laughed a short mirthless laugh. Then a peculiar glint came into his eye. "I'll tell you one thing, though. Whoever finds out might wish he hadn't."

Stacey shivered, glancing around the crypt. Suddenly she knew it was true—that somehow Tanner was right—and she felt a compelling urge to turn and flee, to escape this place and rejoin the world of the living.

She backed out of the entranceway, edging toward the stairs.

"Shall we go? I just remembered . . . I have to speak with the housekeeper. Then I really must get back to the office."

Tanner wandered into the drawing room. He'd seen the look of fear on Stacey's face—an instant of comprehension mixed with dread that she hadn't entirely hidden. Clearly it was an emotion she'd never before experienced in the crypt. But why hide it? Why pretend otherwise and refuse even to discuss it? Her hurried retreat up the stairs had merely been a device to end the conversation. In the foyer she had cut him short—simply left him standing there—and whisked off in search of the housekeeper. Yet her abrupt manner wasn't what bothered him. Nor was he concerned by the look of fright itself. He had the very distinct impression she was frightened of *him*. Or, if not him, then by the fact that he'd unearthed still another contradiction in the paradox of Lucas Brokaw.

Uneasy, lost in thought, he slowly circled the drawing room gallery. He paused from time to time, caught by a splash of color in a Monet or the primitive symbolism of a Gauguin. But his expression was abstracted, vaguely unaware. Though the paintings registered, there was a deeper level of concentration. His mind kept drifting back to the crypt and the curious machine. And Stacey.

Then he came to the portrait of Stephanie Brokaw.

Suspended over the fireplace mantel, it was a large oil, warm and lush, with faint russet hues reminiscent of the old masters. It was hauntingly lifelike, as though the artist had captured on canvas the very essence of his subject. Stephanie Brokaw was an arresting woman, strikingly beautiful, with raven hair and delicate features and an almost ethereal quality of elegance. She was bare-shouldered, dressed in a flowing terra cotta

52

gown, and the claret glow of a ruby pendant sparkled on her breast. Yet it was her eyes that dominated the portrait—deep umber pools, tantalizing and strangely inviting, filled with a spiritual wisdom that transcended time and place and the impermanence of flesh.

Tanner stared up at the portrait, captivated by her gaze. Some inner part of him felt drawn to her, irresistibly beckoned; he couldn't seem to tear himself away. He had the odd sensation of being touched, somehow caressed, as though her eyes plumbed the core of what he was and gently laved it with affection. Slowly, almost imperceptibly, he was consumed within the umber depths of her gaze, the single focal point in a world that had suddenly gone hazy. An exquisite vertigo swept over him, an intensely sensual feeling, and suddenly he was aware of a swirl of color and sound, as if he were no longer alone and somewhere in the distance music played.

She moved toward him then, sweeping majestically down the staircase. She was a vision of loveliness— never more radiant—a creature of stunning incandescence, small and vivacious and graceful. Her beauty was heightened by the russet gown and glittering bloodred ruby he'd given her to mark the occasion—their anniversary.

He crossed the foyer as she descended the last step. Her eyes held him enthralled, brimming with love, and he extended his hand.

"Stephanie . . . thank God! I thought you'd never come down."

"I beg your pardon."

Tanner blinked, the spell broken. The music faded and the voices drifted away. His vision slowly cleared. He found himself staring at Stacey.

"What is it, Warren? Are you all right?"

"Of course, never better." He smiled, suddenly aware of her hand, and released it. "Why, something wrong?"

"No, you just startled me and . . . well . . . there for a moment, you didn't seem yourself."

His smile broadened. "That's because you don't know me well enough yet. But it's an oversight easily corrected . . . if you'll break your rule."

Stacey appeared uncertain, on the verge of a question. Then her expression changed and she merely shook her head. "I'm sorry, but we're running late. Do you mind?"

Tanner stepped aside and she moved past him. There was a look of mild puzzlement on his face, and as she walked toward the door, it occurred to her that the question wasn't necessary after all. He really didn't remember! None of it. Not the words or the name or the tenderness in his voice.

Nor the fact that he'd mistaken her for a dead woman.

V

Logs crackled in the fireplace and a stereo flooded the apartment with gypsy violins. Through an elliptical picture window that overlooked the lee side of Telegraph Hill, lights on the Bay Bridge flickered in the distance. As it did on most autumn nights, the city lay cloaked in a murky haze, punctuated by the basso wail of foghorns and the almost inaudible clang of cable cars. It was a night that invited a toasty fire and dreamy music.

Curt Ruxton lounged back in a huge beanbag chair. He was smoking a joint, drifting lazily on some inner cloud as he watched the blink-blink of lights on the bridge. Beside him, sharing both the chair and the joint, Jill Dvorak hummed softly to herself, lost in an erotic little fantasy of her own. Her cheeks were flushed and her body glowed with anticipation, as she unconsciously carressed and explored, her hand running over him like a rain of softly falling petals. Scarcely aware of her, Ruxton took another long drag, savoring the acrid, grassy taste. Then he pulled the smoke deep into his lungs, passed her the joint, and again focused on the blinking lights.

Across from them, on a plush sofa, Monk Birkhead uncapped a vial of white powder. A small cutting board and a penknife were arranged on the coffee table before him. Carefully, with a slight tap of his finger, he sprinkled a pinch of cocaine onto the cutting board. After sealing the vial, he set it aside, opened the knife, and scraped the powder into a thin line about an inch long. Then he rolled a dollar bill into a tight tube and inserted one end into his right nostril. Leaning forward, he pressed his left nostril closed, positioning the tube over the coke. With a loud snuff, he quickly ran the line, sniffing every last flake off the board. All in one motion, he pulled the tube loose, tossed it onto the table, and flopped back against the sofa.

The effect of his snort was almost instantaneous. A rushing high swept over him, and his skin tingled with a feeling of raw sensuality. The flames in the fireplace became bolder, every color in the spectrum bright and clear and intensely brilliant. A grotesque, lopsided grin spread across his face. His eyes glazed in a look that was at once sinister and lighthearted, a sort of jovial, rapacious lust.

"Anybody wanna fuck?"

The offer was all-inclusive, directed to both Ruxton and the girl. Birkhead was a switch-hitter and by no means a stranger to San Francisco's gay bars. But he generally found all the action he wanted at home. While Ruxton himself wasn't bisexual, Jill's appetites were wholly without inhibition. In bed her entire body became a damp, inviting orifice.

The three of them formed a highly compatible ménage à trois. As roommates they shared one another in the same way they shared a bed—comfortably, without jealousy or jostling, and with very little emotion. Yet however cosmopolitan the arrangement, their needs beneath the sheets were not always the same.

Tonight Birkhead had that weird look on his face— the look that invariably signaled one of his sadomasochistic spells. But at the moment Ruxton simply couldn't be bothered. His own mood was much too mellow to have it spoiled by the big man's whip-and-whimper routine. He ignored the invitation.

"Don't you think you're hitting the coke a little heavy?"

"Hell, this is good stuff!" Birkhead jiggled the vial. "Best I've had since I left Nam, and that's a fact. It's uncut . . . pure as the driven snow!"

"And you're the snowbird that ought to know."

Birkhead gave him a dopey grin. "Yeah, that's me. King of the snowbirds!"

"Which merely proves my point," Ruxton observed. "Keep hitting it the way you have and the inside of your head will look like you inhaled napalm."

Birkhead already had the nasal drip of a cocaine addict, and he sniffed constantly. But his philosophy was live for the instant, and it concerned him not at all that he was slowly incinerating his nasal passages.

"So I'll go down in flames. Who gives a good goddamn? At least I'll be flying high when I take the dive."

"You always were a fatalist, Monk. But unoriginal, sadly unoriginal! All this bunk about live fast, die young, and have a good-looking corpse is pure camp. You think you're into a whole new bag, and all you've really done is take three giant steps backward."

Ruxton's wit, while sometimes charming, often carried a sting. He was inclined to provoke arguments merely to sharpen that sting, for he viewed other people as a foil for his own thoughts. Not surprisingly, this generated a certain irreverence toward the rest of the world. But it wasn't so much contempt as amusement. He found the folly of those about him rather quaint, almost touching, and he had a curious empathy for their struggle to escape the treadmill.

After college he'd spent several years on the treadmill himself, leaping about from job to job in a flurry of disillusionment. Out of his bitterness sprang the conviction that the only way to beat the system was to finesse the men who ran it. So he'd become a stockbroker, and later an entrepreneur, and there he found his true métier in life.

A man of mercurial moods, Ruxton had the look of an aesthetic roué. Lean and wiry, possessed of a massive calm, he had clear, hypnotic eyes, angular features, and dark curly hair cropped close to the skull. Yet it was a deceptive appearance, for he was urbane and glib, with a quicksilver mind and a profound sense of life's absurdities. All of which created an understated air of authority, an advantage he exploited to the fullest.

By contrast, Birkhead was robust as an ox and uncommonly agile for his size. Not slow-witted but simply big and tough, with scarcely any neck, his head fixed directly upon his shoulders. He had a great black ruff of hair, muddy deep-set eyes, and a mouthful of teeth that looked like old dice. His youth had been spent in logging camps, where punishing hours and physical labor had quilted his arms and chest with thick, corded muscle. Later in the army he had acquired a certain worldliness, if little in the way of polish. On occasion he left the impression he was only one step removed from walking on his knuckles.

It was this atavistic quality that fascinated Ruxton even as it revolted him. It was one of the reasons Ruxton kept him around. At times, particularly in their business affairs, it was both reassuring and persuasive to have a neatly groomed Neanderthal backing his demands.

An ex-Green Beret, Birkhead was a master of karate and had a fondness for *mano a mano* brawls. Churlish even at the best of times, he had all the social instincts of a cobra and an absolute genius for the macabre, which was never more evident than when he'd gone too long without a snort of coke. Then he turned brutal, unpredictably vicious, a man to be feared.

But now, like a child rebuked for believing in the tooth fairy, Monk Birkhead grinned sheepishly and averted his gaze. Had anyone else mocked his outlook on life, he would have administered, free of charge, a lesson in brute force. Under Ruxton's haughty stare, however, he simply let it pass and quickly changed the subject.

"Say, talking about three steps backward, that reminds me. What I told you about at the office. You got busy on the phone and you never did answer me."

"Sorry, old buddy, I don't even remember the question. Answer you about what?"

"You know, about whatsizname. The old spook."

Ruxton rolled another joint and lit it.

Several moments passed while he contemplated the fiery coal on the tip. Then he smiled, a lazy sphinxlike smile, as if Birkhead's question were a trifle absurd but he had decided to indulge him nonetheless. At last, having milked the pause for dramatic effect, his words tumbled out in little spurts of smoke.

"Ah, yes, Lucas Brokaw. The riddle of the ages. An ethereal testament to man's supreme gullibility. Part genius. Part ghoul. And the greatest practical joker of all time. A formidable if not altogether lucid combination."

"In a pig's ass!" Birkhead laughed, relaxed now, playing the game. "Save your highbrow routine for somebody else. You just put him down because you're some kind of oddball heathen. Same old think tank mentality."

"Monk, you have a rare and singular talent for the mixed metaphor." Ruxton wagged his head back and forth in mild wonder. "To be more precise, I'm simply your everyday iconoclast who believes in lopping off the heads of all ancient and feeble myths. Which includes everyone's favorite genie, Lucas Brokaw."

"Bullllshit! Lemme tell you something, wise guy. There's more to reincarnation than you think. When I was in Nam I met lots of chicks, and they told me things that'd blow your mind. I mean *real live* spook stories!"

"Now who's doing a number? The only chicks you met in Saigon were hookers. So don't futz me around, old buddy. Whatever they taught you, it didn't have anything to do with your mind."

Jill suddenly stirred, alert as ever to any topic with erotic overtones. She struggled upward out of a glassy-eyed daze and laughed a throaty little laugh. "No fair, you guys! We made a rule, remember? Just the three of us, no outside chicks."

"We weren't talking about chicks," Ruxton informed

her. "Tonight's seminar deals with my impending reincarnation."

"Reincarnation?" Jill batted her lashes, thoroughly disoriented. "I don't get it, luv. Who are you supposed to be?"

"According to our resident scholar," Ruxton made an expansive gesture toward the sofa, "who is a self-professed expert on such matters, I might be none other than old moneybags himself, Lucas Brokaw."

"Oooh wow!" Jill clapped her hands with the greedy savor of a little girl. "Super idea!"

"Monk thought so too. Except that he'd just sniffed a pinch of twinkle-dust, and to put it charitably, he had his head screwed on backward."

"Hey, that's a crock and you know it." Birkhead looked genuinely wounded. "All I said was that you were born on the day he died."

"Wait a minute," Jill interjected. "The day who died?"

"Who we're talking about, juicyfruit. Lucas Brokaw."

"You just lost me again. How did you know that?"

"Hell, I don't know. I just knew. Everybody knows! Besides, it was in this morning's paper. That's what gave me the idea. There was an article about the Brokaw Foundation, and it gave a rehash on the old man. I guess that's the first time I ever really noticed the date. All I did was subtract back and it turns out Curt was born on the night Brokaw died. It's as simple as that."

The newspaper article that morning had been a routine announcement of Warren Tanner's appointment to the foundation staff. But the public never tired of reading about the Brokaw legend; anything concerning his millions, however trivial, created instant world news. An entire column on the front page had been devoted to the story, relating in detail the provisions of Brokaw's will and the fact that his fortune had now swelled to the astronomical sum of $512,000,000. It was this figure that had caught Birkhead's eye and led him to read further.

Jill seldom read anything, particularly newspapers, and the connection still escaped her. "Honestly, Monk, I hate to sound dense, but even if Curt was born that night . . . so what?"

"So nothing!" Birkhead threw up his hands in disgust. "I just mentioned it at the office, that's all. Tried to explain to him that lots of people believe the switch—you know, the reincarnation—takes place at the moment of death. I wasn't even serious, for chrissakes! It was just the date and everything, and . . . well, you'll have to admit, it's a hell of a coincidence."

"Oh, I see!" Jill beamed. "Because of the coincidence there's a chance Curt might be Brokaw. That's what you meant, right?"

"Yeah, right. Except when I bring it up again tonight he starts lecturing me on the yo-yo mentality of anybody who takes it serious. Are you ready for that? Like I'm a fucking missionary or something!"

Ruxton laughed, one eye cocked askew. "Don't try to weasel out of it, you big schmuck. You weren't joking. You were serious, and you damn well know it, too!"

"Easy, tiger." Jill purred a kittenish growl and playfully ran her hand under his shirt. "Monk didn't mean any harm. And besides, maybe the idea isn't so far out after all. You and Brokaw do have the same sign, and there's lots to be said for that." Her lips brushed across his cheek and she smiled suggestively. "Know what I mean, luv?"

"Cool it." Ruxton pulled away, his tone brusque. "We'll get it on later, but first things first. We still haven't settled Monk's zombie theory. Right, old buddy? The mummy walks again and all that."

"Now it's zombies!" Birkhead groaned. "Get your head out, will you? I'm not into that hoodoo voodoo crap. All I'm talking about is the *possibility* of reincarnation. Go on and laugh your ass off, but I'm telling you . . . it's the spooks that'll have the last laugh!"

Jill suddenly rose from the chair, casting Ruxton a hurt look, and glided spectrally across the room, like a small girl playing the role of femme fatale.

But if her smoldering sensuality was an act, there was nothing artificial about her beauty. She had ash blond hair and exquisite green eyes, along with sculptured buttocks, long sumptuous legs, and full youthful breasts. A victim of her own sexual fantasies, she believed that these attributes alone, beauty and flesh, made every man her slave. It was a daydream she had nurtured as a girl on the family farm in South Dakota, and it had worked marvelously well on country boys. Her first year in San Francisco it had even performed wonders on a succession of ultracool executive types. Yet now, like Monk Birkhead, she fooled no one. Not even herself.

Their world orbited around Curt Ruxton, as the earth around the sun, and by tacit agreement it was understood that they were creatures of his will. While he was infinitely tolerant, never obtrusive, he nonetheless exerted that will at his pleasure.

With casual expertise, he had orchestrated a modeling career for Jill and arranged the capital for Birkhead, who held a black belt in karate, to finance a martial arts school. In time, Ruxton had quit his own job as a stockbroker. Employing a mix of business acumen and hucksterism, he had then franchised nearly thirty karate schools throughout the Bay Area. By virtue of franchising fees and an exorbitant percentage of the gross (which were reinvested in a bullish stock market), he had parlayed the public's craze for mayhem into modest wealth. Equal partners in the venture, he and Birkhead were worth something more than $400,000.

Appearances aside, however, there was no partnership either in the business or at home. Ruxton was the catalyst, the element that held it all together. A man of soaring intellect and a flair for the dramatic who forever played to a captive audience. The star of their little threesome.

Jill flopped down on the sofa beside Birkhead and he put his arm around her, patting her rump with a swat of endearment. As she snuggled closer, it occurred to her that Ruxton was baiting the big man, toying with him. And the saddest part of all was that Birkhead went along with it, almost as though he enjoyed it, derived some perverse kick of his own by allowing himself to be mocked.

She tuned out on the conversation, no longer interested. Yet she continued to watch Ruxton with a certain bemused fascination, unable to break the hold. He was like a conjurer, forever dazzling her with his tricks. There was a distant quality about him, never more apparent than when they were in bed. Then, always the man of moods and masks, it was as though his emotional nerve center had been short-circuited, leaving him wholly detached even in the act of love. Which was not the worst of faults, perhaps, considering that he was gentle and protective and so intensely vital the rest of the time.

And of course she loved him. There was always that.

Birkhead's voice, somehow strained and oddly defensive, intruded on her thoughts. She recognized it for what it was—not just a weakening, but that final spasm of capitulation. The way it always happened. With the big man loud and blustering, as if he really hadn't surrendered but was merely conceding a standoff. An amiable truce.

"You know what your problem is, Curt? You're an egghead! One of them pointy-eared whiz kids always trying to make two plus two equal five. Loosen up, for chrissakes. Half the people on this earth believe in reincarnation. Did you know that? Hell, maybe more than half. So don't block it out. Relax! Let your mind expand."

"And the other half," Ruxton noted dryly, "believe

63

in baby Jesus and the pearly gates. So what does that prove?"

"You really wanna know what it proves? It proves what I've said all along. You're not even a card-carrying atheist. You're a heathen. A bloody infidel! And on top of all that, you're the stubbornest sonofabitch I ever ran across."

Birkhead laughed a wild, braying laugh and jackknifed to his feet, dragging Jill along with him. "C'mon, hotpants, time for fun and games." The lopsided grin reappeared, and he gave Ruxton a lewd wink. "How about it, ace? Might as well join us and make it a party."

"No, not now." Ruxton waved them off as if dusting away a cloud of gnats. "Have fun. I'll catch up with you later."

Birkhead shrugged and led Jill toward the bedroom. She glanced back over her shoulder—a wistful, little-girl-lost look—but Ruxton was already preoccupied rolling another joint. As they went through the door, he lit up and took a long drag, inhaling on a deep whoosh of breath.

Embers crackled in the fireplace and a tomblike silence settled over the room. He seemed to fall asleep with his eyes open, but after a while he blinked, focusing on the distant flicker of bridge lights. Suddenly a blurred image came swimming forward in his mind. It assumed shape and substance, and in an instant of recognition, he knew it had been there all along, stuck back in some dim corner, dusty and forgotten, waiting all these years.

A thin smile creased his lips. Then he nodded, inspecting it more closely, mildly astonished that he hadn't seen it before.

Yes, indeed. An extraordinary idea. Not just the way Monk had intended: That was probably impossible. But worth consideration. To be exact, half a billion considerations. After all, it was not without precedent.

Lazarus had done it before him.

VI

Tanner knew the man was a fraud all along.

His name was George Haskell. Unlike most claimants, he had called the foundation beforehand requesting an appointment with the director. That was on a Monday morning a week ago, and his appearance in the office that afternoon created quite a stir.

A man of considerable presence, Haskell had impressed Stacey from the outset. Hardly an eccentric, he seemed respectable and very businesslike. Tall and immaculately groomed, his hair prematurely flecked with gray, he had all the earmarks of a young, upwardly mobile business executive. Which squared perfectly with the details of his personal background. An entrepreneur by profession, he dealt mainly in imports and exports, acting as middleman for various concerns on the world commodities market.

And the tale he told concerning the Brokaw legacy was just offbeat enough to make it credible.

Under constant business pressure, he had recently turned to transcendental meditation as an outlet for stress and mental fatigue—the by-products of success.

According to his guru, he had a latent gift for this ancient philosophy and was soon able to achieve what amounted to a self-induced trance. It was during one of these periods, while chanting his mantra, that he had been transported to the highest level of psychic consciousness. And in a blinding moment of clarity he had seen revealed the vision, an immutable truth from beyond the veil.

By whatever karma, he *was* Lucas Brokaw reincarnated.

What followed was not the most grueling interrogation Tanner had ever witnessed. Yet it was subtle and exhaustive, and cleverly done. Stacey and the director spent nearly two hours grilling Haskell. Working as a team, they badgered and bullied, goading him the entire time. Their technique was to skip back and forth, subjecting him to a barrage of questions concerning both his own life and little-known aspects of Lucas Brokaw's life.

Haskell submitted with equanimity, cooperative to a fault. But while his answers were sometimes fragmented, lacking in detail, they were unable to rattle him. Nor were they able to discredit his claim.

When it was over, Haskell left as he had entered, slightly apologetic and still properly awed by the enormity of what he'd undertaken. The director, on the other hand, was a bundle of nerves. He ordered an immediate investigation into the man's background.

Tanner never for a moment believed Haskell's story. Even as he had observed the interrogation, his sixth sense had begun vibrating. There was something phony about that man. A fixity of speech and appearance that was too pat; the look of an articulated mannequin impersonating the dynamic young tycoon. Worse yet, Tanner had the very disquieting hunch that George Haskell went by many names, none of them his own.

Still, for all his misgivings, Tanner was positively elated by Haskell's arrival on the scene. Since joining the foundation he'd done little to earn his salary; after a month on the job he had slowly come to think of himself as an overpaid gumshoe. Not that there was any dearth of claimants, but his time was consumed investigating an assortment of weirdos and small-time con men. None of them were even remotely legitimate, and he found it difficult to justify either the time or the effort involved. To compound matters, the director's inflexibility merely underscored the deadly routine of the job.

Unless a claimant was certifiable, Hamilton Knox insisted on a cursory investigation at the very least. Tanner's objections were constantly overruled. Thoroughly frustrated, he spent his days constructing files on kooks, petty chiselers, and an occasional religious freak.

Nor was his luck with Stacey anything to rate hosannas. While he'd taken her to dinner several times, she had thawed only by degrees. He had yet to make it past her front door. On their last date, genuinely confused by her ambivalence, he'd put it to her point blank, urging candor. And candor was precisely what he got.

Yes, she admitted, she was interested in him. But her experiences with hard, aggressive men had invariably ended on a sour note—primarily because she refused to play the game—and she was wary of plunging headlong into the same old trap. However attractive she found him (and despite herself, she was attracted), any involvement would have to develop gradually.

It was encouragement of sorts, although far short of what he'd had in mind. But to his own amazement, he didn't press her further, and that's how the evening ended. Nothing resolved. No promises. Merely an agreement to take it slow and see where it led them. She had scuttled his immediate campaign to get her into bed and left him to ponder the vicissitudes of quaint rituals in a liberated age.

So George Haskell had been a ray of sunshine just in the nick of time. Between the frustrations of the job and Stacey's wary attitude, Tanner desperately needed a diversion—something to clear the cobwebs and break the tedium. He was looking forward to a game of wits against a sly and cunning opponent.

All too quickly, however, it proved to be a mismatch. George Haskell was smoother than most, perhaps a better actor, but he still couldn't outrun his past or cover his tracks. In attempting to do so he had merely outfoxed himself.

Tanner accomplished it with nothing more incriminating than a water glass, which Haskell had used during the interrogation. The local police chief was delighted to cooperate, and after the glass had been dusted, the fingerprints were transferred to the FBI in Washington. The government computers went into action, and early next afternoon a complete dossier spewed out of the telex in Palo Alto.

George Haskell was a con man nonpareil, with so many aliases his record resembled a platoon roster. His real name was Alberto Santini, born on the Lower East Side of Manhattan, and his cultured manner was as phony as his business credentials. Although there were no warrants outstanding, Interpol suspected him of several recent capers on the Riviera; the Customs Bureau verified his return to the United States earlier in the year. A quick check revealed that his import-export company, located in downtown San Francisco, had rented a plush suite of offices less than a month later. The firm was conspicuous by its lack of clients.

Clearly George Haskell, né Santini, had organized a legitimate front and done his homework on the Brokaw legend. Then, radiating confidence, he'd undertaken the very scam that had defeated hundreds of his brothers-in-larceny.

Disappointed with the ease of his victory, Tanner was on the verge of exposing the man when he was struck by a sudden inspiration. Why not allow Haskell a crack at the cryptography machine? It couldn't do any harm—scores of claimants had already failed to outwit the machine—yet it would provide Tanner with a personal look at the device in action. In turn, that might shed some light on a riddle which still defied logic: Why Lucas Brokaw had purposely placed the machine in such a vulnerable spot.

So Tanner kept the contents of the dossier to himself. Meanwhile, the director's fidgets increased by quantum leaps, and Stacey developed a severe case of gloom. But they really had small choice in the matter. The claimant had withstood rigorous questioning and a thorough investigation. In short, he qualified for a shot at the fortune. And now, a week to the day since his interrogation, George Haskell stood face to face with the cryptography machine.

Stacey and the director flanked him on either side, and Tanner, leaning against the wall near the entranceway, regarded him with impassive curiosity. The outer chamber was deathly quiet. In the stillness Haskell's breathing was loud and labored. Descent into the subterranean crypt was an unnerving experience, even for a magna cum laude of Sing Sing, and he was obviously struggling to maintain his composure. At last, with a tight grip on his own nerves, the director addressed him in a slow, emphatic voice.

"You may begin when ready, Mr. Haskell. But I caution you once again, you will be allowed only one attempt. Take your time and please be very certain to touch nothing but the keyboard. If you tamper with the machine in any manner, you will automatically disqualify yourself. Are my instructions quite clear?"

Haskell nodded, and frowned uncertainly at the machine. Beads of sweat popped out on his forehead, and the silence suddenly became deafening. Alert, very intent now, Tanner's gaze narrowed as the man placed his fingers on the keyboard.

Nothing happened. The keys failed to depress.

Flustered, Haskell quickly scanned the control panel. Then he smiled sheepishly, and clicked the on-off switch to the on position. The machine came alive with a soft, purring hum. Muttering to himself, Haskell steadied his nerves and then resorted to the hunt-and-peck system. With one forefinger, gingerly, he tapped a single key at a time. It seemed an interminable exercise, with long, reflective pauses between each letter. But finally he stopped, grunted something unintelligible, and stepped back. There was a moment of silence, then the machine buzzed and whirred, emitting three strokes on a bell, and an instant later coughed up a solitary line of plaintext printout.

THIA IS RHE UW5L QM95D V3NCZ

Stacey and the director exchanged a quick glance.

Haskell cursed under his breath, staring at the printout wtih a look of profound aggravation.

Tanner shifted away from the wall, taut and expectant, watching closely. He waited for the machine to self-destruct or disgorge another message. Or perform some startling feat of enlightenment.

But the machine merely purred its soft, rhythmic hum, revealing nothing. Several seconds slipped away. Then the director smiled and flipped the panel switch to the off position.

"I believe that concludes our business, Mr. Haskell." His sangfroid once again intact, Hamilton Knox ripped the printout from the carriage. "Unless, of course, you intend to claim that these jumbled letters somehow spell THIS IS THE REAL LUCAS BROKAW."

"I suspect he's had his fill." Tanner fixed Haskell with a cold, purposeful look. "Haven't you, Mr. Santini?"

"You knew!" Stacey said on an indrawn breath. "You knew all along he was a fake."

The director stiffened, a glimmer of disbelief in his eyes. "Are you telling us that this man is not who he claims to be?"

Tanner ignored them, concentrating on Santini, his voice harsh and cutting, demanding answers. The con man denied everything at first, registering shock, hurt, and righteous indignation. But as Tanner reeled off a chronology of his police record, Santini quickly wilted, and within minutes they had the entire story. He'd spent the past six months devouring everything ever written on cryptanalysis and the development of cryptography machines. And he'd almost succeeded! Gesturing at the printout, he laughed a bitter, defiant laugh and indicated how very close he had come to breaking the code. Given time and another session with the machine, he believed he could still break it. To the letter!

It was sheer braggadocio, but it contained a kernel of truth, and the director glowered at Tanner. "By what authority did you perpetrate this farce? Were you merely indulging a whim, Mr. Tanner, or have you taken leave of your senses?"

"Actually, neither one. I wanted to see that machine in operation, and Santini just happened along at the right time. Even if he'd broken the code, I would have stopped him from going any further."

"Irresponsible! Wholly indefensible!" Knox's tone was clipped and stiff, and he stabbed out at Santini with a bony finger. "This man will go scot-free! Do you realize that, Mr. Tanner? What you've done constitutes entrapment, and we haven't the slightest chance of prosecuting him."

Tanner shrugged. "It was a calculated risk. I needed some answers, and our friend here gave them to me. Offhand, I'd say we came out ahead."

"That remains to be seen!" Knox sputtered to a halt, aware that Santini was listening with rapt attention. "We'll discuss your reasons another time. In privacy." He wheeled around and stalked from the crypt. "Follow me, Mr. Haskell or Santini or whatever it is you call yourself. And if you will, sir, please don't speak to me. I've had more than enough irritation for one day!"

As they went through the entranceway, Stacey moved away from the machine and halted in front of Tanner. She gave him an eloquent look. "I don't know if this is a compliment or not, but you're the first man I've ever met who could make the director lose his cool."

"No harm done. He'll calm down when I explain."

"Then you found out what you wanted to know?"

"Not altogether," Tanner admitted. "But at least I've proved my hunch. Brokaw meant for that code to be broken."

"And I suppose you have a very logical argument to support your theory?"

"As a matter of fact . . . I seem to recall a liquor cabinet up in the study. Why don't I tell you about it over a drink?"

"Isn't it a little early? You know what they say about daytime drinkers."

Tanner laughed. "Let'em talk! Today's special and I feel like celebrating. Besides, the afternoon's half gone anyway."

"Perhaps so, but we really should get back to the foundation. I mean, after all that's happened . . . the director probably . . . I'm sure he'll be expecting us."

"To tell you the truth, I got the distinct impression he'd seen enough of me for one day. Suppose we play hooky and give him time to cool off?"

"Well, since I drove out with you, I guess I wouldn't expect . . ."

"That's right, he wouldn't. And if you need an excuse, just tell him you couldn't let me drink alone."

Stacey hesitated a moment, then she smiled and took his arm. "Why not? You've earned a celebration."

"Damned if I haven't. Come on, we'll hoist one to our friend Santini, and if you twist my arm, I might even take you to dinner."

Tanner led the way out of the crypt, then stepped aside, releasing her arm as she started up the stairs. Stacey glanced at him as she went past, and he caught a hint of something he hadn't seen before. It was a curious look, almost an appraisal. But somehow enticing, a look of promise.

"So as it turned out, all I had to do was keep my mouth shut and let Santini finish his act."

"His act!" Stacey exclaimed. "Oooh no, you're the actor! And I'm not sure I like that very much either. The least you could have done was tell me. Or don't you trust me to keep a secret?"

Tanner caught it again, in her voice this time. Something mischievous and teasing, strangely like a dare. Or perhaps an invitation. But he couldn't be certain. Since entering the study, he'd felt on edge, sensed that she felt it too. There was a peculiar sort of tension between them, like a couple of kids on a blind date, circling warily, drawn ever closer, yet somehow afraid to touch. Still, she kept giving him those glances and her voice seemed . . .

He almost laughed. Coquettish was hardly a term applicable to Stacey Cameron. But there was definitely a change, apparent from the moment he'd aced Knox down in the crypt. A curious blend of intimacy, elusive but sultry.

Then, too, they were already on their second drink, another sign in itself. Tension and jittery nerves acted like a sponge on alcohol, and neither of them had wasted any time on the first round. A thought nagged at him, and while he couldn't discount it, he knew a great deal would be lost if he were wrong. He splashed Scotch into their glasses, still very much in a quandary, and turned back from the liquor cabinet.

She stood by the window watching him. When he handed her the glass, she accepted it with a faint nod. Then he remembered her question. Altogether preoccupied, he'd forgotten to answer, and saw now that she was waiting. He shrugged, offering her a lame smile.

"Sorry, guess I strayed off for a minute. Now, as to your question, the answer is an emphatic, unqualified yes. I'd trust you with my last ten bucks. But—consider carefully now!—if I had told you about Santini, would you have gone along with the idea? Be honest, you won't hurt my feelings."

"I might have." She took a sip of her drink, gazing at him over the rim of the glass. "Maybe it would have taken a little convincing, but then, you're a very convincing man."

"Oh, am I now? And what brought you to that conclusion?"

"The way you handled the director was very convincing."

"How so?"

"I don't know . . . you just seemed so sure of yourself."

"Like I had things under control."

"Yes, exactly. You were very confident and self-assured and . . . well, sort of in command. It's really true, you know, that old adage . . . confidence is contagious."

"So I've heard. Anything else?"

"Now you're fishing for compliments."

"Never!"

"Yes, you are. I'm serious, and all you're looking for is a little ego massage."

"Perish the thought."

"See, now you're making fun of me! And don't deny it, I can tell. You always get that *very* tolerant grin on your face when you're amused by someone."

"Are you really serious?"

"Of course I am. It was perfect . . . the way you set it up and fooled . . ."

"Not that. You know what I mean."

Her expression changed. She tilted her head to one side, very somber now, and searched his face intently. A long moment of deliberation passed in silence, and they both understood she was on the verge of decision.

The light from the window sent flecks of amber and gold dancing through her hair. A warm, smoky look touched her eyes, and once again he was struck by the exotic, wildfire quality of her beauty. Slowly, like the stirring of a faint breeze, he became aware of the scent of her, sensual and cloyed with a heavy musk smell, beyond temptation.

Suddenly he was afraid, unwilling to risk her decision. Not until she knew how he felt. Not unless she trusted him and believed. He took the glass from her hand and set it with his own on a nearby table. She waited, silent and still, watching as he moved closer, touched her hair, gently brushed a stray curl from her forehead. Then his hand cupped her chin, their eyes met, and his voice was barely audible.

"Some things in life . . . you never know unless you try."

Her lips parted and he kissed her, warm and soft, almost tenderly. She trembled. A hot yearning flooded her body and her arms slowly encircled his neck. Then she came up on tiptoe and kissed him with a fierce, demanding urgency. His embrace tightened, banding them together, and he felt the movement of her hips. Suddenly she moaned and pulled away, buried her face into his chest, holding him with a wild, desperate possession.

"Oh, Warren, I want you. I *need* you. I've always needed you."

She pressed against his hardness and he groaned. "Jesus God! It's a two-hour drive back to your place."

"I can't wait. I've already waited too long."

"We could go upstairs. One of the bedrooms."

"No, not there. The housekeeper . . . she'd know."

"The fireplace. There's a bearskin rug . . . I could build a fire."

"Oh, yes. But the door . . . lock the door."

He kissed the tip of her nose, then walked quickly to the door and twisted the key. A whispery, rustling sound filled the room, and as he turned back, her skirt dropped to the floor. Their eyes met, a fragmented heartbeat frozen in time.

Then she smiled and began unbuttoning her blouse.

VII

The sun settled into the ocean with a spray of fire.

As dusk fell over the coastline, bats began stitching through the sky, and Curt Ruxton slowly lowered his binoculars. He was seated in the grove of redwoods that bordered the estate, hidden by the shadow of the forest. On a slight elevation, his position commanded a sweeping view of the grounds and the mansion.

This was the fifth day he'd come here, and it would be his last. The pattern was clear now, confirmed a moment ago when a guard and his attack dog had halted short of the cliffs and turned back along the fenceline. The implications of that single act, at last verified, swept over him so suddenly he felt as if his ears had come unplugged.

It could be done! At night, under the cover of darkness, by way of the sea. Not easily nor without considerable risk. But their vaunted security system wasn't so impregnable after all, and it *could* be done.

His eyebrows drew together in a thoughtful frown, and he examined all he'd learned. Slowly, carefully, he sifted through it for the slightest flaw.

In idle moments, he had toyed with the idea for nearly a month now, but he'd begun thinking of it in earnest less than ten days ago, the day the newspapers had reported an attempted hoax by one Alberto Santini and how he'd been exposed only at the last minute. A slick-talking con man had actually brazened his way into the mansion and the underground chamber. Of greater significance, if the stories were to be believed, he had come within a hair of outwitting the cryptography machine.

To Ruxton, who had analyzed the stories thoroughly,

a couple of things were apparent. Cryptanalysis was not a science to be mastered in a mere six months, and Santini had attempted a caper that demanded not one but several highly specialized skills. Any hope of success was clearly predicated on unraveling the secrets of Lucas Brokaw's crypt *before* approaching the foundation. And an individual, no matter how clever, could never accomplish that alone. The job called for an ultrasecret ferreting operation performed by a team of specialists. Only at the very last, with all the answers committed to memory, could a front man hope to pass himself off as Brokaw reincarnated.

Yet it could be done. He was certain of that now.

As darkness enveloped the land, he climbed to his feet and moved off through the redwoods toward his car. But he'd gone only a few paces when he suddenly stopped and laughed aloud, struck by a thought that had defied words until this very moment.

The fact that Lucas Brokaw could be reincarnated was almost irrelevant. The world was full of weirdos who accepted that as an article of faith. What separated him from the dreamers was logic, intellect, knowledge. Like water slowly formed into an icicle, his fantasy had crystallized and become reality. He had the very thing all the others had missed. The key.

Not only could it be done, he knew *how* to do it.

An hour later he entered the apartment.

Jill was puttering around in the kitchen, apparently overcome by one of her infrequent seizures of domesticity. Birkhead was sprawled out as usual on the sofa. A quick glance confirmed that neither of them was high, and he decided to lay it on them before the evening ritual got under way.

What he was about to propose called for clear heads and straight thinking. So he ignored their greetings, feigning some deep, inner preoccupation, which had the immediate effect of putting them on guard. Whenever he suffered a low mood they had learned to treat him with extreme deference. It was a trick he could now perform at will, and he often used it merely to keep them in line.

Jill tagged along from the kitchen, and he waved her to the sofa while he seated himself before the fireplace. A long silence ensued as he stared into the flames. Then, at last, he turned and leveled them with a piercing gaze.

"I've decided to pass myself off as Lucas Brokaw reincarnated."

His words claimed their attention like a clap of thunder. Birkhead jerked erect, staring at him, and Jill blinked, utterly bewildered, her mouth frozen in a breathless oval. Ruxton waited with spidery patience, allowing time for the shock to wear off. There was something of the phoenix about him—he forever arose anew and revitalized from their debaucheries—that gave him a source of strength his playmates lacked. In moments of reflection, particularly when he was stoned on pot, he often thought of himself as their messiah. Now he awaited their reaction. That they would be dumbfounded and perplexed he never doubted for an instant. Nor was he concerned. He would guide them and instruct them.

It took Birkhead a long while to realize the statement hadn't been made in jest. Finally, he shook his head, one eye cocked awry. "You're serious, aren't you? Honest to Christ serious . . . you really mean it!"

"Never more serious in my life. And I owe it all to you, old buddy. The idea germinated from our little talk about reincarnation. I simply added the finishing touches."

"Then you're out of your gourd! That was over a month ago. And we were all stoned. Hell, you even gave me a big put-down . . . said I was spaced out. Remember?"

Ruxton regarded him with great calmness. "You're

not listening, Monk. I didn't say I've been converted by all that nonsense. I merely said I intend to pass myself off as Lucas Brokaw."

"Oh, is that all?" Birkhead jeered. "Just a quick snow job and zappo! they buy your impersonation. Where's your head at, Curt? People have been trying that ever since Brokaw croaked, and nobody's pulled it off yet."

"You're talking apples and oranges. And in case you've forgotten, I'm not *people*. I function on a whole different level, so let's hear no more garbage about the masses. Got it straight, old buddy?"

"Hey, come on, Curt! Get off my back, will you? I didn't mean anything personal. It just sounds like bad news, that's all. Think about it a minute! Jesus Christ, they could put us in the slammer and throw away the key on a deal like this."

"That's precisely my point. I have been thinking about it. Or, to be more correct, I've already thought it out. What if I told you I've spent the last five days doing a cloak-and-dagger routine on the Brokaw estate?"

Birkhead groaned. "I don't even wanna hear about it."

"And what if I told you I've figured out a way for us to get our hands on the Brokaw fortune? The plan I have in mind is still a little rough around the edges, but essentially it's all we need to get the job done."

"Aww, holy shit! You've got rocks in your head. Those foundation guys are pros, real pros. You try working a scam on them and we'll lose everything we've got. The school and the franchise operation, the whole goddamn show. All of it!"

"One more time, Monk. Same song, second verse, so pay attention. If I had the brains to put all that together—and never so much as a squawk out of anyone—then I've got the brains to steer clear of anything I can't handle. Now quit hassling me for a minute and maybe you'll remember what separates the foxes from the oxes."

Ruxton's point was well taken. Their franchise operation amounted to little more than extortion. Outwardly legitimate, it involved a maze of fine print backed by implied threats that siphoned off a lion's share of the profits to the parent company. While Birkhead nodded, digesting the thought, his gaze settled on Jill. "What about you, kitten? It's one for all and all for one. So don't be bashful, speak up."

Jill hugged herself, suddenly chilled, and gave him a brittle smile. "Truthfully, it scares the hell out of me. And Monk's right, luv. The people at that foundation aren't dumdums. So it could get hairy, especially if we're caught. But on the other hand—"

"Go ahead, don't stop now. On the other hand—what?"

Jill giggled mischievously and hugged herself tighter. "Well, not that I'm greedy or anything, but it's an awful lot of money. And if you have a plan that really would work, then maybe we ought to try it. Just for kicks. You know, like in the movies. A caper."

"Hear that, Monk? The lady votes 'yea' for a caper. So how about it . . . still got the balls for a little action?"

"Don't worry about my balls!" Birkhead flared angrily. "Come on, big shot. Lay it out! We'll see who backs off first."

Ruxton looked like a tiger who had just eaten his keeper. He lounged back in his chair, gazing out the window at the harbor lights, and his smirk slowly widened into a smug grin. Then he told them what he had in mind.

VIII

Again he got that sharp stab of *déjà vu*.

Night was coming on, and to the west billowing clouds scudded across a cobalt horizon. Standing at the window, Tanner watched the dying flare of day disappear into the ocean.

It was as though it had all happened before.

Not yesterday or last week, but at some distant, long ago time he couldn't quite remember. And still it was the same. Precisely as he saw it in his mind's eye. There in the study, looking out over the coastline, mesmerized by a sunset forever quenched in a watery grave.

A sudden chill settled over him and passed just as quickly. Yet it left a residue of uneasiness, some deeper sensation that refused to be shunted aside. It was a feeling he often had these days, vague and disjointed, fuzzy in the way of an elusive dream. Certain parts of the grounds and the mansion now had a haunting familiarity; standing at the study window was particularly disconcerting. Perhaps oddest of all was that he traced it directly to his experiment with Alberto Santini.

Tanner hadn't come away from the incident with anything near the equanimity he pretended. The director had eventually simmered down, satisfied Tanner had acted in the best of interests of the foundation (if not altogether pleased with his secretive methods). And Stacey, vastly impressed by the way he'd handled both the investigation and Hamilton Knox, thought it a marvelous piece of improvisation. But Tanner found himself more troubled than before, disquieted rather than encouraged by what he'd learned.

Curiously, in the aftermath of the incident, he had grown increasingly concerned about the underground chamber. Although his hunch had been confirmed—the code was meant to be broken—the implications were far more sinister than he'd first suspected. The cryptography machine was merely bait! Lucas Brokaw had apparently put it there, exposed and vulnerable, with the very sure knowledge that someone would unscramble the cipher. Which led to an inescapable conclusion.

There was something awaiting an imposter once he got past the machine. Something known only to Lucas Brokaw. And it required no great feat of imagination to conclude that, whatever it was, it was something lethal.

Tanner quickly focused on an obscure clause in Brokaw's will: *Should disaster occur while a claimant is attempting to pass the tests, there is a final, unrevealed secret concerning my crypt. Anyone who later uncovers this secret will thereafter be acknowledged as Lucas Brokaw reincarnated.* With the Santini experience behind him, Tanner had realized that the stipulation was not a catchall clause thrown in to cover the possibility of an accident.

Nothing in the crypt had been designed by chance. It was all very premeditated, in fact, and accident played no part in the obstacle course laid out by Lucas Brokaw. Tanner was certain that the word *disaster* meant a planned disaster. A disaster that merely awaited an unknowing imposter to trigger it off.

Subsequently, convinced that a link existed between the cryptography machine and the disaster clause, Tanner had revamped the security system at the estate. He added another guard whose sole responsibility was to patrol the area immediately around the mansion; in addition, he installed an electronic alarm at the foyer entrance of the subterranean stairway. Several other measures he recommended, particularly closed circuit television in the crypt itself, were overruled by the director as unnecessary and too costly. Since his suspicions were a mix of hunch and supposition, he couldn't justify further expenditure. So he counted himself lucky to have effected any change at all.

Yet his apprehension was very real, and he'd devoted a good deal of time to analyzing the security setup. It was then, during a period of nearly two weeks he'd spent at the estate, that he had begun experiencing those quick flashes of *déjà vu*. They came over him in fits and starts, fleeting glimpses of things he'd seen before, not just as they were at that moment but rather as they had been at some point in the past. A time beyond recollection and by its very vividness all the more baffling.

Uneasy, bemused by the sensation, he had resisted a strong temptation to discuss it with Stacey. However real it was in his own mind, he suspected she would find the notion absurd. Which was perhaps the one risk he couldn't bring himself to face.

And now, watching the dusky horizon, the eerie feeling persisted. He'd seen it before. Not just once but hundreds of times. That exact sunset.

It was enough to make the gooseflesh crawl, but he told himself that it was nothing more than a kind of sensory logic in which his mind absorbed everything, trivia and hard facts and images forgotten long ago. Then, like a blender crammed with random bits of information, his brain concocted what he saw and supplied the rationale for its being there. A product of the subliminal, snatched by the moment from some dark and shadowed corner of his mind. It made perfect sense.

But he never for an instant believed it. Nor was he willing to consider other explanations, however reasonable. He couldn't because none of them was true.

The truth was he'd seen that sunset. *A long time ago.*

On the horizon there was now a watery rim of gold. Then a single streamer of fire split apart, leaping high, and cleaved the darkening sky. It flickered and burst like a fading flare and slowly dissolved into a mere pin-prick of light.

Tanner stood transfixed. His vision blurred and the distant spark became a tiny, pulsating dot within his eyes. A faint dizziness swept over him, grew stronger, beckoned him deeper into a lazy vertigo. Then his vision glazed . . . .

A chill stirring brushed his cheek.

There was a moment before he nodded, eyes fixed in a hollow stare, and turned away from the window. He walked directly to the desk and seated himself in the high-backed chair. Without hesitation, he leaned forward, ran his arm beneath the desk, and pressed a strip of molding behind the center panel. A seam appeared along the back edge of the heavy walnut top, then a spring clicked and a shallow drawer popped open. Narrow and flat, almost a tray, it contained a sheaf of documents.

He removed the papers, slowly scanned the letterhead, and after a long while, he blinked. The glazed look disappeared from his eyes, and his lips parted in a thin smile. He lit a cigarette, inhaled deeply, and settled back in the chair.

Then he began to read.

Shortly after seven, Tanner arrived at Stacey's apartment. She met him in a magenta hostess gown that accentuated the dark sheen of her hair and did little to hide the lovely curves of her figure. Her eyes sparkled, and as she took his hand, her voice was like a warm caress.

"Ummmmm, it's good to see you. Things just aren't the same when you're away from the office. I couldn't wait to get home! Isn't that shameless of me?"

Suddenly he caught her up in a rough embrace and kissed her, then set her down so fast she swayed dizzily. But his hands encircled her waist and her arms went around his neck, pulling his mouth back to her in a long, lingering kiss. She clung to him wantonly, aware of nothing but the man and the moment and the strength of his arms. When at last their lips parted, she burrowed close against his chest, and their silence was as intimate as the touch of hands on naked flesh.

This was how it had been since their afternoon before the fireplace on the bearskin rug. Any vestige of restraint, all her misgivings about office affairs and emotional involvement had simply vanished. She cast aside the cool detachment that masked the woman underneath and admitted what she'd known all along: that he was the man she wanted, the man she meant to have.

It was the same for Tanner. Not so sudden nor nearly so open and heedless of the consequences. He was a very private man, and never before had he laid himself bare to anyone. Yet wherever he turned his restless inner eye these days, she was there, always a part of his thoughts. Perhaps all the more revealing was what the nearness of her did to him. Whenever they were together his iron impassivity simply deserted him; he became someone else, another man—warmer and gentler, not quite so cynical, and for the first time in his life, vulnerable.

Even now, as he held her cloaked in his arms, he knew they might yet hurt one another. This was no casual affair, some transitory sleeping arrangement. Their affinity was too strong, too genuine. So palpable that it had touched their lives in a way neither of them had ever anticipated.

The thought frightened him. Not for his own sake, because he knew he was as capable of absorbing punishment as he was of inflicting pain. He was frightened for her.

Stacey was no less intuitive in her own way. By now she could sense his every mood, and tonight, despite the warmth of his greeting, she knew he was worried about something. Before the moment could be spoiled, she slipped from his embrace. Her smile was disarming, and as she led him toward a small bar in the corner, her voice had a teasing lilt.

"By sheer coincidence, I happen to have a pitcher of martinis freshly chilled. If your day was anything like mine, then I suspect you could use a bracer."

Tanner seated himself on a bar stool while she poured. "What's the matter . . . Knox on the warpath again?"

"No, darling, not *again*. That's much too charitable. I'm afraid our leader is *always* on the warpath."

"Why the switch? I thought you liked the old boy."

"Oh, I do! He's thoughtful and kind, and he believes women deserve equal opportunity and equal pay." She paused, and took a thoughtful sip of her martini. "But sometimes he's so—"

"Don't be inhibited," Tanner prompted her with a smile. "You're among friends."

"Well, I know it sounds bitchy—and I really don't mean it that way—but sometimes he's so insufferably picayune."

"Picayune? Jesus, what a thing to call somebody."

"Not at all. I mean, he did ask us to audit petty cash."

Tanner cocked one eye skeptically. "You're kidding!"

"And later he had an absolute temper tantrum about everyone taking too many coffee breaks."

"Come on. That's a little much even for Squire Knox."

"I agree, but you haven't heard the best part yet. He had the gall to suggest that you were squandering foundation funds by spending all your time at the estate."

Too late, Tanner saw the trap. "And I suppose you agreed with him?"

"Of course. How can I function properly when I never see you any more?" All the while she chattered her eyes had been guileless, but now she tilted her chin and smiled mischievously. "Don't worry though, darling, I covered for you."

"I'll just bet you did. Go ahead, give me the punch line."

"No punch line. I simply told him the truth."

"The truth?"

"Yes. That you feel a very personal bond toward the foundation and the estate. So you're just naturally superconscientious."

"Okay, I'm in this deep . . . I might as well bite. What's the personal bond?"

"Why, that you were born on the fortieth day. To be exact, September 2, 1947. I was curious about your sign—incidentally, I just adore Virgos—so I checked your personnel file. Voilà!"

Tanner gave her a blank look. "I don't get it. The fortieth day of what?"

"What else! The fortieth day after Lucas Brokaw died."

"Terrific. So what's the big deal?"

"Are you serious? You really don't know?"

"Christ, I'm starting to sound like an echo. Know *what*?"

"Oh, I'm sorry, darling. I just assumed . . . well, don't you see, a great many Buddhist sects believe reincarnation occurs on the fortieth day. So, there you have it. Your birthday!"

"Yeah, sure. And Brokaw was convinced it took place on the first day. Which sort of punctures your balloon, doesn't it?"

"Yes, I know. Everyone's confused on that point." She brightened and darted him a sly glance. "But I suppose that's what makes life interesting, isn't it? The forks in the road."

Stacey watched him out of the corner of her eye, enjoying herself immensely. At the office she was precise and efficient, her business day as expertly choreographed as a ballet. Yet in idle moments, alone and dreamy, she felt she had been born out of her time. Quite secretly she yearned to have been the mistress of a nobleman on some vast estate in czarist Russia. To dance to the balalaika and live a life of roses and Dom Pérignon. To ride off into the night and make love astride a fiery-eyed stallion in a moonlit forest. The decor of her apartment even lent itself to this fantasy world. It was an evocative mélange of exotic Oriental and rugged Mediterranean, all brought together with the flair of a true romantic. It provided a glimpse of those dark reveries she kept bottled up within herself.

Tonight, all of it spilled over in a vast outpouring of gaiety and love. She saw before her the czar astride his black stallion. And beyond, beckoning softly, the moonlit forest.

At length, Tanner became aware of the look. Amused but still uncertain, he eyed her quizzically. "You've been putting me on, haven't you? Every word of it. All that stuff about the fortieth day and—"

"No, honestly, that's the truth. Cross my heart."

"Maybe so. But I'll lay odds you didn't tell the director about it, right? C'mon now, 'fess up. That whole routine was strictly for my benefit, wasn't it?"

"Well, of course it was. But where's the harm in a little white lie?" She pouted and glanced aside. "I mean, really, just go take a look at yourself in the mirror. It's obvious you're tired and worried and overworked. So I thought I'd liven you up a bit." Her gaze swung back, and there was a certain bawdy wisdom in her eyes. "Evidently it worked. Not that I'm any wizard . . . but you don't look nearly as worried as you did a few minutes ago."

Tanner's mouth curled in a raffish smile. He twitched his head in the direction of the bedroom door.

She laughed suddenly, spontaneously, and threw her arms around his neck. It seemed to her she could hear the strains of a balalaika. And there was a definite scent of roses in the air.

IX

The sea was choppy and the sky overcast.

A light fog drifted inland, but the coastline was visible a half mile off starboard. The cabin cruiser bobbed on the swells, engines throttled back, as Jill played the wheel to hold it on a heading of north-northwest. On deck, Ruxton was crouched down, arms locked over the side, steadying a Nikon with a telephoto lens. He was shooting fast speed, with an open lens setting to compensate for murky light, and had already put two rolls of film through the camera. Further astern, legs braced against the pitch of the sea, Monk Birkhead was scanning the cliffs through powerful naval binoculars.

Ruxton had instructed Jill to keep the boat at reduced speed until they cleared a jutting promontory north of the estate. In case they were observed from the mansion or by one of the guards, it would appear they were making slow headway in a rough sea. This gave them an unobstructed view of the cliffs for approximately ten minutes. While it was all the time needed to finish filming, it was far less than Birkhead would have liked for his visual inspection. But they dared not draw attention to themselves by anchoring or risk being spotted offshore more than once without arousing suspicion. So this one pass was it. A quick look, along with photo enlargements, would have to do.

Several moments later they rounded the promontory, and Jill eased into full throttle. The cruiser was a thirty-six-footer with an inboard engine and twin screws, and wide open, batted along at almost forty knots an hour. Although it was built to absorb punishment, the ride on choppy seas at full speed was bone jarring. Every time the bottom slapped into a wave, Ruxton and Birkhead were buffeted around in a wild scramble to keep to their feet. Hauling himself hand over hand by the railing, Birkhead made his way forward and with a final lunge threw open the cabin door.

"You dizzy bitch! Throttle down. Now, goddamnit!"

Jill laughed, her eyes glittering with excitement. "Up yours, mate! I'm the captain here. Hang on and enjoy it."

She was above him, on the helmsman's seat, and while Birkhead couldn't reach the controls, he could reach her. He grabbed her ankle and bore down with a viselike grip. "Do it—now!"

The pain numbed her entire leg, and all the color drained from her face. She throttled back so fast Birkhead lost his grip, stumbling across the companionway into the far wall. The cruiser slammed to a halt, wallowing in a trough, then began rocking with the rhythmic slap of the waves. Birkhead caromed off the wall, his face livid, and started toward the girl. Suddenly Ruxton stepped through the door, still clutching the camera, and blocked his path.

"Hold it, Monk. Enough's enough."

"Butt out, man! She's got it coming."

"Not unless I say so." Ruxton held his position, eyes hooded, impassive yet coldly insistent. "We're in agreement on that, aren't we, Monk?"

A moment passed, then Birkhead shrugged, glancing aside. "Yeah, I guess so. But I still say it was a stupid trick! She could've swamped this boat and us with it."

Ruxton turned to the girl. "Monk's right—it *was* stupid. Very dumb and very juvenile."

Jill stopped rubbing her ankle and gave him a huffy look. "Well, the big bastard didn't have to get rough about it. And besides, I was just having a little fun. Where's the harm in that?"

"This isn't a fun exercise. Or did that slip your mind?"

"God, Curt, sometimes you're a real killjoy! I had

this boat under control the whole time and you know it very well."

"Don't do it again." Ruxton smiled pleasantly and patted her leg. "Otherwise I'll let Monk finish the job. Understand?"

Jill understood perfectly. Her expression changed, and she quickly bobbed her head, avoiding his gaze. "Sorry, luv. It won't happen again . . . promise."

"Good girl." Ruxton closed the door and leaned back against it. "You two can kiss and make up later. Right now, let's see where we are." His eyes shifted to the big man. "What about it, Monk? Any problem with those cliffs?"

"Not if you're a goat!" Birkhead grunted coarsely. "In case you didn't notice, they're steep as hell."

Birkhead's opinion was vital. Their entire plan hinged on being able to scale the cliffs to the mansion. As a Green Beret, he had undergone alpine training and he was the only one qualified to make the judgment.

"So they're steep and it won't be easy." Ruxton studied him intently. "But they can be climbed, right?"

"Anything can be climbed if you've got the right equipment."

"That's out. We can't afford the noise, and we can't afford to leave any marks on those cliffs. It has to be done quietly and quickly, with no trace that we were ever there."

"You don't want much, d'ya?" Birkhead sniffed and wiped his nose. "Hell, who knows, maybe we could get by with ropes and fancy footwork. It's hard to say till I get a closer look."

"No sweat there." Ruxton tapped the camera with his finger. "I'll have these films blown up and then we'll paste together a composite. Under a magnifying glass you'll be able to spot every little crack and crevice."

"Big deal! Suppose the rest of the troops have two left feet? What do we do then, carry them up that cliff piggyback?"

Birkhead had a point. The cliffs were merely the first obstacle and could prove less of a challenge than what awaited them inside the mansion. Yet Ruxton had never fooled himself on that score. While the operation revolved around a team of experts, men of specialized skills, all the expertise in the world was of no value at the bottom of the cliffs. And as his planning had progressed, he'd come to realize that the first step was quite literally the longest.

Essentially, what he had in mind was something on the order of a commando raid, to be carried out in utter secrecy, with nothing disturbed and not the slightest hint that the subterranean crypt had been penetrated. Above all, there must be nothing to connect him with the Brokaw fortune. For that reason, he had resisted the temptation to search out building plans or former contractors or anything directly related to the estate itself.

Instead, relying on Jill and Birkhead, he had spent the last two weeks gathering information in a roundabout manner. Through the microfilm repository at the library, Jill had put together a file on everything ever written about the Brokaw legend. Over the years, the press had interviewed former guards and several claimants who had actually seen the crypt; these eyewitness accounts provided an invaluable source of material about the layout of the subterranean chamber. By collating all the bits and pieces, she had arrived at a fairly accurate picture of what they could expect once inside the mansion. Working on another angle, Birkhead had toured the city's nightspots, particularly those with mob connections, and ultimately turned up a name.

Johnny Fallon.

A man of low profile, almost a will-o'-the-wisp, Fallon was a safecracker who had been arrested twenty-three times and never once convicted. This record was all the more extraordinary in that he disdained the use of nitro or a torch. The safes he opened were left exactly as he'd found them, but the secret of how he did it was one of the great mysteries of the underworld.

The cabin cruiser was also Birkhead's assignment. He had leased it in the name of their corporation, rented dock space, and spent several hours every morning instructing Jill in its operation. While they were engaged in these activities, Ruxton had remained in the background, devoting himself to a crash course in cryptology. Not so much a study of the field itself, but rather a detailed examination of known cryptanalysts, those shadowy figures rarely mentioned except in obscure scientific journals who specialized in breaking codes. Only yesterday he'd turned up a name himself, the name of a man no less enigmatic than Johnny Fallon and equally vital to their plan.

All of which brought him back to Birkhead's question. That first step. The cliffs.

His mouth creased in a disingenuous smile. "You'll find a way, old buddy. And if it has to be piggyback . . . well, why not? You've got a strong back."

Birkhead barked a sharp, short laugh. "You're awful damn sure of yourself, aren't you?"

"So sure that tomorrow we start looking for Mr. Johnny Fallon. After all, if we mean to get this show on the road, then it's time we began assembling the cast. The sooner the better, as a matter of fact. One way or another, I have an idea some of them might require a bit of persuasion."

Almost as an afterthought he turned to Jill. "That reminds me . . . you get the role of Mata Hari. I'll admit it sounds like typecasting, but don't let that put you off. It's a very *juicy* part."

Jill gave him a blank look. "Who's Mata Hari?"

"The original foxy lady, that's who! You see, she used her wiles and guiles to seduce men and learn their secrets. Only in this case we don't want the secrets, we want the man."

"You want me to"—her voice trailed off wistfully—"to sleep with someone?"

Ruxton felt nothing. Day by day he'd grown more obsessed with the caper, and lately his sexual needs had fallen off sharply. As though he hadn't the energy to spare, he'd abstained from physical contact for nearly a week. Even now, knowing what he was about to ask of her, his thoughts were on the plan and not the girl. He regarded her curiously for a moment, almost a clinical appraisal. Then he smiled. It was an intimate smile, lacking any great warmth, but tempered by a faint emotional shadow.

"Suppose we head back to the marina. On the way, I'll tell you a little story. It's about a man in Washington. A very special man. I think you'll like him. His name is Chester Wilson."

Jill engaged the throttle and brought the cruiser about, slowly reversing course. As he talked, she listened closely, glancing at him from time to time. But she couldn't fathom his expression, nor did she try. Instead, she concentrated on the words, blocking everything else out. There was a sort of satanic genius to what he proposed, and she found nothing remarkable in the fact that she wasn't surprised. It had to be done, and as he wryly noted, she was the one best equipped to do it. Yet the idea was loathsome, and despite all his glib assurances, she wished the trip really weren't necessary.

Washington in the winter was a bummer. Wet and miserably cold, and so far away. The dark side of the moon.

So lonely.

X

"I must say, Mr. Tanner, you have my curiosity aroused."

"Oh, in what way, professor?"

"Why, the mere fact that you're sitting here for one thing. Not to be blunt about it, but I'm afraid the purpose of your visit isn't quite clear."

"Sorry. I thought I explained that on the phone."

"Hardly. You said you were interested in discussing Lucas Brokaw. That's a reason, Mr. Tanner. Not an explanation."

George Ludmann was too old for diplomacy, and he valued his time far too much to waste it on idle conversation. As professor of the occult sciences, he had become something of an institution at Stanford, holding tenure for nearly forty years. While his color was jaundiced and his hands were mottled with liver spots, there was an ageless quality about him. He was alert and inquisitive, never without a pungent riposte, and still possessed the mental agility that had confounded several generations of undergraduates.

And he wasn't at all taken in by Tanner's story.

Ludmann tilted back in his chair, folding his arms, and stared across the desk. An ancient pipe jutted out of his jaw like a walrus tusk, and he puffed on it in silence, fully prepared to outwait the younger man. He'd asked for an explanation, and before he proceeded further, he meant to have it.

At last Tanner lit a cigarette, took a couple of quick drags, and gave him a lame smile. "To tell you the truth, professor, I don't even have a good reason. I'm here on a fishing expedition."

"Perhaps you could be a bit more specific?"

"No, not really. I'm not even sure what the questions are, much less the answers."

"Then why are you here at all, Mr. Tanner?"

"Well, as you know, I'm with the foundation—"

"Yes, of course. I was aware of that before you called."

"—and I've been investigating certain aspects of Lucas Brokaw's past."

Ludmann blinked and slowly removed the pipe from his mouth. "I beg your pardon?"

"Actually, it's not an official investigation. There are a few loose ends that bothered me, and it's really more a matter of satisfying my own curiosity."

"I'm not sure I follow you, Mr. Tanner. What loose ends?"

Tanner sensed he'd struck a nerve, but he decided the oblique approach was still best. "Little things, professor. As an example, why did Brokaw suddenly become a convert to reincarnation? By his own admission he'd been a practicing agnostic all his life."

"I take it you find that strange?"

"Not just strange. Highly paradoxical! Everything indicates he was converted shortly after learning he had cancer. That's further substantiated by the fact that he began construction on his underground crypt almost five weeks to the day after receiving the prognosis from his doctor. So there's definitely a link."

"I see." Ludmann knocked the dottle from his pipe, thoughtful a moment. "Anything else?"

"Well, it's obvious something extraordinary happened during those five weeks. Something that turned Brokaw's life completely around. I also have reason to believe it affected the way he died."

"Is that conjecture or fact?"

"A little of both, I suppose. But consider the circumstances. He died on the night of his birthday, within hours after signing his will, and exactly one day after

98

construction was completed on his crypt. Taken together, that sort of strains the law of coincidence."

Tanner paused, stubbing out his cigarette in an ashtray. "I think Brokaw killed himself. Probably with an overdose of drugs."

"For a man seeking answers, you seem very well informed, Mr. Tanner. May I ask how you came by your information?"

"The same way I came by your name, professor."

"Oh? And how was that?"

"Brokaw kept all his personal papers in a secret drawer of his desk." Tanner smiled, alert to the slightest reaction. "Let's just say I stumbled across it."

Ludmann met his look squarely. "Then you know."

"Yes, professor, I know."

Tanner was convincing. His offhand manner, backed by a confident smile, suggested he knew everything. Yet he was actually at a dead end, and despite his bold demeanor, he was bluffing.

The trail that led him to George Ludmann had been long and frustrating. True, the records he'd unearthed had provided him with dates and names previously unknown to anyone except Lucas Brokaw. By piecing together unrelated bits of information, he was able to establish a sequence of events for the last weeks of Brokaw's life. But the records themselves led him nowhere. The physician who had attended Brokaw was in a mental institution. Edgar Pollard, the attorney of record and Brokaw's sole confidant, was deceased. Two of the three contractors who had worked on the crypt were also deceased, and the third man had simply vanished. Approval or permits had not been sought from the county planning board, and as far as Tanner could determine, blueprints of the crypt either never existed or else had been destroyed by Brokaw.

Nearly two weeks of legwork had brought him roughly full circle. Except for a name. Professor George

Ludmann. And a curious grant of $2,000,000 donated by a dummy corporation and untraceable to anyone without access to the private files of Lucas Brokaw.

Now, seated across from Ludmann, he lit another cigarette and waited. Beyond the fact that the grant had been made, he knew absolutely nothing. Nor was he willing to speculate and expose his hand. The important thing was what the professor *thought* he knew. With a little luck and a bold front it might be enough.

Ludmann took a long while loading his pipe. Although rattled, his hand was steady and he appeared to be playing for time. At length, after he'd fired up the pipe, his eyes narrowed in a reflective squint.

"Frankly, Mr. Tanner, I find it hard to believe that Lucas Brokaw would have left those records so . . . unprotected."

"As a matter of fact, they're quite heavily guarded. I just happen to have unrestricted access to his study."

"I see. And other than yourself, who knows about your discovery?"

"I assume you mean the grant . . . the two million?"

The figure jarred Ludmann. Several moments passed before he could speak. "Yes, Mr. Tanner. The grant."

Tanner saw the look and decided to try a shot in the dark. "Professor, you knew Brokaw as well as anyone—perhaps better—so let me ask you a question. Do you think he would have wanted this information made public?"

"Good God, no!" Ludmann was obviously appalled by the thought. "One of the last things he said to me was that the whole affair must be kept confidential."

"Then I'll make a deal with you. Fill in the holes for me—the details of what happened during those five weeks—and I won't tell anyone about the grant. You have my word on it."

"Your word! Come now, Mr. Tanner. Do you really expect me to accept the word of someone who has just rifled the files of a dead man?"

"That's hardly the point," Tanner corrected him. "We're not debating my use of expedient methods. The fact is you don't have any choice. Do you, professor?"

Ludmann pursed his lips, seeming to deliberate, then slowly let out his breath. "Very well. But I warn you, it's far easier to pull the cork than it is to put the demon back in the bottle."

"You're wasting your time, professor. I don't believe in witchcraft or demonology or anything else related to the occult. So save your warnings and just give me hard facts."

"Hard facts are my stock in trade, Mr. Tanner. That may appear to be a contradiction in terms, but I assure you, it's not so difficult to convert the skeptic as you might believe."

There was a moment of calculation, then Tanner frowned. "Lucas Brokaw?"

Ludmann swiveled around in his chair. The wall behind his desk held row upon row of built-in bookcases extending from floor to ceiling. Several hundred tape casettes were stacked on the lower shelves, and Tanner could hear him muttering to himself as he rummaged through the collection. At last, with a satisfied grunt, he swung back around. In his hand was a sixty-minute cassette. He leaned forward, opening the cover of a tape recorder on his desk.

"This will answer all your questions, Mr. Tanner. The original became somewhat fragile, so I've transcribed it, but I can vouch for its authenticity."

Ludmann inserted the cassette into the recorder and pressed a switch. "Allow me to introduce you to Lucas Brokaw."

XI

. . . and then . . . oh God, I couldn't believe it. Not the general! Stuck that pistol upside his head and . . . and just blew his brains out. I wanted to puke. Only nothin' come out. It was like I had the dry heaves. Like my guts was up in my throat but something was lodged in my craw, and I couldn't get my mouth open. I just stood there and they rode him down. Hundreds of 'em . . . rode right over him. I couldn't move . . . felt cold and sick . . . froze up inside. So I stood there watchin'.

You saw Custer fall and . . . go on. What happened next?

Like I told you, I froze plumb to the marrow. I seen it and I knew it was real, but it weren't right. Gawddamn, he weren't no pisswillie. Not him. He was a soldier!

So you felt as though he'd taken the coward's way out?

Bet your rusty butt that's what he done. We'd been in a tight fix lots of times . . . hell, durin' the war we must'a been surrounded a hundred times . . . and we always fought clear. But up there on that hill, he lost his nerve. Don't you see, he showed the white feather!

And in your view that was inexcusable.

Worse'n that. It was a gawddamn blasphemy! Went against everything he stood for. Everything he'd taught me since I joined up 'fore Bull Run. Weren't no way for a soldier to die. Specially a general. Just showed he was yellow the whole time. Nothin' but a blowhard!

Yes, I understand. So go on . . . after he killed himself?

Why, I looked up and saw this big red booger ridin'

*straight at me. Had one of them war clubs, the kind
with a spike stickin' out of the top. Anytime else, I
guess it would've curdled my milk. But I just squared
up . . . sort of come to attention . . . and gave him
the old evil eye.*

You didn't try to run? Or fight back?

*Wasn't no need. Don't you see, it was like I'd already
cashed in my chips. After I saw what the general done I
just didn't give a shit. I was good as dead anyway, so
what the hell? Figgered the least I could do was show
that red heathen that somebody in the outfit had a little
guts.*

*And he . . . that is to say, the warrior . . . what
did he do?*

*Near as I recollect, he snuffed me out with that club.
Not that I exactly remember it, you understand. But the
last thing I saw was that big spike comin' down, and
then . . .*

*Yes, don't stop. You saw the club, and then what
happened?*

*Well, I don't rightly know. It's like I was lost for
awhile, and then all of a sudden I was just . . . sort of
wanderin' around.*

Where were you?

*That's hard to say. I know it was light, though. Light
and clear, real bright.*

Was it a place?

Not just a place. It was . . . it was more like space.

Did you know you were dead?

Oh, sure. No doubt about that.

Did it bother you . . . knowing that you were dead?

I was sad. Not unhappy, but kind of discontent.

Were you aware of the passage of time?

*Not especially. I was aware of . . . I guess it was
sort of like waiting.*

*This place where you were . . . was there someone
in authority? Anyone who took charge?*

Yeah, but not the way you mean. I felt bound by . . . someone.

Did he take form . . . the form of a person?

No. It was a power.

Who had the power?

It came from somewhere . . . higher.

Did you ever see the power?

Not just exactly. I saw . . . all I saw was the light.

Above you?

Beyond. Way far off.

Did you speak to the light?

Yeah, lots of times.

And did it answer you?

Sure.

What did it say?

It said to be patient.

Did it tell you how long you had to stay there?

No, not outright. It always said I could . . . could go on farther.

The voice from the light said that?

Yeah.

What did it tell you . . . precisely?

It told me I could choose . . . if I stopped feeling sorry for myself. That I could go ahead.

Did the voice tell you where that was?

Not in words. I just knew it was final . . . real peaceful.

What happened then?

I searched for a long time. Searched for someone . . . him.

Did you ask the light to help you find him?

No, I just waited.

And finally you came back?

That's right.

Now, when you came back . . . do you remember how you were born?

I felt it was time. I was . . . shown.

What steps did you go through?

None. No steps.

How did you enter the world . . . your new self?

I didn't. I was just there.

And what did you remember?

Nothing.

At that moment . . . the instant you were reborn . . . were you still troubled about your previous life?

No, it was all dark. There was lots of noise. Like a twister . . . black and that loud rushing noise.

Did you see anything?

I told you, it was dark.

But did you see anything . . . anything at all?

No. It was done. All over.

And did you hear the voice again?

I couldn't. I left it behind . . . in the light.

So you remember nothing else?

Nothing. Not after the darkness.

I see. Very well, Sergeant Hughes, I believe we'll stop there. When I count three, you will awaken. One . . . two . . . three . . . .

Christ, I must've dozed off. What happened? Did you put me under?

In a sense, Mr. Brokaw. To be more precise, I took you back in time.

To the dream?

Yes, to the dream. And beyond that . . . farther back. Would you like to hear it?

Course I would. What the hell you think I'm here for . . . thirty winks?

Quite so. But first, let me ask you . . . do you remember anything we discussed? Anything at all?

Not a word. Say, listen here, none of your mumbo jumbo. Was I under or wasn't I?

Suppose you judge for yourself, Mr. Brokaw. Please bear with me while I rewind the tape.

CLICK

Tanner shook his head. "That's eerie stuff. I suppose it sounds trite, but it was like hearing . . ."

"A voice from the grave?"

"Yes, exactly. Only there were two voices. At the end there, when you woke Brokaw, it was almost as if you were talking to another man."

"I was, Mr. Tanner." Ludmann regarded him impassively. "Under hypnosis, the subject invariably assumes the mannerisms and speech patterns of his former incarnation. In this case, I was talking with Sergeant John Hughes . . . through Lucas Brokaw."

"Then Brokaw wasn't an isolated case?"

"Hardly. I've documented dozens of such cases over the years. Contrary to what many people think, reincarnation isn't a rare phenomenon. It's really quite common."

"Was that why Brokaw came to you . . . because of your reputation?"

"Partly. And of course the dream."

Tanner nodded, silent a moment. "When was this tape made, professor? The date?"

"January 26, 1947."

"By rough estimate, that would have been three weeks or so after his doctor informed him he was terminal."

"Three weeks and five days, to be exact."

"And approximately ten days before construction was begun on his crypt."

"As I recall, that's correct."

"So this tape was the turning point. It confirmed everything he'd seen in the dream, and once he heard a replay, he never looked back. That's what you meant about converting a skeptic, right?"

"I prefer to think of the tape as a catalyst. Actually, a good deal had already transpired when Brokaw came to see me."

"You mean the dream?"

"Not altogether. Of course, the dream was a nightly

recurrence—precisely the same in every detail—so Brokaw began to suspect something abnormal long before he contacted me. In a manner of speaking, he established his own bridge with the past. I merely guided him across and helped confirm what he found on the other side."

"I'm afraid I don't follow you, professor. What bridge?"

"That's something of a story within itself, Mr. Tanner. Really quite remarkable." Ludmann's pipe had gone cold, but he scarcely seemed to notice. He continued to suck on it, his expression abstracted, gazing off into space. "Keep in mind, Lucas Brokaw was a man of action and he knew he had only six months to live. So he took a direct and highly perceptive approach to this matter of the dream. Let me explain."

With time at a premium, Brokaw had hired an entire team of historical researchers. It required whirlwind planning and immediate access to the National Archives, not to mention a monumental fee. But their assignment was without precedent and of such magnitude that it seemed doomed to failure.

Less than a month later, however, Brokaw's hunch paid off with spectacular results. The researchers established that there had been *one* sergeant with Custer in those final moments on the knoll above the Little Big Horn—Sergeant John Hughes.

Then, virtually overnight, the research team established corroboration from a most unlikely source. The Indian version of Custer's Last Stand had been preserved by Red Horse, a Sioux war chief who participated in the battle, in the form of crude drawings etched on deerskin. These obscure pictographs, lost to scholars for nearly seven decades, were discovered in long forgotten storage vaults beneath the Smithsonian Institution. Red Horse had illustrated the battle from beginning to end. His final drawing was the clincher. It depicted Yellowhair Custer committing suicide, while in the foreground a pony soldier sergeant stood stiff as a ramrod while a Sioux chief brained him with a war club. In a verbal account of the battle (conveyed in sign language and transcribed by an army surgeon in 1881), Red Horse identified himself as the war chief and recalled with amazement how the sergeant had stood there as if in a trance, almost as though he welcomed death.

Still another mystery had been solved at the same time. Of the 215 dead men littering the battlefield, only Custer and Sergeant John Hughes had not been scalped. In his statement, Red Horse observed that Sioux warriors never took the scalp of a man who had destroyed himself, such as Yellowhair and the sergeant who embraced death. The scalps of such men were cursed, according to Red Horse, as was the man himself, who would forever wander through the afterlife without his soul. It was a chilling thought, made all the more personal for Lucas Brokaw by the vividness and brutal clarity of his dream.

Yet, even with seemingly irrefutable evidence at hand, Brokaw hadn't been satisfied. He was a practicing agnostic, a devout skeptic with the methodical mind of a scientist. So he had gone one step further. He had contacted George Ludmann at Stanford to undertake a hurried course in reincarnation. There he discovered that experiences such as his were by no means unprecedented and that dreams were the most widely accepted manifestation of a previous life. Ultimately, he allowed the professor to hypnotize him and then regress him to that fateful day on the Little Big Horn. It was then that Sergeant John Hughes retold the horror of his death and the wonder of his rebirth *on the very same day.*

Lucas Brokaw's birthday.

Afterward, listening to a playback on the tape recorder, Brokaw had at last been convinced. Neither the words nor the voice were his own. But it had all been spoken through his mouth, and with the zeal of a convert, he had quickly set in motion an intricate plan for his future life. The result was the Brokaw Foundation and a legend that had captivated the world for the past thirty years.

"So there you have it, Mr. Tanner. The complete and unabridged version of Lucas Brokaw's final days on earth."

Tanner was stunned. "Jesus! It's no wonder he was convinced he'd be reborn on the night he died."

"Indeed, how could he have believed otherwise?"

"And the grant . . . the two million dollars?"

"An outright bribe. He anonymously funded a chair of occult science here at the university, with the proviso that my role in his personal affairs would be kept confidential. A vow I've faithfully maintained until today."

"There's something about that." Tanner faltered, at a loss for words. "I don't know why, but it bothers me. As far as I can determine, Brokaw didn't make mistakes. Unless it was an intentional mistake, meant to throw you off the track. Yet he left evidence of the grant in his files, and then went out of his way to hide this business about the researchers. It just doesn't add up."

"Oh, and what leads you to that conclusion, Mr. Tanner?"

"Because the transactions are not only related, but they both lead directly to you. Think about it, professor. If he really wanted to eliminate any chance of a connection, then why didn't he destroy the material concerning the grant?"

Ludmann shifted in his chair and looked away. He seemed distracted. "Perhaps I should have mentioned it, but frankly, I find the thought a bit . . . unsettling."

"What the hell, we've gone this far. Let's go all the way."

"Very well. But I'm afraid it raises more questions than it answers, Mr. Tanner. You see, my agreement with Lucas Brokaw was conditional. At our last meeting, he instructed me in very precise terms that I was to *break* my vow of silence if ever I was contacted by a third party."

"By a third party? That's sort of nebulous, isn't it? I mean, after all, a third party could be anyone."

"I think not. As you so aptly noted, Lucas Brokaw wasn't a man to make mistakes."

"That's ridiculous!" Tanner scoffed. "Don't you see what you're suggesting?"

"Indeed I do, Mr. Tanner. I'm suggesting you're the third party."

Tanner stared at him, nonplussed. After a while, Ludmann chuckled and lit his pipe. Then he tilted back in his chair, squinting through a cloud of smoke, and grinned.

"I warned you! It's difficult to put the demon back in the bottle."

XII

"Ask him again, Monk."

Birkhead backhanded him across the mouth. Joey Pike's lip split, spurting blood, and he lurched backward. His arms came up to ward off the blows, but Birkhead feinted, ducking low, and chopped him in the kidneys. His knees sagged and the big man grabbed a fistful of shirt, holding him erect, then cuffed him on the head. A jagged cut appeared over his eyebrow, and his mouth flew open in a hoarse moan as Birkhead slammed him into the wall.

"Hold off a minute!" Ruxton moved in closer and lifted his chin. "You're really a mess, Joey. How about it? Feeling a little more cooperative?"

"Please, you gotta believe me." Pike's left eye was swollen shut and blood trickled from the corner of his mouth. "Honest to Christ, you're making a mistake."

Ruxton sighed, fixing him with a weary look. "You're not listening, Joey. I told you before. We know that Fallon fences all his hot stones with you. Got it now? We already know! So stop with the dummy routine and save yourself a lot of grief."

"But that's what I'm trying to tell you!" Pike blurted. "I never heard of this Fallon. On my mother's head! Never."

"It's your funeral." Ruxton shrugged and backed away. "One more time, Monk."

All in one motion, Birkhead let go of the shirt and drove upward with the butt of his hand. Pike's nose flattened in a spray of blood, and as his head bounced off the wall, the big man kicked him in the kneecap. He slumped forward, clutching wildly at his leg, and Birkhead clouted him behind the ear. The force of the blow knocked him off his feet, and he dropped to the floor in a heap. He shivered, gasping for breath, and wet his pants.

"No more! Please, no more." Pike covered his head, sobbing piteously. "Just call him off. I'll tell you. I swear it!"

Birkhead grunted and walked away, inspecting his skinned knuckles. After a moment Ruxton smiled and knelt beside the fence.

"So tell me, Joey. I'm listening."

"Oh, Chester, I just love it."

Jill swirled around the sitting room while Chester Wilson stood rooted in the middle of the floor. It was the smallest suite in the Mayflower and dismally lacking in decor. But her eyes glowed and she kept uttering little squeals of delight, as if it were all somehow beyond belief.

"Honestly, Chester, you're so clever. I never dreamed anyone could make a hotel look like a home. But that's what you've done." She paused, sweeping the room at a glance, and threw her arms up in a speechless gesture. "It's . . . well, it's just *you!*"

"Really, it isn't much." Wilson beamed with pride, slightly drunk yet totally unaware his speech was slurred. "I simply gave it . . . made it comfortable . . . that's all."

"Don't be modest." Jill wagged her finger at him and suddenly burst out in laughter. "Oh, Chester, I'm so happy you asked me out again. Washington can be so lonely when you don't know anyone. And now the evening's perfect!" She took a step closer and smiled engagingly. "Can I tell you a secret?"

"Why, of course you can. I'm really quite good at secrets."

"Well, I know it sounds brazen, but I was so afraid you wouldn't invite me up for a nightcap. Literally petrified! Isn't that terrible of me?"

"Not a'tall. It's . . . it's wonderful . . . that's what it is."

Chester Wilson was bewitched by the girl's loveliness. They had met in the elevator three nights ago, and while it was all quite proper, his life hadn't been the same since. She seemed so helpless, a bit awed to find herself alone in the capital. Full of questions about politicians and bureaucrats and society figures, all the things an old Washington hand took for granted. Their conversation carried over from the elevator to the lobby, and before he realized it, he'd somehow invited her to join him for dinner.

And then again the next night, and again tonight.

Normally, Wilson trudged through life with the metabolism of a sleeping bear. He was a quiet pedantic man, tall and bony, with sallow skin and lusterless eyes, almost cadaverous in appearance. A confirmed bachelor, somewhat shy around women, he was dedicated to his work. As one of the foremost cryptanalysts at the State Department, he had position and prestige, and seldom gave any thought to his rather bleak personal existence. He took his meals at the Mayflower, where he'd lived for nearly fifteen years, and his leisure time was devoted exclusively to the study of hieroglyphics and ancient cryptograms.

But all that had changed. Since meeting Jill he was a new man, vitalized by feelings he'd never before experienced. With her on his arm, he felt suave and debonair, a man of the world. And protective. Intensely protective. An emotion he hadn't allowed himself in all the years since his mother's death.

Tonight he'd consumed enough wine to embalm a mummy. His head reeled with his own good fortune, but he couldn't quite decide on the next step. Jill's eyes shone and her lips were moist and inviting. He wanted desperately to touch her, yet his feet had turned to stone and his nerve had suddenly deserted him. He felt awkward and clumsy, not at all the sophisticated man about Washington.

Then, scarcely able to believe it was happening, he saw her move across the room and pause in front of him. Her hands came up, resting on the lapels of his coat, and her features softened in a little girl look.

"Chester, I was wondering."

"Ummmm." He thought her the most exquisite creature he'd ever seen. "Wondering what?"

"Do you ever come to the West Coast?"

"I've always wanted to."

Her eyes were downcast. "Maybe you could take a vacation sometime and . . . well, you know . . . visit me."

"Visit you?"

"Yes, wouldn't that be fun?"

"Are you serious?" His tongue felt numb. "You want—me—to visit you?"

"Of course, silly! I wouldn't ask if I didn't mean it, now would I?"

"No, it's not that! I was just surprised . . . what I mean to say . . . well, I'm delighted."

"Oh, good! I'll show you San Francisco and you can meet all my friends and . . . oh, Chester, I'm so happy!"

She loosened his tie, and he blinked, groping for words. "Your friends?"

"You know, my business associates. The ones I told you about. But don't worry, we'll have loads of time to ourselves." She began unbuttoning his shirt. "Naturally I want them to meet you . . . oh, they'll be green with envy . . . and then we'll drive down to Big Sur. Or maybe north to the redwoods." He stared at her hands, utterly fascinated as the buttons popped open. "Which would you prefer . . . hmmm lover . . . warm beaches or snuggly coves?"

A bead of sweat trickled down his forehead and he

licked his lips. "Either . . . both . . . I . . . uh . . . I really . . ."

"Yes, both! That's a wonderful idea, Chester. We'll have a long, scrumptious holiday . . . just the two of us."

Her hands snaked inside his shirt, caressing warm flesh, and he shuddered. She kissed him, and for a moment he continued to stare at her, completely spellbound. Then her hips moved, grinding slowly but eagerly, and she thrust herself against him.

His eyes closed and her tongue darted into his mouth. He moaned and his arms went round her, and suddenly he was lost.

"Sorry, chum, no dice. I work alone."

"That's why I'm here." Ruxton smiled with false cordiality. "You work alone. You've never been caught. And you have a reputation for keeping your mouth shut. Those are the qualities I'm looking for."

Fallon's gaze remained flinty and remote. "Look, no offense intended, but you guys are obviously a couple of amateurs. You breeze in here with some dippy proposition and lay the strong talk on me like I was a hit man. Jesus! Didn't anybody ever tell you that you don't put out a contract on a safe?"

"You disappoint me, Fallon. I just got through saying I don't want to peel it or blow it or leave a mark on it. In short, a clean job. Nothing disturbed and no trace we've ever been there. That's hardly the request of an amateur."

"So get yourself a Ouija board. I'm not interested."

They faced each other across a kitchen table in an apartment as barren as a monk's cell, sizing each other up. Birkhead stood off to one side, arms folded across his chest. His expression was oxlike, cold and impersonal and menacing. Fallon glanced at him from time to time, but the look was flat and guarded, a wary look, without reaction, carefully concealing his thoughts.

Johnny Fallon was a wiry feist of a man. There was an astringent quality about him, harsh and uncompromising. His lips scarcely moved when he talked, as if his jaws had been wired shut, and his small, flaring eyes, set close together above splayed cheekbones, gave him the visage of a sullen dog, ugly and unpredictable.

Fallon was worried. If a couple of small-time punks could track him down, then he'd become too sloppy for his own good. It was time to pull a vanishing act. Change contacts, get himself a new fence, and lay low for a while.

Ruxton sensed his mood, and although stung by the man's sarcasm, he couldn't afford the luxury of anger. Not at this stage of the game. He needed Fallon, and before it was too late, he decided to try anther tack.

"We'd like to have you with us, Fallon. Everyone says you're the best box man in the business. And believe me, on this job, nothing but the best will do." He paused, suddenly very earnest. "It's big, bigger than anything you've ever tackled before. A once-in-a-lifetime deal."

Fallon's gargoyle features split in a grin. "Listen, sport, don't try to hustle me, okay? You show up out of the clear blue," he gestured at Birkhead, "with King Kong there, and hit me with a line of bullshit, and I'm supposed to kiss your ass. Thanks all the same, but don't do me any favors. First off, I'm not looking for work. And in the second place, I don't know you guys from a hole in the ground. Hell, you might even be the heat!"

"Not a chance!" Ruxton waved his hand negligently, as if dusting away the thought. "Come on now, Fallon, be honest. Do we look like cops?"

"I'll say this for you, you've got balls." Fallon's laughter sounded like a death rattle. "No names. No info on the job. In for a dime, in for a dollar. Just like that! Right?"

"Yeah, but look at it from my side. Until you commit

yourself, I've got no choice. Besides, what you don't know can't hurt you. So at this point it's really better to keep you in the dark."

"In the dark? Come off it! You're asking me to step in blind as a bat." Fallon shook his head. "No way, chum. Those aren't my kind of odds."

Ruxton smiled without warmth. "Your fence—what's his name—Joey Pike? He said you had nerves like steel cable. But I don't know, maybe he was wrong. You keep making noises like a man who can't get his act together."

Anger flashed in Fallon's eyes. Then his chin came up and his mouth set in a hard line. "Okay, hotshot, let's lay our cards on the table. You say you've got the score of a lifetime, right? And unless I heard wrong, you just got through telling me that once I'm in then there's no way out. Now if I went for a deal like that, it'd have to be sweet. Damned sweet! So why don't we quit playing games and get down to the bottom line— what's in it for me?"

"How about five million dollars?" Ruxton paused, allowing him to digest the figure. "Would that be sweet enough?"

"Sugar sweet," Fallon agreed gingerly. "If it's on the level."

"Like you said, we're a couple of amateurs. So if it weren't on the level, how could we expect to hustle an old pro like you?"

"I guess you couldn't. But suppose I agree to listen and the job don't strike me as kosher. Then what?"

"Then you have to deal with my friend. And if you need references, Joey Pike will tell you he's even meaner than he looks."

Fallon's gaze flicked across to Birkhead, then swung back. "You did say five million, didn't you?"

"Five million," Ruxton nodded. "All in dollars."

A long silence fell over the room. None of them moved, and the tick of a battered old alarm clock sounded deafening in the stillness. Fallon stared across the table, impassive and unafraid, but clearly wrestling with himself. After a while his mouth quirked in a hard smile. Then he laughed and threw up his hands.

"What the hell! Cut the cards and deal."

XIII

After dinner they came back to her apartment. Tanner took a seat on the sofa while Stacey fixed drinks. The evening had been strained, one-word questions and monosyllabic answers, and even now the tension persisted, as if they were strangers forced to make conversation.

And neither of them wanted to make it worse.

Stacey brought him a snifter of brandy and placed it on the coffee table. Her smile was tentative. Without a word, she settled herself on the sofa, tucking one leg underneath the other. Tanner lit a cigarette, painfully aware of the silence, and averted his gaze. She watched him for a long while, quietly sipping her brandy. Then she frowned, mimicking his dour expression, and lowered her voice in a gruff drawl.

"Drink up, pardner! No need to look so glum. Long as the cat's got your tongue, your secrets are safe."

"Very good," Tanner remarked dryly. "Can you do Bogart, too?"

"No, but I do a terrific Cagney! What if I snarl and poke you in the chest . . . would that scare you into talking?"

"Not likely. Besides, I've already told you all there is to tell."

"Oooh sure! And this sudden interest in reincarnation is all in the line of duty. Right?"

"To some extent . . . yes. Along with plain old curiosity. Why do you find that so unnatural?"

"Because I know you, that's why."

"Sorry. I'm afraid *because* isn't an answer."

"Darling, please! After weeks and weeks of digging,

you still insist you haven't learned anything. Nothing at all?"

"So I drew a blank. Jesus, nobody ever said I was Sherlock Holmes."

"Bull!" She cocked her head in that funny little smile. "Granted, I have a few blind spots where you're concerned . . . but gullible I'm not."

Her bantering tone wasn't altogether convincing. Under normal circumstances, their laughter came easy and their silences were never awkward. Yet tonight everything was out of sync.

Tanner had been brooding for the past week. He wasn't sullen or grouchy, he just seemed sunk in disgruntled introspection. And secretive. Stacey was certain he'd learned something about Brokaw. But whatever it was, he refused to disclose it. Which left Stacey all the more intrigued. She *had* to know; he wouldn't tell her, and she'd never been more infuriated in her life.

To compound matters, he couldn't even explain the reason for his silence. Having given his promise to Professor Ludmann, there was no way to tell her part of the story without telling her all. So he told her nothing.

Instead he exhibited a sudden and wholly unexpected interest in reincarnation. His rationale was simple if somewhat suspect. When she asked, he told her that his investigation of Brokaw had led nowhere, so he'd decided to work backward. By understanding the man's beliefs, he hoped to gain some clue to the man himself. But his quest for knowledge was overdone, too intense. Often he read till dawn, and in less than a week, he'd polished off every popular book on the subject in the university library. All the rush and urgency smacked of something far more serious than mere curiosity. It was more like an obsession.

Tanner felt a bit guilty about the whole business. She had a right to know, and several times he was tempted to break his promise to Ludmann. By the end of the week, however, he found himself distracted by a new problem. The deeper he probed into reincarnation, the greater the riddle became. Buddhists believed one thing; Hindus believed another. And both had a bewildering array of sects with beliefs all their own. It was like a Chinese box that opens and reveals ever smaller boxes inside. There was no single answer. A man could believe almost anything and still find some authority for his belief.

So his brooding manner wasn't so much the result of secrecy as confusion. He hadn't lied to Stacey; he had genuinely hoped to unearth further clues to Brokaw's character. All he'd discovered was an enigma within an enigma.

Even worse, his efforts had left him not just baffled but deeply disturbed. While he knew it was foolish, he couldn't shake a very real sense of being guided. Led onward step by step, almost as though he were merely an instrument in some greater design. Yet he also felt like a grave robber, a bumbling ghoul who had intruded on something—or someone—by uncovering ashes of the past.

Nor was his mood tempered by Stacey's dogged insistence. She sat perfectly still, watching him with a look of open skepticism. It was a look that demanded candor, and inwardly he knew she was entitled to hear it all. Every last scrap, whether fact or fancy. But there was nothing he could tell her. Nothing. Not until he'd made sense of it himself.

"Do me a favor, will you? Let it drop for now. I've told you all I can."

"All you can," she countered, "or all you will?"

There was a mute eloquence in his shrug, at once furtive and apologetic. "Take your pick. I suppose it amounts to the same thing."

"Hardly." She smiled, but it was a faint outline, lacking humor. "Now really, darling, am I asking for so much? If you won't explain, then at least give me a reason . . . an excuse . . . anything!"

"I can't! Don't you understand that?" He leaned toward her, all earnestness and gravity. "I just can't."

She recoiled as if he'd slapped her. He saw anger and resentment, even a trace of fear in her eyes. "No, I don't understand. You see, there shouldn't be anything hidden between us, Warren. Not now! It's too late for that. I'm sorry, but it comes down to a matter of trust . . . either you're honest with me or you're not."

"Your words, not mine." He inspected his cigarette as if he'd never seen one before. Then a muscle in his jaw twitched, and something odd happened to his voice. "I guess we're at an impasse."

"Yes, I suppose we are."

The distance between them seemed to widen abruptly. He realized that what he'd done was inexcusable. He'd fobbed her off by resorting to word games, semantics, a device that belittled all he felt for her, denied everything he'd led her to believe. Inexcusable, perhaps unforgivable, yet still necessary.

Until he knew why he'd been selected. And by whom.

There was nothing left to say, no way to ease the hurt he saw in her eyes. He stubbed out his cigarette and rose from the sofa. "Maybe it's best if I run along. I'm pretty poor company tonight. Might even make things worse if I stayed over."

"Perhaps you're right. We could both use some time to think."

"Yeah . . . sure. Good idea. I'll let you know if I get a brainstorm."

Tanner bent down and kissed her. A fleeting kiss, almost a formality. Then he turned and walked from the apartment. Her eyes clung to him as he went through the door, imploring him to come back, to stay and talk it out. Even as the door closed, something weak and treacherous told her to run after him, to cajole and submit, not to risk losing him. But she didn't move. Nor did she call his name.

That way, it would never have a chance. Not if she had to beg. So she took hold of herself and did the only thing she could do, the one thing that might bring him back.

She let him go.

. . . he ripped the printout from the machine. His lips moved, like a child repeating the alphabet, and several minutes passed as he stared intently at the characters on the slip of paper. At last, he pulled a cigarette lighter from his pocket. The printout burst into flames and he dropped it to the floor. A moment later it was reduced to a charred crisp, and he ground the ashes underfoot.

Then he swung the steel door open and entered the vault. He walked directly to a wall safe on the left. His movements were skillful and precise, and in a matter of seconds, he finished wiring an explosive charge to a mousetrap device. In turn, he wired the device to a flange on the inside of the door. Quickly, without lost motion, he moved to the safe on the right and repeated the process. Nodding to himself, he took two envelopes from his coat pocket, scrutinized them carefully, then placed an envelope on the upper shelf of both safes. Again moving left to right, he spun the combination knobs and closed the safe doors.

Standing back, he studied the safes for a few moments. A crooked smile spread over his face and he grunted with satisfaction. Then he turned and walked from the vault into the outer chamber . . . .

The stirrings penetrated his sleep. Tanner moaned, thrashing wildly at the bedcovers, and slowly groped his way to wakefulness. The room tilted crazily before his eyes, whirling and spinning. He retched and bolted upright, head churning. He flung the covers back and sat up on the edge of the bed, planting his feet firmly on the floor. Then he hung on, clutching the mattress with both hands, waiting for the dizziness to pass.

Gradually his head cleared. The vertigo faded. He looked about the darkened room, confused and still slightly disoriented, but aware of his surroundings and comforted to find himself in his own bed. He was not quite sure what had happened.

Then he remembered. All in a flash, vividly detailed.

It was the crypt. A man moving around in the crypt. Working on the cryptography machine and the safes. The wall safes!

Inside the vault. He'd been *inside* the vault.

Wiring explosives: *The booby traps.*

Leaving envelopes: *The secret questions. A list of answers.*

Closing the safe doors: *The combination locks. Set and rigged to explode.*

A man. Working alone. An old man. Tall. Shock of gray hair. Ruddy and smiling, but not well. In pain. Limping.

Limping back and forth between the wall safes. Inside the vault. The vault door wide open and he was . . .

Lucas Brokaw.

Tanner blinked and, staring into the darkness, watched it again in his mind's eye, concentrating on the face, that hard, cynical face he'd seen so often in the portrait hanging on a wall at the mansion.

There was no doubt. None at all. It was Brokaw. The night he had sealed the vault. The last night. The night he'd died.

An icy sensation came over Tanner. Suddenly he remembered something else—a snatch of conversation, all out of context and fuzzy. Something Professor Ludmann had told him. It had been meaningless at the time, a bit of trivia. But now—tonight? His brow seamed in a frown, and he tried to recall the words. To remember exactly.

Something about dreams. Lucas Brokaw's dreams.

XIV

"In a word, there's no margin for error."

Ruxton studied their faces a moment, then turned back to the display. On portable easels were arranged a photo composite of the cliffs, beside that a diagram of the estate grounds, and last, a floor plan of the crypt itself. Using a pencil for a pointer, he moved from easel to easel as he talked.

"Jill will anchor a half-mile out and wait. We'll go ashore in a rubber boat at precisely 10:05. That gives Monk an hour to get us up the cliffs and inside the house. Our only leeway is the fifteen minutes it takes the guard to patrol the house grounds. We have to be inside within that exact time frame."

"What's the rush?" Fallon inquired. "Hell, we've got all night."

"Wrong. We've got fifteen minutes. Otherwise we run the risk of being delayed by the change of guards at midnight."

"So what? Give or take a few minutes, you're talking about an hour."

"Wrong again. Come on, Fallon wake up! You're supposed to be the pro in this group, so use your head. The old guard will be on the tail end of an eight-hour shift. Which means he'll be tired and bored, and a lot easier to slip past than his replacement. That's when we go. Any objection?"

Fallon shrugged indifferently. "Just checking you out. Never hurts to take a closer look."

"All suggestions welcome." Ruxton's smile was strained. "If you think you can punch holes in it, be my guest."

"Okay, one more thing. So we're inside the house . . . what about the servants?"

"Creatures of habit. Every night the lights go out at precisely ten on the dot. Which is still another reason to start up the cliffs at 10:05. By the time we get to the top, that guard will be bored stiff."

"Yeah, that's something else you sorta skipped over. Just how the hell do we get up those cliffs, anyway? Looks to me like—"

"Jesus Christ!" Birkhead overrode him in a loud hectoring voice. "Quit asking so goddamned many questions and worry about your own job."

"Chum, unless you get me up those cliffs, I can't even do my job. So the question's not out of line."

"Go ahead, Monk," Ruxton winked and nodded. "Set his mind at rest."

"The method we'll use," Birkhead growled, "is called a prusik sling. Tomorrow I start giving lessons on that," he jerked his chin at a high beam in the cathedral ceiling, "so don't sweat it. You'll get to the top."

"Never thought otherwise. Like I said . . . just checking."

"Well, I'll tell you something, Charlie Brown. That works both ways. So far, all we've had out of you is a bunch of hot air. I think it's about time we got the dope on how you mean to crack those safes."

Fallon eyed him with a gargoyle grin. "It's called the Fallon method. Satisfaction guaranteed or your money back. No demonstrations, though. Not till you get me up those cliffs in one piece."

Ruxton tapped the diagram of the crypt with his pencil. "Since we're on the subject, let's double-check that. You said you could open all three safes within an hour. Now, is that a guesstimate or a hard fact? There's a difference, and it could affect the logistics of the entire operation."

"I never guess, pal. You told me those safes were built in 1947 or before, right?"

"That's right. But don't forget, we have to assume they were custom-built to Brokaw's specifications."

"So it's six of one and half-dozen of another. With the technology they had in them days, all you'd need is a can opener and a corkscrew."

"Even though they're wired with explosives?" Ruxton persisted. "That won't slow you down?"

Fallon's expression was wry and enigmatic, almost a grimace. "Take my word for it. I'll open 'em up like they had zippers."

Throughout the conversation, Jill and Chester Wilson had observed silently from the couch. Wilson appeared catatonic. He clung to Jill's hand and stared straight ahead in a glassy-eyed trance. None of it seemed real. The words. The people. The house. Least of all his own involvement. It was as though he had dozed off during a horror movie on the late show and then suddenly awakened to find himself strapped to the vivisection table of a diabolic madman.

Scarcely a week ago he had followed Jill to the coast. With a month's leave from the State Department—the first vacation he'd taken in years—he had visions of a romantic tryst in the sun. Perhaps even marriage. But quickly enough, he'd learned that Jill's body was an instrument of emotional blackmail. She used it to reward and punish, and however much he detested himself, he discovered he hadn't the strength to deny her. It was as if she had cast a spell over him and he was helpless to resist.

Then he met her friends, and it quickly became real-life horror. Ruxton terrified him. Nothing overt. No open threat. Yet behind that glacial calm he sensed there was neither conscience nor mercy. Instead there was a cold ferocity as elemental as nature itself.

Nor was there ever any question of defiance. Ruxton's offer was both straightforward and generous: Break the code and receive $5,000,000—all in cash and tax free, unrecorded and untraceable. Implied if unstated was still another consideration. By accepting, Wilson would be allowed to go on living. The alternative was obvious and required no explanation.

But the clincher was Wilson's blinding infatuation. Though he'd been duped, he was convinced that Jill, like himself, was merely another pawn in this deadly game. She seemed no less terrified of these men—her fear was unmistakable, contagious—and his belief held firm that she genuinely cared for him. With the money and a fresh start they might yet find their life in the sun.

Jill, of course, pandered both to his fantasy and his fear. She was playing the role assigned her with consummate skill and thoroughly enjoying the performance. Still, she hadn't deceived herself. She knew Wilson was a dead man if he refused to go along, and in the end, she'd gulled him with a budding sense of compassion. To the point that she had agreed to live with him—at Ruxton's insistence—until the job was finished.

While she was gone, Birkhead had rented a secluded house on the outskirts of Sausalito. Only a short drive from the marina, it was an ideal location for their planning sessions. Off away from the neighbors, situated in a grove of trees, it eliminated the chance of their being spotted and later linked together.

Like a seductive black widow, luring her mate ever deeper into the web, it was there she had brought Chester Wilson. Her body and her guile, along with his fear of Ruxton, kept him there. Curiously though, his calf-like adoration and his dread had been fueled by his own greed. If he was a victim, then it was apparent to everyone except himself that he was a willing victim. A collaborator, however unwittingly, in his own corruption.

Tonight, seated next to Wilson, Jill regarded Ruxton as if he were a magician engaged in some staggering sleight of hand. All of them, herself included, were like rabbits who materialized on cue and performed as ordered. Always there was some new and startling feat in his repertoire, but the magic he worked had little to do with illusion. His commanding presence, the very force of his will, was no trick. It was tangible, almost animate.

Just now his attention had strayed from Fallon to the cryptanalyst. He smiled, aware of how desperately Wilson clutched the girl's hand, and when he spoke, it was in a mild, jovially menacing voice.

"Well now, Chester! I suppose that brings us around to your shtick."

"Beg pardon?" Wilson mumbled.

"A show biz term. Shtick, as in speciality." Ruxton's pencil rapped the diagram like a drumhead. "In your case . . . how long will it take you to unscramble Brokaw's code?"

Wilson jerked erect, abjectly uncomfortable under the younger man's scrutiny. A long silence ensued while everyone stared at him, and he in turn stared at the small dot that represented the cryptography machine. At last he licked his lips, then sighed and shook his head.

"I haven't the slightest idea."

Ruxton's smile vanished. It was as if a shutter had fallen, and what remained was a mask. "Try again, Chester. You're here by virtue of your expertise . . . remember?"

"Yes, of course. I understand. But don't you see, it depends on an almost infinite number of variables. How many rotors did Brokaw engineer into the machine? And what system of wiring did he use? And the sequence? And the monoalphabetic substitution factor is critical to—"

"Please, Chester!" Ruxton halted him with an upraised palm. "Spare us the lecture. Just an educated guess. Your best estimate."

"Two hours?" It was less a statement than a request. "Perhaps less."

"Will you need any special equipment?"

"No, not really. Just a screwdriver."

"A screwdriver?"

"Yes. A small screwdriver." Wilson grinned weakly and darted a nervous glance around the room. "And a camera might be helpful. If it's not too much trouble."

"No trouble at all. Any special brand?"

"Well, a Minox would be nice. With a flash attachment."

"Fine. Thank you, Chester." Ruxton switched his gaze to Birkhead. "Okay, Monk? Add a Minox to your shopping list."

"One Minox," Birkhead nodded stolidly. "And a small screwdriver."

"What about the rest of the stuff?"

"Already got it. Clothes. Ropes. Tennis shoes. The whole ball of wax. Everything but the ski masks. I'm having a helluva time finding them in black."

"Then I suggest you get busy. We go for broke Thursday night."

Everyone in the room was stunned speechless. Several moments passed as they stared at him, unable to believe he was serious. Then Fallon finally got his tongue untracked and came up on the edge of his chair.

"Jesus, that's pretty quick, isn't it? I mean . . . in case you've forgotten . . . this is Tuesday. What's the big rush?"

"Time and tide, my friend. Mother Nature's stopwatch."

"Terrific. That's a real pearl of wisdom. But for us slower types, would you mind spelling it out?"

"Not at all. We land Thursday night. Low tide on Friday morning is at 4:27. Which means we have to be back in the water no later than 4:22."

He paused and the others waited, hushed and expectant. A static charge swept over the room, then he smiled and riveted them with a look.

"That gives us six hours and five minutes. To the second!"

XV

A patch of sunlight inched across the wall. The movement was almost indiscernible but constant, and at last it touched the edge of a gilded picture frame. Then it exploded in a burst of gold.

Stacey blinked, startled by the reflection, and looked away. Her expression was pensive and vague. It took a moment for the meaning to register. Her eyes went to the desk clock, then shifted back to the wall.

She'd been watching that spot of light for nearly an hour.

It was almost noon and she still hadn't opened the morning mail. A Danish and a cold cup of coffee sat untouched on her desk, exactly where her secretary had put them down earlier. Hours ago! Somewhere before ten. But afterward—nearly half the morning?—was a blank. She'd been sitting there in a funk all that time, like some dizzy sophomore with a schoolgirl crush.

Her hand moved toward the phone, but she quickly pulled it back. She pushed the coffee aside and threw the Danish in the wastebasket. Then she riffled through the mail, scarcely able to concentrate, and slammed it down on the desk. She felt harried and out of sorts, thoroughly exasperated with herself. Yet the thought was there, and she couldn't seem to suppress it. Finally, swallowing her pride, she lifted the receiver and dialed the receptionist.

"Hi, Laura. Has Mr. Tanner come in yet?"

"No, he hasn't, Miss Cameron. But he called in."

"Called . . . from where?"

"The estate. He said he could be reached there all day if anyone wanted him."

"Oh, of course! It completely slipped my mind. Thank you, Laura."

Stacey carefully returned the phone to the cradle and sat there glaring at it. Her eyes stung and a knot pulsed at her temple. Her hand tightened in a hard fist.

Damn! Always the estate. That damned estate!

She continued to glare at the phone. Wondering what to do. Where to turn. How to help. She was not even sure he would accept help. How could a man be helped when he refused to discuss the problem?

Nearly two weeks had passed since their quarrel, but even now she knew little more than the night he'd walked out. He still refused to confide in her, and though she'd managed to coax a few things out of him, what she had heard was more than enough to frighten her. Some of it in the middle of the night when he awoke bathed in sweat, hollow-eyed with what he'd seen. Or perhaps what he had lived through.

She shuddered, thinking of last night. Her stomach felt queasy, and she tried to put it out of her mind. But the image persisted, bright quick flashes of pain. The look on his face. That inhuman moan . . .

"Ooo Jesus! No more. Noooo!"

"Warren . . . honey, it's all right. You're dreaming. Understand, just another . . ."

"I saw him, Stace. I was there. I could've reached out and touched . . ."

"Darling, listen to me." She took him in her arms, and cradled his head against her breast. "It was a dream, that's all. A bad dream."

"No, he was in the crypt. Sealing the vault and—"

"Who?"

"—rigging that goddamned machine again."

"Who, Warren? Who was in the crypt?"

Silence. His breath warm on her breast. Very still now.

"Warren, answer me. Was it the same as before?"

136

"Yes. It's always the same."

"And the man . . . who was it you saw?"

A long beat, then muffled, almost a whisper. "Him."

"Say it, Warren. Go on . . . tell me his name."

Nothing. His lips moved, but there was no sound. A mute agonizing that recoiled from the words, paralyzed speech.

"It was Lucas Brokaw, wasn't it? Say it, Warren! Say his name . . . Lucas Brokaw."

"Yes."

"No, not yes. Say it!"

"Brokaw." Then softly, "Lucas Brokaw."

"And Lucas Brokaw is dead, isn't he? Darling, look at me . . . he's dead! And it's not him or a message from the grave or anything else. It's a dream."

His mouth opened and closed, then he glanced away. "I don't know."

"Oh, Warren . . . sweetheart, what else could it be? Surely you don't believe . . ." She paused, thoughtful a moment, felt her heart quicken. "Darling, are you telling me everything . . . all of it?"

"There's nothing else. It never changes. The crypt and him limping around . . ."

"No, not that. Something else . . . something besides the dream. The way you act . . . you're too upset . . . there has to be something else. Something you haven't told me."

He lay rigid, immobile, cold stone against the warmth of her breast. "Nothing else. It's the dream, Stace. Don't you see? In the dream he's . . . not dead. He's there, in the crypt. We're there together. I'm . . . oh Christ, why can't you understand? *I'm there with him.*"

Stacey pressed her fingers hard against her temples. The words still echoed through her mind, fully as frightening this morning as they were last night. Perhaps worse, for in retrospect, the hell of last night and all the nights before suddenly culminated in a single thought, the very thing she'd sensed after last night's dream.

It was just too real even for a nightmare.

Like most people, Stacey had read a good deal about psychic phenomena. She knew of reputable scientists, funded by prestigious universities, who were actively engaged in experiments dealing with parapsychology and telekinesis. On one occasion, at a faculty gathering, she had even allowed herself to be drawn into a discussion of the occult in which Professor George Ludmann had argued his case persuasively. An erudite man, unperturbed by skeptics, he had buttressed ancient myths with data from controlled experiments and in the end left his kibitzers not quite so cocksure.

All things considered, though, Stacey remained a doubter. Jaded by her daily involvement with weirdos and religious freaks, she simply couldn't muster any great belief in the paranormal. The whole idea seemed riddled with contradiction; despite her streak of romanticism, she found it difficult to accept superstition and old wives' tales as fact.

Yet she couldn't ignore the dreams. Warren's hellish nightmares. All the more frightening because he believed the old man to be Lucas Brokaw.

But if it wasn't paranormal—or some dark figment of his psyche—then what was it?

Suddenly she felt in need of advice. Another opinion, a sympathetic shoulder, if nothing else. Someone whose view was unclouded by emotion. Someone honest enough to tell her the truth rather than what she wanted to hear.

Swiftly, before she could change her mind, she stood and walked from the room. Crossing the hall, she took a deep breath, straightened her skirt, and rapped on the door of the director's office. A muffled voice called out, and she opened the door a crack, peeking inside.

"Sorry to barge in on you," she edged through the door, "but could I speak with you a moment?"

"Of course, my dear. Come in." Knox smiled and indicated a chair. "Silly of you to ask. Besides, you're interrupting nothing that won't wait."

"Well, it isn't exactly business." She saw his expression change as she took a seat and immediately regretted her choice of words. "That is to say, it is and it isn't. It does involve the foundation . . . in a manner of speaking."

"My, my! Sounds mysterious. Nothing wrong, I trust?"

"Oh, no. Not really. It's just that—" She faltered, suddenly at a loss for words, then decided simply to blurt it out. "To be perfectly frank, it's Warren. I'm worried about him. In fact, I have been for some time. Perhaps I should have come to you sooner, but I thought the . . ."

Her voice trailed off. There was no way she could mention the dreams. By any interpretation, the whole thing smacked of instability, or worse. Nor could she admit how she'd learned of the dreams. Sleeping with Warren was one thing. To openly confront the director with it was another matter entirely. Flushed, searching for a way out, she dismissed it with a lame gesture.

"I thought it would pass. Whatever it is that's . . . troubling him."

"I see." Knox steepled his fingers, studying her a moment, then smiled reassuringly. "Why don't you tell me about it?"

"I'm not really sure I can verbalize it. You know Warren. He rarely confides in anyone until after the fact. But it's . . . well, it's almost as if he has a fixation about the estate. Especially the security system."

"I thought we settled all that after our little mishap with that Santini fellow."

"So did I. But it only seems to have gotten worse. Lately, Warren is out there every day. Sometimes he doesn't come into the office at all."

"Yes, I knew he was spending a good deal of time at

the estate, but . . . well, as you say, that's a bit much, isn't it? Exactly what is it that has him so concerned? Or hasn't he told you?"

Stacey hesitated, choosing her words with care. "I gather it's the crypt. He seems to think there's some danger of . . . I don't really know. Of it being broken into, I suppose. Violated in some way."

"Violated?" Knox arched one eyebrow and looked down his nose. "I daresay he does have a fixation. Sounds as if he thinks he's guarding the Pharaoh's tomb."

"I know," Stacey murmured uneasily. "That's why I'm so worried."

Hamilton Knox was a man who saw the world through a prism of his own attitudes. He'd been aware of Stacey's affair with Tanner almost from its inception. Though he disapproved, it had never ocurred to him to interfere. As long as everyone did his job, he was willing to overlook these mundane liaisons. But now he was keenly disappointed. Stacey no longer seemed the cool, crisp executive assistant he valued so highly. And he secretly wondered if she hadn't fallen victim to a suppressed maternal instinct. Her concern was touching but absurd, almost childlike in its simplicity. Yet it wouldn't do to criticize, not when she was upset and clearly suffering a fixation of her own. Instead, for the time being, he made a mental note to keep a closer watch on the situation. Particularly on Warren Tanner.

"Actually, there's nothing to alarm ourselves about." His remark came after a long pause, eyes narrowed in a reflective squint behind his glasses. "What we have here is a classic case of job stress. Warren is extremely conscientious, as we both know, and I suspect he's taking this matter of security a bit too seriously. I'll have a little chat with him. All quite discreet, of course. No need for him to know we've talked. Would that set your mind at rest?"

"Yes, it would. Definitely." Stacey smiled, but she

was a poor liar. "Thank you, Mr. Knox. Warren respects you, and I'm sure he'll listen to your advice."

"Think nothing of it, my dear."

With as much grace as she could manage, she beat a hasty retreat back to her own office, feeling like a traitor. It was debatable that she'd fooled the director, but she certainly hadn't fooled herself.

Warren wouldn't listen. Not to her. Not to Knox. Not to anyone. Nor would he stop haunting the estate night and day.

Not while he still dreamed.

XVI

Birkhead went up the cliff first.

His ascent looked almost effortless. He moved with the swift grace of a circus acrobat. His legs provided thrust and his powerful arms the necessary upward pull; he had the knack of balance, his body scarcely touching the rock, weight evenly distributed on his feet. His climb had been memorized to the smallest detail, and he scampered from ledge to crack to ledge, zigzagging upward in a fluid burst of motion.

It took him eleven minutes to scale the cliff.

The others watched from below, where the rubber boat had been secured on a small beach. A quarter moon dimly illuminated the cliffs, and they were able to track Birkhead's progress without difficulty. This in itself vindicated Ruxton's decision to stage the raid tonight. Last night the moon had been too bright. Tonight it was perfect. There was adequate light for scaling the cliff, but hardly enough to betray their movements on the open ground above.

Once on top, Birkhead quickly set about rigging the climb for those below. He unslung two ropes, crisscrossed over his chest like bandoliers, and laid them on the ground. Both were Perlon ropes, stout fiber core with a woven sheath, specially constructed to withstand the sawing effect of rocky cliffs. He tied one end of the shortest rope around a nearby tree, then hurled the remainder off the cliff. This was the ascent rope, which would support the prusik sling of each climber. The longer rope was to be used as an upper belay, a lifeline of sorts. With one end fastened to carabiners on a rappel sling, which in turn was attached to the climber, Birkhead could provide independent support during the ascent. It was a makeshift arrangement, expedient if unorthodox, combining elements of various alpine techniques.

Birkhead felt embarrassed by the whole rigmarole, as though he'd violated every tenet in the mountaineer's handbook. But it was unavoidable, since the rest of the team were inexperienced climbers.

Tonight they couldn't afford an accident.

On the beach, Fallon prepared himself for the climb. Along with the others, he'd spent hours practicing on the prusik sling. A stepladder affair, the sling consisted of three loops of rope attached at intervals to the ascent rope. One loop went around the chest for balance, and the other two served as footsteps. The knot used on the loops had a unique feature: It remained in place when weighted, but easily slipped up or down when unweighted. To ascend, the climber stood in the lowest loop while raising the knot on the upper loop. Then he stepped into the top loop and slid the lower loop to his new position. By repeating the process, shifting the loops higher one step at a time, he was able to climb a vertical rope with little more effort than required to shinny up a tree.

Lithe and ferret-quick, Fallon took slightly less than fourteen minutes to scale the 200-foot cliff. Chester Wilson was nowhere near as quick or coordinated, and required considerable assistance from Birkhead to get up in twenty-one minutes. Ruxton was slowed by the drag of a nylon rope attached to his belt, but he managed the ascent in sixteen minutes. As he crawled over the edge of the cliff, Birkhead began tugging at the nylon rope and quickly hauled a knapsack containing their equipment to the top. After unstrapping himself from the slings and ropes, Ruxton checked the luminous dial on his watch: 11:07.

Thirteen minutes to elude the guard and get inside the house.

Birkhead again led the way, with Ruxton bringing up

the rear. The only one who was armed, Birkhead carried a Colt Python .357 Magnum fitted with a silencer. If they were detected, either by the house guard or the servants, the pistol would ensure their escape. Fallon now lugged the knapsack, leaving Birkhead free to handle any emergency, and Wilson trotted along in the middle of the group.

The men were almost invisible in the bluish murk of darkness. Covered from head to toe in black—ski masks to tennis shoes—they catfooted across the lawn without a sound. Four minutes later, they darted into the shadows of the entrance pavilion.

Fallon went to his knees beside the front door, pulling out a packet of rubber gloves and a small leather case from a pocket of the knapsack. None of the men spoke as they slipped on the gloves, nor was there any need to stress urgency. Fallon already knew they were running late, that the house guard could appear at any moment. He took a locksmith's pick from the leather case and inserted its slim, flat tip into the door lock. Gently, working by feel, he probed and tested; time seemed protracted, but in less than a minute there was a distinct *click*. Fallon rose and turned the doorknob as footsteps sounded on the driveway. Without a word, the four men hurried inside the mansion.

The guard strolled by, stifling a yawn, an instant after the door closed.

XVII

A waning moon dimly lighted the bedroom.

Stacey lay curled alongside him, an arm thrown over his chest and her head nestled in the hollow of his shoulder. His breathing was rhythmic, shallow and even; he lay sprawled on his back, arms and legs flung wide, deep in a trancelike sleep. His eyelids fluttered and his lips moved, then he mouthed a silent cry of recognition.

. . . *he walked from the vault into the outer chamber. Cautiously, quite deliberate in his movements, he avoided touching the door handle and swung the steel door closed. He waited, listening for the muffled thud of the lock bolts; then he twirled the combination knob. Wheeling around, he crossed to the entranceway and mounted the stairs.*

A clock tolled as he emerged from the upper landing and limped across the foyer. At the stroke of nine the house again went silent, and a moment later he entered the study. Without hesitation, he walked straight to the liquor cabinet, took a vial from the top shelf, and emptied it into a glass beaker. His hand steadied, and he held the beaker to the light, squinting at the opaque liquid. A soft grunt became a raspy chuckle, and he nodded to himself.

Bright shafts of moonlight flooded the room, and as if drawn by impulse, he moved to the window overlooking the coastline. His expression was tranquil yet oddly jubilant, and a long while passed as he stood gazing down on the cliffs. Presently his eyes mellowed and a mystic look of reverence illuminated his features.

Then he turned up the beaker . . .

The dream coalesced into an anguished dread. A disembodied face floated past, exaggerated and distorted, as if seen in a carnival mirror. It chilled his drowsy fitfulness and jolted him into sharp awakening. The image surfaced, vividly fixed in sensory reference, and for an instant he was numbed by what he saw. His eyes popped open, dull and sightless, turned inward on something too terrible for speech.

Suddenly he grasped it. Understood. Knew that what he'd seen was the final moment. An irreversible step into the unknown. Lucas Brokaw's ultimate act of belief in his own immortality.

Yet it was still incomplete.

Why had he been chosen to have the dreams? To what purpose were these things revealed? Was it a message? Some spectral nudge he'd failed to comprehend? And after all these weeks—reliving the same dream over and over again—why at last was he shown that final moment in the study?

Why indeed? Why not last night, or the night before? Why tonight?

The hair bristled on the back of Tanner's neck. An image flitted across his mind—*Lucas Brokaw at the vault door*—and unaccountably, he felt compelled to visit the estate. He knew he had to see the crypt. Tonight! Tomorrow morning wouldn't do. It had to be tonight.

Now. Before it was too late.

Tanner shifted sideways, freeing his arm, and gently eased Stacey back onto the pillow. Then he rolled out of bed and padded barefoot to the closet. As he opened the door, groping in the dark for his shirt, Stacey awakened. Her hand searched his side of the bed, moving sleepily over the empty space. After a moment it registered, and she turned her head toward the bathroom.

"Warren?"

"Over here."

"Where?" She rubbed her eyes and peered across the room. "What are you doing?"

"It's okay. I'm just getting dressed."

"What's wrong?"

"Nothing's wrong. Forget it and go back to sleep."

"Then why are you getting dressed?"

"I have to go out for a while. Turn over and go back to sleep . . . get your beauty rest."

"Out?" Suddenly she bolted upright in bed. "Out where?"

There was a deliberate pause before he spoke. His words were almost inaudible, so quiet she had to strain to hear. "The estate . . . something I want to check out."

"In the middle of the night! Warren, what is it? What's wrong?"

"I told you, nothing's wrong. Nothing at all."

"I don't believe you." She snapped on the bedside lamp and gave him a suspicious look. "You're upset about something, I can tell. Was it the dream?"

He glanced at her, on the verge of answering, then seemed to change his mind. Quickly, he began stuffing his shirt into his pants and turned back to the closet, avoiding her gaze.

"That's it, isn't it? You had another dream. And it upset you enough to make you rush out there in the middle of the night."

Still no answer. He zippered up his pants and buckled his belt.

She threw off the covers and jumped out of bed. In one motion she whipped her nightgown overhead and flung it aside. Then she hurried toward the closet.

"I'm going with you."

"No!" Tanner replied sternly, facing her. "You're staying here, that's final."

She smiled and brushed past him. "Let's not argue, darling. I said I'm going with you . . . and I am."

Her tone was pleasant but firm, and her nakedness

lent a curious note of defiance to her words. Tanner chewed on his lip and stared at her backside for a moment. Then he sighed and turned away as she began rummaging through the closet.

XVIII

The house was dark and still.

Huddled together, the men waited just inside the door, listening intently, until they were certain the guard had continued on his rounds. At last, Fallon flicked on a rose-lensed penlight and led them across the foyer. He halted at the stair landing and dropped to his knees. Quickly and expertly, he examined both sides of the stone arch. Then he smiled, nodding to himself, and spoke over his shoulder, sotto voce.

"It's infrared. We'll have to crawl under. Do like I do."

He went to the floor, stretched out flat on his belly, and pushed the knapsack ahead of him onto the landing. Then he slithered through, hugging the cold stone, and climbed to his feet on the other side. Birkhead went next, wiggling through with the same snakelike crawl; then Wilson, and finally Ruxton. Gathered on the landing, they peered down the cavernous passageway, warier now than before. A moment passed. Then, according to plan, Fallon again took the lead. His first job was to get them safely through the alarm systems. Failing that, the entire operation would be scrubbed.

Their descent along the winding staircase was painstakingly slow. Not only was Fallon checking the hewn steps and the walls for hidden alarms, but all of them felt a sense of entering another world, an eerie subterranean abyss stretching endlessly into the bowels of the earth. There was a dank, fetid quality to the spiraling corridor, which grew worse as they approached the innermost depths of the cliff. Though the air was cool and clammy, all four men were sweating heavily by the time they reached the bottom landing.

After a quick inspection of the entranceway, Fallon signaled all clear and stepped into the outer chamber. The others crowded close behind, then abruptly pulled up short, made momentarily speechless by the sight. While they'd known generally what to expect, it was far more impressive than any of them had imagined, an excavation feat of such scope that suddenly they were forced to consider, after all, whether they were a match for the man bold enough to have envisioned such a crypt.

Then Ruxton chuckled, mocking himself, struck by the absurdity of grown men being intimidated by a ghost. Later, looking back, he would remember the moment and regret the chuckle. But now, feeling devilishly clever, he ripped off his ski mask and cocked his head in a smug grin.

"My friends, I congratulate you. It went off like clockwork."

Everyone smiled except Fallon. He was staring around the room, his forehead wrinkled in a frown. As if thinking out loud, he grunted and wagged his head back and forth.

"You know, it's funny. After somebody went to all this trouble, you'd think they'd have the place loaded with TV cameras or laser beams or some damn thing. But there's nothing . . . zilch! Beats the hell out of me why some clown hasn't ripped it off before."

"Let's not have any famous last words," Ruxton commented. "I seem to recall a little matter of explosives in there," he jerked his chin at the vault, "not to mention opening the door itself."

"That!" Fallon sneered. "Hell, that's a piece of cake."

"I suggest you save your bragging for later. And remember what I told you . . . we take *nothing* for granted. Brokaw had a very tricky mind, so we operate on the premise that nothing is as it appears to be. Now, suppose we go to work." He glanced at his watch. "We have precisely three hours and four minutes to get the job done and get out."

Fallon grumbled something to himself, then knelt down and began loosening the straps on the knapsack. Opening it, he took out an oilskin pouch containing the camera and a set of screwdrivers and handed it to Wilson. With considerably more care, he then extracted a bulky object that was wrapped in several layers of foam rubber. He pulled slipknots on the thongs holding it together and slowly removed the padding. Underneath all the spongy rubber was an object that appeared at first glance to be a portable television set. It was something else entirely.

The device was a marvel of space age technology and one of a kind. It had been built for Fallon by a former physicist on the Apollo Project. Not surprisingly, the physicist had met with an untimely and fatal accident shortly afterward, which gave Fallon a monopoly on the machine and had thus far kept him out of jail.

Weighing some twenty pounds, the device was roughly a foot square and perhaps eight inches in width, with handles projecting off either side. On the front was a steel disk embedded with crystal sensor elements. On the back was a monitor screen that produced an electronic graph similar in appearance to an electrocardiogram. The guts of the machine consisted of an ultrasonic transducer powered by a nuclear energy cell. The transducer emitted signals through the sensor elements; these ultrasonic signals penetrated the mass of any target object to the depth of its opposite side. The signals then bounced back to the monitor screen, producing a graph of the internal structure of the target object. It was an ultrasonic scanning device that gave the operator a glimpse of the inner workings of the object under scrutiny.

As Fallon had remarked, the steel doors found on bank vaults were a piece of cake. Of equal significance, the device came equipped with a unique and rather revolutionary attachment. It allowed him to listen to the ultrasonic bleeps, which translated to a form of eavesdropping on the tumblers inside a vault door.

Birkhead was fascinated by the device, as was Ruxton; for a while they hovered around watching Fallon's every move. But it required several tests to make the device operational, and Ruxton finally grew bored. While Fallon continued to fiddle with the control knobs, Ruxton turned away and walked back to the cryptography machine. Wilson was already busy at work with his screwdriver, very methodical and very careful, at great pains not to scratch the metal cover. Humming softly to himself, he slowly worked his way around the machine, treating it with the affection another man might have lavished on a woman. Ruxton stopped beside him, observing quietly for a moment, then smiled.

"How's it going, Chester? Any problems?"

"Not, not at all. She's being very cooperative. A perfect lady. And an extremely unusual design, I might add. Quite advanced. Knew that the instant I saw the control panel."

"Excellent. Now you'll be able to find out for yourself, won't you . . . about Brokaw's reputation as a genius?"

"Yes indeed! By all means. In fact . . . we're about to see what makes this little lady work."

Wilson removed the last screw and laid his screwdriver on the table. With a sort of loving tenderness, he lifted the cover and swung it aside, bending forward to examine the innards of the machine. Suddenly his face blanched, and he rocked back on his heels, staring incredulously at what he'd uncovered.

"Oh, my God! Look, Curt! Look what he's done."

XIX

Tanner drove like a man possessed.

His eyes were glued to the road and he kept the speedometer hovering around ninety. Stacey huddled in the corner, watching him nervously, thankful there were so few cars on the freeway. Since leaving Palo Alto, she hadn't spoken a word, fearful of distracting him. But as they approached the outskirts of San Francisco, she couldn't contain herself any longer.

"Warren, why not slow down a little? At least until we're through the city. If you get stopped for speeding, we'll lose all the time we've gained."

Tanner tromped the accelerator. "To hell with 'em! I haven't got time to spare. Any cop gets on my tail, he'll just have to take his chances."

Stacey fell silent a moment. There was a fixity of expression on Tanner's face that bordered on desperation. She sensed now that he was beyond reason and knew it was useless to try. Yet he seemed rational, and if she got him talking, it might have a calming effect. Finally, with the needle pushing a hundred, she decided that distracting him might be the lesser evil.

"You're afraid, aren't you, Warren?"

"Afraid! Jesus, how'd you come up with that?"

"I'm serious. You're afraid of what we'll find at the mansion. It's written all over you."

"And you know an open book when you see one, is that it?"

"No, that's not it. But I do know that something . . . strange happened tonight. You had a different dream, didn't you?"

His eyes flicked at her in a quick, sideways glance. "What makes you think that?"

"Darling, please, give me a little credit! What else could explain this madness? Do you realize you could get us both killed the way you're driving?"

"So?"

"So unless you have a very large death wish—which you don't—then something happened to set you off."

"And you figure it was the dream?"

"Not *the* dream. Another dream. Or at least a variation—something new—something you hadn't seen before."

"Nice deduction. You should've been a detective."

"Then it's true . . . isn't it?"

"You're the one with all the answers. You tell me."

"No, I have a much better idea, darling. You tell me." She leaned across the seat and gently stroked the back of his neck. "You've been lying to me by omission for weeks. Don't you think it's time you took me into your confidence—*before* we get to the mansion?"

"You mean the dream . . . what I saw tonight."

"I mean all of it, everything you've been hiding. The way you act, it's a very big load, and I believe I've earned the right to help carry it, don't you?"

There was a long reflective pause while Tanner thought it over. Tonight's dream had shaken him far more than he cared to admit, and he realized it was a burden he could no longer manage by himself. He needed someone he could trust, someone who would listen and believe and help him sort it out. Someone who wouldn't think he'd gone off the deep end.

So he told her everything.

Those odd, almost surreal flashes of *déjà vu*. The investigation that led him to Professor Ludmann. The chilling voice of Lucas Brokaw—and his former incarnation—on a tape unheard by anyone for the past thirty years. Then the dreams, commencing the very night he'd listened to the tape, explicit in every detail but curiously abbreviated, like a film clip from an old movie. Until tonight, when at last he'd seen how Lucas Brokaw ended it. Which left only one question. Perhaps the most disturbing question of all.

Why him? Why Warren Tanner?

Stacey listened, appalled by the enormity of what he'd discovered, but she had no ready answer. It was too much too quickly. She needed time to analyze it, for the only common denominator was Lucas Brokaw and that led inevitably to the very question Warren himself had raised. Why indeed had he been selected?

But there was no time. Even now they were less than two hours from the estate and—God! The thought struck her with the force of a polar wind, chilled her to the bone. She had accepted it! Without question, never once conscious of it while he talked, she had accepted the only premise that made sense. Lucas Brokaw existed, dead yet not dead! An unseen force, perhaps even a presence, returned from the grave.

At last, too astounded to lie, she simply blurted out the truth. "You believe it was a message, don't you? That tonight's dream was some sort of psychic vision."

"Let's just say it was too strong to be ignored."

"And you believe the crypt is being violated . . . tonight! That's it, isn't it?"

"Stace, I don't believe . . . I *know*."

Tanner hit the accelerator and roared down off the expressway. Before them loomed the Golden Gate Bridge, and beyond, the darkened hills of Marin County. High in the sky, obscured by westerly clouds, the moon drifted seaward and the ebb tide lay still.

XX

Ruxton had expected to encounter problems tonight, and Wilson's shock came as no great surprise. But he knew that technology alone would never solve those problems; to succeed, the operation required guidance and a steadying hand. So he kept his own expression bland, as, bending closer, he peered into the machine. Though he'd read a good deal on the subject and understood the basic principles of cipher machines, he was startled by what he saw. Inside the machine was an incomprehensible maze of wiring and fittings, ratchets and gears, and several oddly constructed wheels, a bewildering array of hardware. But he merely nodded and smiled, seemingly unruffled, and finally glanced up at Wilson.

"Very interesting, Chester. Looks a little complicated, doesn't it?"

"Complicated? Good lord, it's much more than that! No offense intended, but the word hardly does Brokaw justice. It's a marvel, Curt. An absolute marvel! The man was light-years ahead of his time."

Wilson was in his element, enjoying his authority. For a moment the complexity of the machine had unnerved him, but lecturing Ruxton was a new experience, one that quickly restored his confidence. Using his screwdriver as a pointer, he indicated the row of wheels arranged side by side within the machine and connected together by hundreds of wires.

"These are the rotors—the codewheels. Their function is to transpose plaintext into ciphertext. Normally, five rotors are considered sufficient to scramble any message. But you will notice that Brokaw engineered *eight* rotors into his machine. The ramifications of those extra rotors are all but incalculable. Here, let me show you."

The rotors were hard rubber disks approximately four inches in diameter. Around the circumference of all eight rotors—on both sides—were twenty-six electrical contacts. The contacts on one side of the rotor were wired at random to contacts on the opposite face; this created a double alphabet on every rotor. Thus an electrical impulse might transpose the letter *b* on one side of the wheel to the letter *z* on the other side. Since the rotors were wired together, the electrical impulse jumped from wheel to wheel, traversing a maze of sixteen scrambled alphabets in one burst of current. Any plaintext letter on the keyboard went through this profusion of alphabetic changes and appeared on the ciphertext printout with no relationship whatever to its surrounding letters.

"We call this the monoalphabetic substitution factor. Translated, it means that the number of ways all these letters and wheels can be wired together is practically infinite. In the case of Mr. Brokaw's machine, I venture to say these eight rotors are capable of producing somewhere in the vicinity of 20,000,000 cipher alphabets. So as you can see, it really is a marvel."

Ruxton looked properly impressed. "You've made your point, Chester. I'm convinced! Which sort of takes us back to square one . . . how do you solve it?"

"Oh, we're very fortunate," Wilson chortled. "Very fortunate, indeed. You see, a cryptanalyst normally has only the ciphertext to work with, and it might take him months to break the code. I not only have the full plaintext message, I have the machine itself! In a sense, I'll be working backward, but it simplifies the task enormously."

Briefly, Wilson outlined the procedure. Since he knew how the rotors were wired, he could establish numerical equations that would then be fed into a digital computer. Using such esoteric tools as stochastic processes and matrix theory, the computer would program a mathematical model of the cryptography machine and simulate its operation. The end result would be a reconstructed encipherment, producing a printout of Brokaw's original codetext message.

"Quite simply," Wilson concluded, "you will memorize the codetext, then type it into this machine, and it will deliver the plaintext message that identifies you as Lucas Brokaw."

"Not to steal your thunder, Chester, but that was the purpose of this drill from the beginning. Now, let's forget all the professional gobbledygook. You've seen the machine and you know how it operates, so in words of three syllables or less, how long will it take you to reproduce the codetext message?"

Wilson blinked, aware that his lecture had been cut short. He cleared his throat, suddenly uncomfortable, and averted his eyes. "Well, of course, we'll have to rent time on a computer. But I suspect that won't pose any problem in San Francisco. Perhaps we can find a monolithic system. Quite remarkable, real workhorses! Perform over a million calculations a second. It's done with logic circuits that—"

"How long, Chester?"

"A day. Perhaps less. I would like to program it several times to—"

"That's fine. We can certainly afford a day. Now, suppose you take your photographs and do whatever it is you have to do, and I'll see how Fallon's coming along. Okay?"

Wilson gave him a waxen smile and went back to tinkering with the machine. Quickly absorbed in the task, he began tracing through the maze of wires, and Ruxton left him muttering to himself. Apparently it was none too soon, for as he turned away, Fallon exploded, cursing fluently.

"Sonofabitch! Can you believe that? The dirty old scumbag rigged it. Suckered us!"

Birkhead glanced across at Ruxton and shrugged, clearly dumbfounded by the outburst. Fallon stood stock-still, reduced to baffled fury, glaring at the vault door. Ruxton approached and halted beside him, careful to betray none of his own apprehension.

"What's the problem, Johnny? Brokaw throw you a curve?"

"You bet your ass he did!" Fallon growled. "The bastard booby- trapped that door handle."

"The *vault* door handle?" Ruxton studied it a moment, thoughtful. "That's odd. Nothing was ever mentioned in his will about the vault being rigged. How can you be so sure?"

"Screw him and his will! You don't believe me? Watch!"

Fallon grasped the handgrips on the scanning device and directed it at the vault. Slowly he moved the device in a vertical path from the door handle to the top of the door and along the wall above the door. A jagged, bleeping pattern appeared in the center of the monitor screen. Then he raised the scanner overhead and ran a line across the ceiling to the entranceway. There he lowered the device and scanned the wall directly above the entranceway opening. The telltale pattern, dancing blips that varied in configuration, was apparent on the monitor the entire time. Finally, he switched off the scanner and his expression became pensive. He stepped aside, his eyes flicking from the entranceway to the vault and back again, clearly lost in thought. At length he grunted, and his features twisted in an ugly smile.

"You know, that Brokaw must've been a beaut! A real pisscutter!"

"I assume the machine told you something," Ruxton interjected. "Now suppose you tell us."

"I'll tell you one thing, he was a sneaky old bastard. It's real cute. A classy piece of work, and I thought I'd seen 'em all."

Fallon quickly briefed them on what the scanner had

shown him. A steel plunger, specially engineered within the vault door, was connected to the door handle and ran on a vertical line to the upper wall. Throwing the door handle, which normally released the lock bolts, would thrust the plunger upward, driving it into the wall above the door. There it broke the seal on a hydraulic system and rammed the fluid through a tube across the ceiling. What appeared to be a massive stone slab was suspended over the entranceway, held in place by explosive bolts. The hydraulic fluid activated a piston, which in turn set off the explosive charges and sheared the bolts.

". . . and when that happens, the stone slab drops into place and seals the entranceway. There's also a string of wires running off the entranceway, and I'll lay odds it activates an alarm system. So we'd be trapped in here like a bunch of rats till the guards came to let us out."

"And haul our butts to the slammer," Birkhead added sourly.

Ruxton's gaze traveled across the ceiling to the entranceway. "You're right, Johnny. Mr. Brokaw was even more devious than I suspected." His eyes narrowed and he swung back to the vault. "Are we stalemated or not? Can it be opened?"

"I'd say it's a toss-up." Fallon walked to the vault. "I've scanned this whole area between the door handle and the combination lock, and there's nothing that connects them. So if we stay away from the door handle, we're probably in the clear."

"Probably. That seems to be the operative word." Ruxton mulled it over a while, staring at the vault, and finally shrugged. "Why not? We're here, and the only alternative is to walk away empty-handed. Let's give it a try."

Fallon opened a pocket of the knapsack and took out the final accessory for his machine. It resembled a stethoscope fitted with stereo earpads and had an electri-

163

cal jack connected by a length of wire. Kneeling, he placed the scanner on the floor beside the vault and plugged the jack into its receptacle. Several quick adjustments calibrated the instrument for external operation. Then he licked the tip of the audio bell, which was rimmed with a suction cup, and stuck it on the side of the door. At last, everything in order, he slipped the earpads over his head and began slowly rotating the combination knob.

It took eighteen minutes until the last tumbler rolled into position. Fallon pulled the suction cup loose and removed the earpads. Stooping down, he switched off the scanner, laid the stethoscope apparatus to one side, and then straightened to face Ruxton.

"The combination is six left, twenty-five right, eighteen left, seventy-six right. Other than that, I can't guarantee a damn thing."

Ruxton merely nodded. "A bit like Russian roulette. But then . . . what isn't? Go ahead, Johnny. Try it."

Fallon dialed the combination and hastily backed away from the vault. A sudden stillness fell over the chamber. The men waited, staring intently at the door. Seconds ticked past in leaden silence. Yet nothing happened. The tension became oppressive, mirrored in their drawn faces. Time was suspended, an interminable quiet that held them immobile, scarcely able to breathe. Then, with an abrupt jolt, it ended.

There was a muffled thud and the lock bolts were withdrawn. Precisely one minute had passed, and on the second, the door swung open. Beyond, empty and waiting, stood the vault.

"I *told* you he was cute!" Fallon laughed, shaking his head. "The sonofabitch built it to open automatically . . . but with a time lapse. Anybody that wasn't wise would've grabbed the door handle instead and bingo!"

Ruxton glanced at his watch, collecting himself. When he spoke, it was with renewed authority. "Hustle it up, Johnny. You've got two safes to open, and we're running short on time. To be exact, an hour and fifty-eight minutes and counting."

Fallon's mouth again crooked in that grotesque smile. Without a word, he gathered his equipment and entered the vault.

During the next hour Fallon slowly lost his smile, along with his good humor. But what he discovered inside the vault did nothing to lessen his respect for Lucas Brokaw. If anything, he grew more cautious by the minute. In fact, he was becoming unnerved. Gradually, as he moved back and forth between the wall safes, it dawned on him that he'd met his match at last. Except for the scanner, he would have been a dead man.

After he had checked and double-checked and then checked it all again, he finally accepted what he'd found. The scanner had never lied to him before, and he knew it hadn't lied to him now. Yet it seemed somehow unfair that he had to stake *his* life to prove the point. As he walked back to the door, where Ruxton and Birkhead waited, it was the thought uppermost in his mind.

"I'll give it to you short and fast," he informed them. "Damn near everything in Brokaw's will was pure bullshit. Just for openers, those safes aren't wired together. The wall between them is solid rock. No wires, no channels, no nothing. So it makes no difference which one we open first."

"That's hard to believe," Ruxton said flatly. "His will was explicit. If you open the *answer* safe first, then they'll both blow up simultaneously."

"Take my word for it, chum. It'll never happen. But if you can't hack that, wait'll you try this on for size." Fallon rapped the vault door with his knuckles. "You remember the combination for this—it's the same for both safes in here."

"Are you serious?" Ruxton demanded. "Come off it, Johnny. That's absurd! I think you better test that scanner before you get us all killed."

Fallon's jaw clenched so tight his lips barely moved. "Since it's me that has to open 'em, it's not exactly the kind of mistake I'd make. And you haven't heard the half of it yet. See, regardless of what the will says, there's nothing peculiar about those locks. They're not wired to anything—least of all explosives. If you want, you could fiddle with the combination all day."

"Wait a minute! Are you saying it's all a smoke screen? Some sort of diversion?"

"Yeah, that's exactly what I'm saying. Brokaw put a bunch of crap in his will just to throw everybody off the track. Then he rigged his booby traps completely *opposite* to the way he said he'd done it."

"Opposite? Are you trying to tell me it's—"

"That's right, chum. It's the door handles again. I don't know for sure how he did it, but there's some extra metal on the back of both doors. Centered square behind the handles. It shows up real clear on the scanner. Looks to me like that's how he rigged it—to the door handles."

"Do you think there's another time release—on the doors?"

"Hard to tell. He was so goddamned tricky, maybe that's what he wanted us to think. The only way to find out is to try the combination. Either the door opens or it doesn't."

"And if it doesn't . . . then what?"

"Yeah. I've been asking myself the same question. And you know, I keep coming back to one idea. Most people wouldn't give it a second thought, but the handle on a wall safe normally moves in only one direction—down. You couldn't force it up with a crowbar. So if the door doesn't open on its own, then I'd say the odds favor trying to turn the handle *up*."

A strange look came into Fallon's eye and he grunted. "One thing's for damn sure! I wouldn't try turning the handle down if you offered me the U. S. Mint and a one-way ticket to Rio."

"Perhaps it's too logical," Ruxton countered. "Suppose Brokaw carried it to the same conclusion? Then it blows if you turn it up."

"Like you said, it's Russian roulette. You go with your best hunch or you don't go at all."

"Then let's go, Johnny. We're too close to quit now."

Fallon grinned and turned away quickly. He knew it had to be done fast, almost mechanically, before he had a chance to change his mind. He walked to the safe on the right, and without an instant's hesitation, dialed the sequence. Then he waited, eyes on his watch, counting the seconds.

A minute passed. Then another. And nothing happened.

Birkhead and Ruxton quietly eased away from the vault door. Wilson joined them, eyes glazed with fear, and the three men flattened themselves against the wall of the outer chamber. Inside the vault, Fallon was sweating bullets, his gaze fastened on the safe in a look of petrified desperation. He filled his lungs with a deep breath, held it a moment, steadying himself, and exhaled slowly. Then he reached out and took a firm grip on the door handle. All thought suspended, operating on nerve alone, he twisted the handle upward.

There was an audible *clunk* as the lock bolts disengaged.

Fallon gently opened the door a mere crack. Holding his penlight to the slot, he clicked it on and peered inside. His face went pale and he nearly dropped the light. But again he steadied himself, breathing hard, and eased the door ajar to a handspan's width. Cautiously, an inch at a time, he slipped his arm into the safe. Working by feel, every movement slow and deliberate, he located a loop of wire hooked over the metal flange and carefully removed it. Then his knees turned to jelly, and as he swung the door open, he had to brace himself against the wall.

Ruxton stuck his head around the corner, darting a

quick peek into the vault. Fallon managed a weak grin and jerked his thumb at the safe. "Plastique. About ten kilos. Enough to blow this whole goddamn cliff into the ocean."

The extent of Lucas Brokaw's ingenuity was apparent when they inspected the safe. Only by the slimmest of margins had Fallon second-guessed him on a booby trap rigged with diabolic cunning. Turning the handle down would have engaged the metal flange, stretching the wire taut, and pulled the pin on a mousetrap detonator. Simply opening the door before unhooking the wire would also have triggered the device. Had Fallon done anything, one single act, in the normal fashion, nearly thirty pounds of plastic explosive would have gutted the crypt, killing them all.

Vastly relieved, but pressed for time, the men worked at a feverish pace during the next half hour. After the second safe was opened, the envelopes were unsealed with a solvent specially mixed by Wilson. The cryptanalyst claimed to have learned the formula from the CIA. Ruxton then photographed the question-and-answer lists with the Minox; the envelopes were resealed and returned to their respective safes. While Fallon again activated the booby traps, Wilson and Birkhead packed their equipment in the knapsack. The last step was the vault door, and when Fallon closed it, turning the combination knob to zero, the others were waiting for him in the entranceway. Ruxton crossed off the final item on his checklist and made a quick visual inspection of the outer chamber.

Then they turned from the crypt and filed silently up the stairs.

XXI

Outside the house, Birkhead again took the lead, instructing them to wait while he scouted ahead. Without a sound, he ghosted down the walkway to the forward edge of the pavilion. Suddenly, headlights flashed on the driveway and he whirled back, hissing between his teeth. The other men instantly separated and vanished into the shadows. Birkhead went down on one knee, hidden behind the base of a massive column beside the steps. He raised the Colt Python to shoulder level and clamped it hard in a two-handed combat grip.

The car skidded to a halt in front of the mansion, and Tanner jumped out, running toward the pavilion. Stacey hurried after him, fumbling with a key ring in the dark. Tanner mounted the steps two at a time and moved quickly to the door. He twisted the handle and found it locked; wheeling around, he cursed, gesturing impatiently. Stacey caught up with him, and he stood fidgeting as she tried to insert the key in the lock.

Birkhead kept the pistol trained on his chest, slightly below the sternum, while Tanner stood sideways to the door, hovering over Stacey, urging her to hurry. But suddenly he stiffened, alert to some unseen threat, and looked around. It was nothing tangible, but rather a moment of blind instinct, an odd sense of being watched. His eyes flicked about the pavilion, probing the shadows, and for a brief instant settled on the column near the steps. Birkhead steadied the pistol, waiting for him to move or cry out, finger curled tightly on the trigger. Then Stacey finally found the lock, and there was a faint click as she opened the door. Tanner hesitated, some sixth sense still nagging at him, and she turned back, tugging at his sleeve.

"Warren! Come on, it's open."

A moment passed with no response, and she became aware of his watchful manner. Her voice dropped to a whisper. "What's wrong?"

He squinted harder into the darkness. Birkhead slowly squeezed, ready to touch off the trigger. Stacey edged closer and darted a quick glance around the pavilion.

"Warren . . . say something . . . what is it?"

A long beat of silence, then at last he shook his head. "Nothing . . . just my imagination. Let's go."

Stacey began a question, abruptly changed her mind, and stepped through the door. With a last look about the shadows, Tanner turned and followed her into the house.

Birkhead waited until the door closed, then he eased around the column, crouched low, and checked the driveway. There was no sign of the house guard, and he quickly motioned the other men forward. All but invisible, like chunks of black smoke, they melted into the darkness, moving toward the cliffs.

It was 3:07. They would have to race to beat the tide.

Inside the mansion, Tanner crossed the foyer, motioning Stacey back, and paused before the subterranean stairway. Kneeling, he inspected the electronic alarm and briefly searched the stone landing for fresh scuff marks. There was no indication of tampering; he frowned, studying the entrance a moment longer. Then he rose and walked to an armored knight standing in the far corner. He opened the visor on the helmet, ran his hand inside, and flicked a switch that deactivated the alarm.

Turning, he nodded to Stacey and moved back to the stairway. She joined him and they stood for several seconds, peering down the winding corridor. At length he shrugged, indicating silence, and crossed the upper landing. They began a slow descent into the netherworld stillness below.

Several minutes elapsed as they cautiously inched down the stairs, but what they found was perhaps the last thing Tanner had expected. Standing just inside the entranceway, they surveyed the outer chamber with a kind of bemused apprehension. It was empty and still, apparently undisturbed. Yet there was a sense of suppressed violence in the crypt. A quiet foreboding, unnatural and somehow ominous.

The feeling was so intense that neither of them spoke for a long while. Tanner walked forward and slowly circled the cryptography machine. Again he found no indication of tampering, and his frown broadened. Then he inspected the vault door for any telltale sign, quickly checked the setting on the combination knob, and knelt down for a closer look at the fittings around the door handle. Finally, he rose and moved back to the entranceway. He glanced at Stacey, clearly baffled, and shook his head.

"Nothing. It's like . . . it's never been touched."

"Maybe it hasn't. After all, if there aren't any . . ."

"No! Someone's been here. I can tell."

His certainty jarred Stacey, and the harsh look on his face momentarily unnerved her. The menace of the crypt, unlike anything she'd ever felt here before, only made it worse. Confused and frightened, she tried to collect herself, to restore some sense of balance and perspective. The dream tonight had triggered something—goaded him into coming here—and perhaps the answer was to be found in that. Yet it wasn't the place to start. Better to lead up to it slowly, one step at a time.

"The *déjà vu?*" She kept her voice casual, low-key. "Did it show you anything in particular about the crypt . . . maybe stress one part more than another?"

"No, as a matter of fact," He pulled at his ear reflectively. "Now that you mention it, I never saw anything in the crypt. That's damned strange when you stop and think about it."

"Nothing at all?"

"Not a thing. It was always in the study or the gardens. Especially at sunset. And once I got a strong impression down at the graveyard."

"Where Brokaw and his wife are buried?" he nodded, and she quickly glanced aside. "What were you doing down there?"

"Just poking around. Looking things over."

"The impression . . . what was it you saw?"

"I suppose it sounds odd, but I saw water . . . an open grave filled with water. Then I saw a headstone . . . a blank headstone, nothing on it . . . and the water disappeared. All of it seemed sort of . . . I don't know . . . somehow out of place. Not the way it was supposed to look."

She walked to the cryptography machine, thoughtful a moment. Circling the table, she stopped behind it and looked up. "So you never actually saw the crypt until after your session with Ludmann, when the dreams began?"

"That's right." He appeared distracted, staring intently at the vault door. "But it wasn't the crypt. It was always the inside of the vault. Or at least it was until tonight."

"Perhaps Ludmann hypnotized you too. Gave you a posthypnotic suggestion. It can be done."

Tanner shook his head. "Ludmann's sharp, but he's no witch doctor. Besides, he's never seen the inside of the vault himself."

"Are you sure of that . . . absolutely certain?"

"Absolutely. Once he found out I had Brokaw's papers, he played it pretty straight. The tape itself is a good example. He could have kept quiet about it and I wouldn't have known the difference."

"I've been wondering about that. If the tape was sup-

172

posed to be such a big dark secret, why would he volunteer to play it? You said he'd all but sworn a blood oath to keep it confidential."

"Except to a third party."

"Third party? I don't understand. What third party?"

"Brokaw gave him an out. If he was ever contacted by a third party, then he could break his silence."

Tanner paused, thinking back, and finally dismissed it with an idle gesture. "According to Ludmann, I'm the third party."

Stacey felt a surge of adrenalin, then a sudden loss of sensation, as though all her nerve ends had been cauterized.

"That's not . . . possible." Her conviction fell away on the last word. "Don't you see, that would mean it was preordained . . . somehow destined."

"Yeah, I know. Kismet with a little assist from Lucas Brokaw."

"Warren, you're not serious—are you? You couldn't be!"

"I don't know what to believe any more. All I've got to go on is what I see in those dreams." His gaze flicked past her to the vault, and his voice took on a note of defensive gruffness. "As much as I hate to admit it, they're pretty damned convincing. It's like someone—hell, I know it sounds crazy—but it's like he's trying to warn me of something."

"Warn you?"

"Yeah, about the crypt. How it works and the way it's . . . rigged."

Stacey flinched from the thought, but it was inescapable. Tanner's talk was no longer about dreams; it was bordering on the supernatural. That slip of the tongue—*he's trying to warn me*—meant only one thing. He'd convinced himself that Lucas Brokaw had *summoned* him to the crypt tonight.

Her reaction was spontaneous yet carefully staged. A

challenge. She turned away and walked directly to the vault. Then she slowly reached for the steel door handle.

"*Don't touch it!*" His words were chips of ice. "*Back off—now!*"

She stepped back from the vault and faced him. "I had to know. You really do believe it, don't you?"

"I suppose I wasn't sure . . . not until tonight. But there's no use kidding myself any longer."

His eyes glittered, alert yet somehow remote. "I've believed it for a long time. Now I know why." His hand moved, indicating the vault. "Remember the disaster clause in Brokaw's will? The one I could never figure out?"

Stacey merely nodded, unable to trust her voice.

"Tonight he showed me. That door handle's it . . . the disaster."

XXII

Tanner sat off to one side. An observer thus far, he hadn't yet joined in the interrogation. Instead, he merely listened, watching the man closely, reminded somehow of a cat. The similarity was remarkable.

Not once had Stacey or the director been able to rattle him. Throughout the grilling he had maintained a ready smile, his eyes cold and opaque, almost indulgent. The look of a man who tolerated people, perhaps found them a bit gauche. Yet infinitely patient, willing to endure almost anything if in the end it served his purpose. The look of a cat.

"Now, Mr. Ruxton, if you don't mind," the director paused, emphasizing the words with a sharp glance, then resumed, "suppose we move on to a few specifics. As an example, would you happen to know the name of Lucas Brokaw's father?"

"Hiram."

"And his mother?"

"Elizabeth."

"Back to Brokaw himself," Stacey prodded. "Where was he born?"

"Denver. A hospital in Denver."

"And his wife's name?"

"Stephanie."

"Her maiden name?"

"Gilchrist."

"What was the nature of her death?"

"Tuberculosis."

"Who was the architect Brokaw commissioned to build his mansion?"

"Foucart. Louis Foucart."

"You're no doubt familiar with the Brokaw art collection. Can you tell us the first major painting he bought?"

"I have no idea. There were so many."

"Perhaps you could tell us the name of Lucas Brokaw's most trusted adviser?"

"Edgar Pollard."

"And his title."

"He had no title. He was a lawyer. An attorney."

"Lucas Brokaw's wife had a pet name for him. A name only she used . . . when they were alone. What was that name?"

"I believe you're mistaken. Stephanie Brokaw was a lady. She never stooped to pet names."

That was true. It had been a trick question. On the other hand, the answer might easily have been a good guess. Other claimants had researched the Brokaw legend, many of them more thoroughly than the man being questioned today. But neither Stacey nor the director could recall one out of all the thousands who was so unflappable, so utterly in command of himself.

Curt Ruxton had appeared at the office shortly after lunch. In answering Stacey's preliminary questions, he was polite if somewhat reserved, but firmly insistent on the key point. He was Lucas Brokaw reincarnated and he could prove it. The statement had a ring of conviction. The man himself could not be discounted. He was educated, clearly in possession of his faculties, and seemed determined to press his claim. Stacey held a brief conference with the director, after which Tanner was summoned, and they all came to the same conclusion. The man sounded legitimate, and at the very least he deserved a hearing.

The story he told was unusual, but hardly farfetched. During a session with his psychiatrist, while under hypnosis, he had stumbled upon a previous incarnation. Only later, after a series of dreams, had he been able to deal with the situation rationally and accept it as a literal truth. He was Lucas Brokaw reincarnated.

176

Stacey and Tanner were astonished beyond words. Dreams were indeed revealing, as they both knew. Then, too, Tanner experienced a curious aversion to Ruxton the moment he entered the room. It was an odd sensation, deep and visceral; he had felt it the instant they shook hands. Afterward, Ruxton had avoided his gaze, addressing himself to either Stacey or the director. But Tanner couldn't shake the feeling; the longer he listened, the more uneasy he became. His reaction to what he heard was one of raw animosity.

The director was altogether unfazed by the story. He'd heard every fairy tale ever concocted during his thirty years with the foundation; his initial interest was with the man rather than the fantasy, and he proceeded to explore Ruxton's background, a line of questioning that led him into a blind alley. If Ruxton was to be believed, he was moderately wealthy, the major stockholder in a flourishing corporation, and a businessman of impeccable credentials. Hamilton Knox reversed course, directing his questions to the Brokaw legend, and by that time Stacey had regained her composure.

Now the interrogation accelerated. Their questions were pitted in counterpoint to his answers, and they gave him no time to think or choose his words. It was hard and fast, bluntly done. The facade of etiquette splintered; all pretense was forgotten.

"I find it unusual," Stacey began, "that you have such a wealth of information about Lucas Brokaw. Perhaps you could explain that, Mr. Ruxton."

"Part of it was revealed to me in the dreams." Ruxton's smile was one of disarming candor. "And as you may have surmised, I've been doing a lot of reading in the past few weeks."

"I daresay!" the director fixed him with a baleful look. "Now, as to these dreams you've been experiencing, Mr. Ruxton. If I understand correctly, they began after your second session with a psychiatrist?"

"The same night as a matter of fact."

"And your reason for seeking psychiatric help?"

"A month or so ago, I began suffering periods of severe depression. It had me confused and disturbed because there was no reason to be depressed. Nothing adverse had occurred in either my business or personal life. I felt I needed professional advice."

"So you went to a psychiatrist and he hypnotized you. Isn't that unusual—that he would resort to hypnosis so quickly?"

"Not at all. I understand it's common psychiatric procedure these days. Apparently it allows the psychiatrist to probe the subconscious, to go directly to the root of the problem."

"Perhaps you could clarify that point," Stacey interjected. "Exactly what was your problem?"

"I'm afraid we never found out. The doctor attempted to regress me back to my childhood, but he inadvertently went too far. That's how it all started. He somehow regressed me to a former incarnation."

"And you claim this former incarnation was Lucas Brokaw?"

"That's correct."

"Do you believe in reincarnation, Mr. Ruxton?"

"To be frank about it, no. At least I *didn't*. Not until that day. After listening to the playback of the tape, I began to have second thoughts."

"Precisely what did the tape reveal?"

Tanner suddenly became very alert, his senses attuned to the slightest nuance. Ruxton appeared uncomfortable for the first time, as if the memory were distressing. "It was the voice of a man in great pain, dying of cancer. But a man who had conquered the pain—and his fear of death—through a profound belief that he would be reborn. Reincarnated. On the tape he identifies himself as Lucas Brokaw."

"Would it be possible for us to hear the tape?"

"No, I'm sorry. The tape also reveals certain details about Lucas Brokaw's crypt. In fact, part of it deals with the cryptography machine and the coded message. So I think you'll agree, it wouldn't be in my best interests to allow anyone to hear that tape."

"Then perhaps you would allow us to speak with your psychiatrist," Knox's voice was unnaturally harsh and aggressive, "merely to substantiate the validity of your statement."

"I hate to seem obstinate or uncooperative. And believe me, I have no reason to suspect your motives. However, every man has his price, even a reputable psychiatrist. It's unlikely, but still possible that he could be induced to break the rules of doctor-patient confidentiality. As you can see, that would seriously jeopardize my position."

"How can you be sure he won't come forward on his own? Contact us directly?"

"Several reasons. I demanded the tape after our second session, and I never returned. So he knows nothing of the dreams and probably wrote me off as a hyperneurotic of some sort. More to the point, he doesn't know I'm here. Nor does he have any reason to believe Lucas Brokaw would contact me again."

"By further contact, I presume you mean the dreams?"

"Yes. To be specific, twenty-three dreams spaced over the period of a month."

"Very impressive. Suppose you tell us a little about the dreams."

"You place me in an awkward position, Mr. Knox. What I saw in those dreams convinced me that I am Lucas Brokaw reincarnated. But the information is so detailed—of such a technical nature—that even the smallest disclosure would jeopardize my claim. I believe the secrets of Lucas Brokaw were meant for my ears and my ears alone."

Stacey frowned skeptically. "Pardon my bluntness, Mr. Ruxton, but if everything you say is true, then why have you waited so long to come forward?"

"Quite simply because the final secret was revealed to me only last night." Ruxton paused, his expression very intent and very earnest. *"I am now prepared to enter Lucas Brokaw's crypt."*

The impact of his statement visibly startled Stacey and the director. Neither of them responded, and a hush fell over the room. Tanner lit a cigarette, thoughtful a moment. He was convinced the man was an impostor; he had a gut feeling the story was riddled with fabrication. On top of his certainty that the crypt had been violated, Ruxton's timely appearance also seemed rather too coincidental. Yet there was something inscrutable about Ruxton, a sort of personal insensitivity that concealed whatever truth lay behind the urbane mask. Abruptly, with a sense of nothing to lose, Tanner decided to join the interrogation.

"Not to change the subject, Mr. Ruxton, but I wonder if you could satisfy my curiosity on a couple of matters?"

Ruxton turned, facing him, and something unspoken passed between them. A kind of mutual recognition, the wary respect of duelists about to engage each other with a yard of cold steel. Ruxton nodded, the catlike smile impassive. "Certainly, Mr. Tanner. What is it you wish to know?"

"Does the Battle of the Little Big Horn mean anything to you?"

"Are you talking about Custer's Last Stand?"

"Yes."

"No, it doesn't. Why do you ask?"

"How about the Smithsonian Institution?"

"Nothing."

"Perhaps you're familiar with a Sioux war chief named Red Horse?"

"Sorry. My knowledge of the Sioux is limited to Sitting Bull."

"None of it rings a bell? You're sure?"

"Quite sure, Mr. Tanner. But I fail to see the connec-

180

tion. Do your questions have some relevance to the Brokaw estate?"

Tanner smiled, equally impassive, his expression sphinxlike. "One last question. Would you allow yourself to be hypnotized again—by someone who knew Lucas Brokaw intimately?"

"I'm afraid not." Ruxton met his gaze and held it. "Please understand, Mr. Tanner. I want to be cooperative, but it's necessary to establish certain limits. Above all, I refuse to divulge what I've been shown in the dreams. Not to you. Not to anyone. On the other hand, you have the means to substantiate everything I've told you."

"You're referring to the crypt."

"Precisely. Allow me to demonstrate that I *am* Lucas Brokaw reincarnated."

Tanner gave him a bored look and slowly blew a smoke ring. "Talk to Mr. Knox. He's the one you have to convince."

Knox rose to his feet, hurriedly ending the interview. "Thank you for dropping by, Mr. Ruxton. We'll give it every consideration, and rest assured—you will hear from us within the week."

"I appreciate your courtesy." Ruxton stood, nodding to Stacey and Tanner, then walked to the door. "By the way, there's no danger involved for whoever accompanies me into the crypt. Lucas Brokaw was quite explicit in his instructions."

The door closed behind him, and Hamilton Knox flushed red to his hairline. "Well! Of all the impertinence! I must say, the fellow certainly doesn't lack confidence."

"Far from it," Stacey murmured. "I got the impression he was already counting the money."

The director collapsed into his chair. "And of all the confounded luck, he had to be born on the night Brokaw died! That complicates matters greatly."

"Don't let it upset you too much," Tanner remarked. "I've got one of my hunches."

"Hunches are hardly admissible! Which reminds me. What was all that nonsense about Custer and the Smithsonian?"

"Just a shot in the dark." Tanner flicked a warning glance at Stacey, then smiled. "I thought I'd feed him a few sucker questions and see how he reacted."

"Like Mr. Ruxton, I'm afraid I fail to see the connection." Knox pursed his lips, silent a moment. Then his eyes turned grim, hidden in a nest of wrinkles, and he suddenly leaned forward in his chair. "I want the man thoroughly investigated. Use every means at your command, Warren. And do it with dispatch. Quickly!"

Tanner suppressed the urge to laugh. He hardly needed to be told. Long before the interrogation ended, he'd already made up his mind about Curt Ruxton. Their verbal sparring had merely confirmed it. They drew sparks, and their antagonism had little to do with the foundation. It was personal. One on one.

A thing born of dreams.

XXIII

Tanner's investigation lasted five futile days. By Friday morning all he had produced was a blizzard of paperwork. Wherever he turned, he'd been unable to discredit Curt Ruxton.

The misgiving he had about Ruxton was like a barb that worked deep and slowly festered. But the antidote—tangible proof of a hoax—wasn't to be found. Tanner obtained a full and comprehensive report from Dun & Bradstreet. The San Francisco police allowed him unlimited access to their files, and they quietly circulated inquiries among their street contacts. Through an old friend at the FBI, he collected voluminous data from the IRS, the CIA, and the bureau's mammoth computer repository. As a last resort, he even questioned Ruxton's neighbors and personally visited several of the franchised karate schools. The result was always the same, whatever the source. Nothing.

Or at least nothing incriminating. Early on, he had uncovered Ruxton's kinky relationship with Jill Dvorak and Monk Birkhead. But it was a discreet arrangement, and while revealing, not all that relevant in terms of the investigation. A man's sexual habits, however outlandish, hardly disqualified him as a claimant.

Finally, late Friday afternoon, Tanner called it quits. Having exhausted every available resource, he had no choice but to admit he was stymied. Almost as though it was a personal defeat, he met with Stacey and the director and reluctantly delivered his report. Curt Ruxton was nothing more nor less than he claimed to be—a legitimate businessman.

Stacey accepted the news with a look of resignation, but the director nearly bit the stem off his pipe. He regarded Tanner with a dour expression and made little more than a token effort to hide his displeasure.

"That's it? A bedroom peccadillo and nothing more? Come now, Warren. Surely no man is that spotless."

"I didn't say he's spotless. I said there's no indication of fraud."

"Are you sure, though? Absolutely certain?"

"No, I'm not sure! Quite the opposite, in fact."

Tanner was still plagued by a nagging suspicion, bothered by Ruxton's failure to acknowledge the connection between Lucas Brokaw and the Little Big Horn. Of course, his own dreams hadn't dealt with Custer either. But, then, he wasn't claiming the Brokaw fortune. His instincts told him he was right, and he saw nothing to lose by getting it on the record.

"As far as I'm concerned, Ruxton's as phony as a three-dollar bill. But I can't prove it. Except for his playmates, he's the original Mr. Clean."

There was conviction behind his words, but the director dismissed it with an abrupt gesture. "I've told you before, Warren. Hunches are not admissible. We need hard facts. Proof!"

"In that case, my report stands. Those *are* the facts. You could investigate till hell freezes over, and it won't change his record. On paper, he's a solid citizen. Obeys the law, pays his taxes, and never had so much as a traffic violation."

They lapsed into silence, and a long while passed before Knox threw up his hands in disgust. Then he hunched down in his chair, as though he'd reconciled himself to the inevitable, and a pallid cast settled over his features. He glanced across at Stacey.

"Very well, my dear. Call him. Arrange it for Monday."

Tanner stood woodenly apart.

Over the weekend his mood had steadily darkened, and this morning his face was congealed in loathing. On the ride out to the estate he hadn't once spoken to Ruxton, and his grim look became all the more pronounced upon entering the mansion. Outwardly, he had control of himself, but inside he was gripped by a sense of bitterness and rage. Descending the staircase, his mood had grown worse. It was as though he personally was being violated. Not the crypt or its secrets but him! — some part of his inner self.

The feeling was so strong that he had to turn away from Ruxton when they first entered the crypt. It was insane. Paranoid. An instant of blind, ungovernable fury, unlike any emotion he'd ever known. Only by imposing an iron will was he able to restrain it, and several moments passed before he got hold of himself. But when he finally turned back, it was still there. An urge to kill provoked by some monstrous need to survive.

The others were much too preoccupied to notice his behavior. Watching them now, Tanner was struck by a sense of impending doom. Stacey and the director were positioned on opposite sides of the cryptography machine, and Curt Ruxton stood directly in front of the table. Knox concluded his instructions, warning that only one attempt would be permitted, but Ruxton gave no indication that he'd heard. His eyes appeared glazed, fixed in an intensely vacuous look, and he stared spellbound at the machine, like a holy man locked in a trance.

Tanner thought it an act. A very good act, but nothing more. It seemed to him less of a trance than the look of a man in deep concentration, trying to remember something very involved and very complicated. Like a code.

After a while, Ruxton blinked, as if awakening from a heavy sleep. His hand went to the control panel and, without hesitating, he flipped the on switch. The machine purred to life with a rhythmic hum. Then he placed his fingers lightly on the keyboard and slowly, one letter at a time, began typing. Twice he paused to reflect, clearly in no rush, but his pace was steady, very deliberate. Though it seemed longer, less than two minutes elapsed before he removed his fingers from the keyboard.

A momentary hush fell over the crypt. Everyone stood frozen, eyes glued to the machine. Suddenly it erupted. There was a muted buzz, followed by three strokes on a bell, and the machine spat out a single line of plaintext:

THIS IS THE REAL LUCAS BROKAW

Stacey and the director were literally flabbergasted. Their mouths popped open and they gaped at the printout in stunned disbelief. The unthinkable had finally happened. The very thing neither of them had ever believed possible. Yet it was there before them in black and white.

Tanner evinced no surprise whatever. He'd known all along from the minute they entered the crypt that today was the day the code would be broken. His only uncertainty was where it would end. How far could Ruxton go without getting himself killed? And perhaps, in the process, killing them all.

Ruxton apparently saw nothing to be gained by delay. Assured, quite confident now, he spoke to the director, indicating the vault. Knox's reply was unintelligible, but he managed to bob his head in assent. Ruxton walked to the vault and paused, fingers pressed to his forehead, trancelike. Then he nodded to himself, opened his eyes, and began dialing the combination.

Watching him, Tanner suddenly remembered the door handle. Without a word, he grabbed Stacey and pulled her back through the entranceway. It offered protection of sorts, and there was always a chance they could escape up the staircase. But this time Ruxton fooled him. Instead of turning the door handle, he moved aside, motioning the director to stay back, and waited. Everyone again stood motionless, as if mesmerized, trapped in an instant of deafening quiet.

There was a loud *thunk* and the vault door swung open.

Tanner couldn't believe it. He swayed backward, confused and disoriented, jolted by the shock of what he'd seen. *Ruxton hadn't touched the door handle.*

Stacey and the director seemed momentarily paralyzed. Utterly dumbstruck, they stared wide-eyed into a vault that was last seen thirty years ago.

By Lucas Brokaw.

After a casual inspection of the vault, Ruxton turned in the doorway and regarded them with a diffident smile. It was a look of profound empathy, almost as though he was commiserating with their dismay. Yet the look was contrived, all part of the act, and he could scarcely conceal his contempt. He decided to press the advantage while they were still in a state of shock.

"Shall we proceed?" Ruxton inquired calmly. "I believe the next step is to open the question safe."

The director darted a quick glance into the vault. His mouth twitched in a nervous smile, and his voice was strained. "Yes, of course . . . the safe. Quite right, Mr. Ruxton. Please lead on."

"No!" Stacey cried.

Surprised, the two men turned from the doorway. Stacey's hand went out to the director, her eyes pleading with him. "There's no need for you to go in there. Let him open the safe by himself! Then you can ask him the questions."

Knox smiled, touched by her concern, but shook his head. "I'm sorry, my dear, but the will is quite specific as to procedure. I can't shirk the responsibility now. Not after all these years." He nodded to Ruxton and took hold of the door. "If you will, please step inside and allow me to close the door."

"I'm afraid that's impossible," Ruxton informed him. "The door can't be opened from the inside."

"Oh! And why not, Mr. Ruxton? The will made no mention of the door."

"Look, just take my word for it, all right? It's a specially built door, and that's the only way it works. Believe me, I know what I'm talking about."

Tanner stiffened, glaring at him.

How the hell could he know that? Unless . . .

Knox shrugged, motioning for Stacey and Tanner to remain where they were, and then followed Ruxton through the door. From the entranceway, their view into the vault was restricted; the inner edge of both safes was visible, but little else. Knox halted in the center of the vault, directly in their line of sight, and Ruxton moved to the wall safe on the right. It was apparent the instant he touched the combination knob. The director began fidgeting, and great pearls of sweat trickled down over his forehead.

Unable to look away, Tanner and Stacey braced themselves, waiting for the explosion. Absolute silence descended on the crypt, and for what seemed an eternity, they stared at the director in morbid fascination.

Then Ruxton's hand appeared, holding an envelope.

The director sighed, almost resigned now. He accepted the envelope, tore it open, and slowly scanned the contents. At last, clearly puzzled by what he'd read, he looked up.

"Mr. Ruxton, I will now ask you the questions."

He took out a pen, ready to jot down the answers, and glanced at the sheet of paper. "The combination knob on the vault door was set at zero. What is the symbolism of that setting?"

"Life is an endless circle, and our karma guides us safely along the path of each new cycle in the journey."

"The combination on the vault door and on both safes was the same: 6–25–18–76. What is the meaning of this sequence?"

"It is the date of my birth. June 25, 1876."

"State the full name of my previous incarnation."

"John Roger Hughes."

"Now state the exact date of his death?"

"June 25, 1876."

"What is the significance between my date of birth and the date of John Hughes's death?"

"It was a sign that the circle would be joined on the day of my birth. An omen that I would be reincarnated on the day of my death."

The director stared at the paper for several seconds, seemingly transfixed. Finally he drew a long breath and nodded. "Very well, Mr. Ruxton, you may open the second safe."

It took Ruxton less than three minutes to disarm the booby trap and open the door. He reached into the safe, extracted the envelope, and silently handed it over. The director ripped it open and placed the two sheets of paper side by side. A slight tremor tugged at his fingers, rattling the paper, and his eyes flicked from page to page. Then his features drained of color and his lips moved in an incredulous whisper.

The answers were a perfect match, word for word.

Abruptly, he turned and walked away. His motions were jerky and disoriented, like a straw man tottering clumsily in the wind. He stepped through the door and halted, staring vacantly across the room. His face was ashen and his voice trembled as he held out the papers.

"It's him—he's come back! This man is Lucas Brokaw."

XXIV

The first check was for $51,228,649.

Yet the money was secondary in public interest. Of greater interest by far was the reincarnation of Lucas Brokaw; the story created a worldwide sensation. Newspapers and television reports quickly labeled it The Second Coming. The Vatican and various Christian organizations strenuously objected, but the allusion stuck. Prominent religious scholars, Occidental and Oriental alike, were unanimous in their verdict. In all of recorded history, never had there been a more clearly documented instance of a dead man being reborn.

By the terms of the will, Lucas Brokaw reincarnated was to regain control of his fortune over a period of six months. The transfer was to be accomplished as expeditiously as possible, but without placing undue hardship on the foundation. Since the bulk of the inheritance was invested in debentures and tax-free municipal bonds, the paperwork alone was expected to consume several months. The initial payment had been made in cash, as specified in the will, and represented 10 percent of the fortune. The balance would be transferred in successive increments on a month-to-month basis.

Current market value: $512,286,493.78.

Curt Ruxton was catapulted from obscurity to international fame within hours of the first news release. Virtually overnight he became the living symbol of man's search for immortality; his name swiftly attained the status of a household word around the globe. Newscasters, reporters, and photographers descended on San Francisco by the planeload. They besieged his apartment, clamoring for interviews, swarming over him like a pack of famished jackals whenever he emerged on the street.

Finally, on the following Monday, the deed was properly recorded and the Marin County estate was transferred to his name. With Jill and Birkhead, he fled across the Golden Gate Bridge, hounded all the way by a caravan of taxis and rent-a-cars filled with reporters. Once inside the front gate, however, he was safe. The guards were now working for him, and he issued orders that no one was to be admitted without an appointment. Privately he was somewhat amused by the irony of the situation. This time he was on the right side of the electric fence.

And it was *his* fence!

The servants were another matter entirely. Ruxton wanted no spies under his own roof, and neither the housekeeper nor the caretaker could be trusted. Their loyalty would always remain a question mark; things they overheard might very well be reported to the foundation, which made their presence in the house a definite liability. So he wrote out checks for three months' severance pay and instructed both of them to be off the estate before dark. Until his plans were firm, Jill could look after the house and Birkhead could hire day laborers to maintain the grounds.

The rest of the afternoon they spent exploring the mansion, like tourists on a holiday. Their mood was festive; they wandered from room to room, laughing and excited, as though inspecting the ruins of some ancient castle. The one sobering moment in their tour was the crypt. Ruxton and Birkhead knew its secrets and were reminded that they'd come perilously close to failure. Jill was simply frightened. Even the outer chamber gave her the shudders, and despite a good deal of coaxing, she refused to set foot in the vault. Nor was she interested in hearing Birkhead's monologue on booby traps. She hung back near the entranceway, scarcely listening, and the men finally got the message. Ruxton suggested they leave.

Upstairs their festive mood returned. With the servants gone, they had the house to themselves, and everyone agreed that a celebration was in order. Ruxton and Jill retired to the drawing room while Birkhead went off to loot the wine cellar. He came back shortly with several bottles of vintage champagne, and the party began. After they'd toasted one another, Ruxton rolled a couple of joints, lighting one for Jill, and the big man fixed himself a quick snort of coke. Then, in dazzling good humor, they drank to their benefactor and resident spook, Lucas Brokaw.

Laughing, Jill swept airily around the room, a joint in one hand and a glass of champagne in the other. Her hair was drawn back on the nape of her neck, accentuating the sleek contours of her face; her eyes were large and expressive, animated with a kind of childlike wonder as she gazed at the art collection on the walls. She felt giddy and foolish, intoxicated by the sheer opulence of the room, pausing from time to time to stare at a Renoir or a Degas, all the while marveling to herself that they had pulled it off. That it was over. That all of this was theirs at last.

Watching her glide about the room, Ruxton thought he'd never seen her so happy. Not even the night he'd come home with the check. In a curious sort of way, it was as though the nesting instinct had asserted itself. To her, the mansion, the estate, and the gallery of paintings represented permanence, a tangible reality. The money was still an illusion, a truth so abstract and of such magnitude that she hadn't yet accepted it as fact.

He glanced across at Birkhead. The big man was twisting and squirming in an ornate Victorian chair, trying to find a comfortable position. It appeared to be a losing battle, and Ruxton sensed that they were of one mind about the mansion. However grand, it simply wasn't their style. A whole new world awaited them once they had control of Brokaw's fortune—and perhaps tonight was the night to reveal the final step in his plan. After a while he caught Birkhead's eye and jerked his chin toward Jill.

Birkhead studied him a moment, then nodded. He wasn't certain what the look meant, but he'd suspected all along what Ruxton had in mind. If he was correct, that left only Jill to be convinced.

"Quite a layout, isn't it, Monk?" Ruxton lifted his champagne glass in a grand gesture, indicating the room. "All the comforts of home."

"Like hell!" Birkhead grunted sharply. "It's a goddamn mausoleum."

"Oh, it's not!" Jill laughed, arms thrown out, and pirouetted toward them in lazy circles. "It's wonderful! The most wonderful house I've ever seen."

"Yeah, it's really great." Birkhead grinned, baiting her. "Especially if you're a vampire. Tell you the truth, I about halfway expected to find Dracula stashed down in the wine cellar."

"Honestly, Monk! That's your whole problem. You have no appreciation for the finer things."

"No, he's got a point," Ruxton countered. "There's a funereal atmosphere about this place. Could get very depressing."

"Then we'll redecorate!" Jill responded brightly. "After all, it's ours now, isn't it?"

"Oh, it's ours, all right. But it won't be for long."

"It won't?" Jill cocked her head in an inquisitive frown. "I don't understand. Why won't it?"

"Because we're going to sell it."

"Do you mean—are you talking about the house?"

"The house. The paintings. The whole ball of wax."

"But why, Curt? We just got it."

"And in a few months we're going to unload it. Just as quickly as I get my hands on the rest of Brokaw's money."

194

"But what does the house have to do with the money?"

"Because I want to travel. See the world. London. Paris. Rome—"

"The Orient!" Birkhead interjected.

"And I don't want this albatross hanging around my neck. As a matter of fact, when we take off, I don't want *any* encumbrances left behind."

Jill gave him a quick, intent look. "You aren't talking about the house, are you? You're talking about something else."

"Someone else," Ruxton corrected her. "In a word, our silent partners."

To avoid complications, the rest of the gang had dropped out of sight the night of the raid. Chester Wilson was sequestered in the house north of Sausalito, and Johnny Fallon had a new hideout in the Mission district. They were to lie low and talk to no one while Ruxton attempted to pass himself off as Lucas Brokaw. If the plan succeeded, it was prearranged that Birkhead would deliver a first installment of $1,000,000 exactly two weeks after the foundation issued a check. Since the event had made world news, there was no need for further contact. Fallon and Wilson knew precisely which night to expect delivery.

Now Birkhead suddenly jackknifed out of his chair. He slammed a fist into his palm and uttered a jocular bark of laughter. "By God, I knew it! All along I kept telling myself you had a surprise in store for those bastards. Just flat-ass knew you wouldn't—"

"But *why*?" Jill cut him off, her eyes wide with horror, fixed on Ruxton. "It's not necessary, Curt. We've got it all, everything! So why—*that?*"

Ruxton shrugged. "Why waste $10,000,000?"

He paused, reflective a moment. When he spoke again, his voice was charged with malevolence. "Let's face it. Neither of them can be trusted. They'll keep

195

quiet only until they've been paid off. And at that point, they'll get greedy. Especially Fallon. He'll start brooding on the half billion we got and his share will begin to look like peanuts. Then he threatens to blow the whistle, and we'll end up paying blackmail the rest of our lives."

Jill began a protest but he stopped her with an upraised palm. "Don't hassle me on this. It has to be done and that's it!" She blinked, staring at him through a prism of tears, and finally looked away. Then his gaze shifted to Birkhead.

"Let's make it permanent, Monk. Permanent silent partners."

XXV

"I admire your tenacity, Warren. But I question the—"

"Save the lecture! You're wasting your breath."

"Yes, I daresay I am. Be that as it may, however, I do question the soundness of your judgment. After all, it's been two weeks now, and you've uncovered nothing to alter the situation. Forgive my candor, but that has all the earmarks of a lost cause."

"And you've got all the earmarks of a man who's lost his stomach for a fight."

"You needn't be rude, Warren. I'm merely trying to point out the futility of carrying it further. Ruxton has established himself as the legitimate heir, and we're bound by the terms of the will. Those are the facts. There's nothing to be gained by turning it into some sort of personal vendetta."

"He'll slip. His kind always slips. Sooner or later he'll make a mistake. And when he does, I'll be standing right there waiting!"

The director glanced at Stacey, and she shook her head helplessly. Their concern was evident, yet neither of them seemed able to reach Tanner. Over the past week, his behavior had become aberrant. One moment he was withdrawn and unresponsive, aware of little that went on around him. The next he was surly and belligerent, given to violent outbursts of temper, almost as though he'd suddenly gone schizoid. It was unnerving to watch, and as he became more erratic, their apprehension had steadily mounted. He blamed himself for Ruxton's success, considered it a personal failure of the worst sort. Today, despite all their arguments, he still refused to admit defeat. And he also refused to close the file on Ruxton.

If not irrational, it was certainly unrealistic, and they were no longer merely worried. They were frightened.

Tanner stood at the window, gazing out across the campus. There was a faraway look in his eyes, as if he was staring toward something dimly visible in the distance. Quite the contrary, his thoughts were very much on the problem at hand. Hamilton Knox.

The director was demanding an end to his investigation. Yet he knew Ruxton was an impostor. Not just a hunch, but hard fact. Unwittingly, Ruxton had tripped himself that day in the crypt—by spieling off the name John Roger Hughes, when only a week before he'd disavowed any knowledge of Custer's Last Stand or the Little Big Horn. Lucas Brokaw had been intimately familiar with Sergeant John Hughes and the manner of his death. And Lucas Brokaw reincarnated would have made the connection instantly.

So it was quite obviously another of Lucas Brokaw's crafty little tricks. He'd purposely deleted the word *sergeant* from the question-and-answer lists, aware that its omission would ultimately force an imposter to betray himself. Which was precisely the case. Tanner now knew that it was Ruxton who had somehow gained entry to the vault—and escaped undetected. But he'd come away with only half the story. The half that branded him a fraud.

Perhaps it wouldn't hold up in court, but it was proof enough for Tanner. He felt outraged and vindictive—personally defiled by the hoax—and he knew he wouldn't quit until he'd exposed Ruxton. The more immediate problem, of course, was Hamilton Knox.

Oddly enough, Tanner had no explanation for his own secretiveness. It certainly wasn't the result of his promise to Professor Ludmann. Stacey already knew of the Brokaw tape, and with the foundation on the way down the tube, it served no purpose to withhold information from the director. But he still couldn't bring himself to divulge the entire story.

Stacey was confused and upset. Only last night, in a bitter argument, she had accused him of becoming paranoid. And while he agreed, he'd again extracted her promise not to talk until he had devised a way to trap Ruxton. So perhaps the director was right after all.

Perhaps it *was* a vendetta. Very personal and very private. A matter to be settled solely between himself and Curt Ruxton.

And Lucas Brokaw.

Several minutes passed in silence while Tanner stared out the window and the director stared at Tanner. Stacey, loyal to one and in love with the other, couldn't bring herself to look at either man. Presently, determined on a last-ditch effort, the director cleared his throat.

"Warren, let me be frank with you. By continuing to poke about in Ruxton's affairs, we've come dangerously close to charges of conflict of interest. You must realize that you've placed us all in a highly untenable position. Lucas Brokaw's will is unequivocal. Our responsibility is no longer to the foundation, but rather to his legitimate heir."

"Jesus Christ!" Tanner wheeled away from the window, fists clenched, and advanced on him. "Do you seriously believe Ruxton is—that he's Lucas Brokaw?"

"Please refrain from shouting, Warren. And bear in mind that my personal views on reincarnation are totally irrelevant. We deal in facts—nothing else! Curt Ruxton has established his claim and we *will* comply. Do I make myself clear?"

"Perfectly clear. But if you think I'm going to back off now, you're mistaken. Ruxton will get everything coming to him all right, but it'll be more than he bargained for. A helluva lot more!"

"Then you leave me no choice, Warren." Knox's voice was grave, subdued. "I want your investigation terminated today. That is a direct order, and you may consider it effective immediately."

"Tell you what you can do with that order . . . turn it sideways and see if it'll fit."

Hamilton Knox was too astounded to reply. Tanner turned and stalked toward the door, nodding to Stacey as he crossed the room. There was no need to ask where he was going or what he intended to do. She already knew. Over the last two weeks his routine had become as regular as clockwork. Every night he vanished shortly before dark and returned sometime during the early morning hours. But today there was a difference. Some almost imperceptible change she couldn't define. Then she caught it out of the corner of her eye. A fleeting glimpse as he went through the door.

He was favoring his right leg, as though he had a sprained ankle or perhaps a stone bruise. Yet there was something odd. . . .

The door slammed and he was gone.

XXVI

Tanner lit a cigarette and slouched lower in his chair.
There was a prolonged silence, and he shifted uncom-
fortably, aware of the older man's scrutiny. At last, with
a bleak frown, he sighed and looked away.

"That's it, professor. Everything that's happened."

"I wish you had come to me sooner, Mr. Tanner. To
be quite frank about it, I was afraid something like this
would happen."

"Well, I thought I could handle it myself, but this
afternoon everything went to pieces. When I told Knox
to stuff it, I knew I needed some advice. And damned
fast."

"Actually, Knox was little more than a catalyst. In
light of what you've told me, I believe we can conclude
that your anger was directed solely at Curt Ruxton."

"Even so, why should I feel that strongly about him?
Hell, he's nothing to me. Not personally, anyway. But
it's like an obsession. I can't let go! Something keeps
pushing me to go after him, break him."

Across the desk, George Ludmann methodically
filled his pipe. Then he struck a match, puffing smoke
as he pondered the question. Tanner was desperate, on
the verge of losing control. Yet it was all too obvious
that the reason still eluded him. Or perhaps he was beyond reason, past the point of no return. Considering
the story he'd told, it was a distinct possibility.

The solution had occurred to Ludmann almost immediately, but he knew it must be approached with caution. He stuck the pipe in his mouth and leaned back in
his chair. He was determined to take it step by step,
eliminating the alternatives as he went along. Suddenly
he knew where to start.

"I presume you've heard of Carl Jung."

"The psychiatrist?"

"Yes, but a man with an open mind . . . despite his training. Along with Freud and a few others, he displayed a genuine interest in the occult."

"Interest or belief?"

"It's a moot point." Ludmann made a small gesture of dismissal. "The important thing is a theory Jung developed. He believed that the unconscious contains collective instincts common to mankind, but he postulated that these instincts are *never* exposed to the conscious mind. Thus the collective unconscious could appear in the form of dreams or hallucinations, and since there's no awareness of its origin, we immediately label it strange and uncanny . . . paranormal."

"Sorry," Tanner interjected. "I don't see the connection."

"It's really quite simple. Jung's theory provides an intellectual explanation for everything you've experienced. By projection, it could also account for your animosity toward Ruxton."

"Professor, there's no rational explanation for the things that have happened to me. And I think we both know it. So don't waltz me around with that intellectual number."

"Very well. Suppose we try another tack." Ludmann fussed with his pipe, thoughtful a moment, then glanced up. "Have you noticed any outward change in yourself . . . either physical or emotional?"

"No, why?"

"Because these outward manifestations are often the direct link to a previous life. If a man begins to exhibit unusual behavioral characteristics—a dramatic personality change—then we have grounds to suspect it's a former incarnation asserting itself."

"Hold it!" A querulous squint. "Are you telling me a former incarnation can actually take over the . . . new body . . . the living person?"

"Of course. I wouldn't say it's common, but it's by no means rare. There are numerous cases on record, and all of them are heavily documented. As a matter of fact, our studies indicate that the transition accelerates enormously once the living person starts to recall places and events from his previous existence."

"You're not talking about dreams, are you?"

"Dreams and recurrent nightmares, but more importantly, visions. These are all part and parcel of a former incarnation asserting itself. Curiously, a subject who has visions of a past life generally died a violent death in that previous existence."

"Like the dreams Brokaw had about Sergeant Hughes?"

"Yes . . . and the dreams you've had about Lucas Brokaw."

"Are you suggesting . . ."

"I'm suggesting nothing, Mr. Tanner. It's merely an observation. And perhaps not altogether relevant, at that. You see, in cases involving violent death, we generally find direct recall of some sort. Either visions or spells of involuntary memory."

"So dreams and *déjà vu* don't really count?"

"Oh, it all counts," Ludmann informed him. "In the paranormal we're hardly limited to one method of scorekeeping."

"What about the premonitions I've had—" Tanner hesitated, unsure exactly what he wanted to say. "The premonitions about the crypt. How does that tie in with dreams and the rest of it?"

"Actually, there are no hard and fast rules in terms of the occult. Clairvoyance and precognition are accepted phenomena in virtually all instances. It could be another means of a previous incarnation asserting itself. On the other hand, it might easily be the spirit of Lucas Brokaw transmitting a telepathic message."

"Wait a minute, are you talking about ghosts?"

"Spirit, ghost, haunt—the terms aren't incompatible.

The critical factor is the message, whatever its source. Within the last few years, we've gathered sufficient evidence to indicate that telepathy *does* cross the gap between living and dead. Generally, it's all quite spontaneous—a product of the unconscious—which further indicates that the spirit chooses the time and place to make his thoughts known."

"Very enlightening, professor. But you still haven't answered my question. What does all that have to do with these premonitions?"

Ludmann studied his nails, pedantic now. "One of the constants we find in clairvoyance and precognition is the crisis factor. The spirit frequently sends a telepathic message while undergoing a crisis, and the living person then exteriorizes that message in a form apparent to the senses."

"You're saying Lucas Brokaw knew of the danger to his crypt and flashed me a message about the impending crisis. Is that it?"

"Precisely."

"Bullshit!"

"Not at all. In your case it resulted in a highly visible paranoia concerning the crypt. And a form of paranoia, I might add, not unlike that which afflicted Lucas Brokaw himself."

"Jesus Christ. It's like a candy store: there's something to suit everyone's taste. First, you hint that I'm Brokaw reincarnated, and now you say it might be Brokaw's spook working some sort of voodoo on me. Any more goodies?"

"Yes, now that you mention it, there is another possibility." Ludmann tamped the dottle in his pipe and lit a match. "Let's go back for a moment to your feelings of animosity toward Ruxton. You admitted yourself that it was a strange reaction; I believe the word you used was inexplicable." He puffed smoke, blew out the match, and tossed it in an ashtray. "Yet, I wonder . . . doesn't it strike you as the very reaction Lucas Brokaw would experience?"

"I don't follow you, professor. What's the point?"

"I'm merely theorizing, you understand, but it suggests the possibility of a possession."

"Possession?" Tanner shook his head, astounded. "I thought that only had to do with demons . . . the devil. Isn't that what exorcism is all about, drive Satan out and purify the soul?"

"Not entirely, although that's a common belief. In point of fact, exorcism had its origins long before the birth of Christ. Among ancient cultures, it was the accepted purgative when an alien spirit gained control of a man's mind and body. Even in the Middle Ages, after Satan became the symbol of evil, priests were frequently called upon to exorcise lesser demons—the alien spirit."

"So according to your theory, the alien spirit—"

"In this case, Lucas Brokaw."

"—is trying to take possession of my soul and . . . do what?"

"Force you to become the instrument of his will. By controlling your mind, he could then use your body to exact retribution. Assuming, of course, that Ruxton is the imposter you claim and that Lucas Brokaw does feel the need for vengeance."

"Oh, Ruxton's a phony, all right. But what if I resist?"

"How so?"

"What if I won't cooperate? Suppose I refuse to act as Brokaw's instrument of vengeance . . . then what?"

"Then Lucas Brokaw might very well take matters into his own hands. I've told you before, it's difficult to put the demon back in the bottle."

"Are you saying Brokaw could act on his own . . . somehow do it himself?"

"I'm saying it's one of several possibilities. There are documented cases of a spirit doing exactly that, just as there is documentation of clairvoyance and possession.

Not to mention countless instances of a person assuming all the traits and physical manifestations of a previous incarnation."

"Then it really is a grab bag, isn't it?" Tanner demanded. "Sort of an any-or-all proposition."

"Given the circumstances, I would discount nothing. Lucas Brokaw was a vindictive man, and I see no reason to believe that death would have altered that in the slightest."

"In other words, you believe he's already come back . . . in one form or another."

"I never thought he was gone, Mr. Tanner. He's been here all along . . . merely waiting."

"For what?"

Ludmann chuckled. "Why, for you of course. The third party we discussed on your last visit. Or had you forgotten?"

Tanner averted his gaze, silent for a time. Then he straightened in his chair, tight-lipped, his voice brusque. "So what's your considered opinion, professor? Is he after me, or has he already got me?"

"We could find out easily enough."

"How?"

"Through hypnosis."

"Thanks, but no thanks."

"There's nothing to fear."

"Maybe not, but the answer's still no."

"Mr. Tanner, to paraphrase your own statement . . . either you are Lucas Brokaw reincarnated or else he means to possess your mortal soul. Wouldn't it be wise to find out which it is . . . while there's still time?"

"It's a bad idea, so let's forget it. I came here for advice, nothing else."

"That is my advice. In fact, it's perhaps the one step that . . ."

"Goddamn, are you deaf?" Tanner rose, towering over the desk. "I said no, and that's final! Now, have you got the message, or do you want me to spell it out?"

"I understand perfectly, Mr. Tanner." Ludmann met his look. "You fear the unknown far less than you do the truth. Isn't that about the gist of it?"

Tanner glowered down at him a moment, seething with anger, then turned and marched toward the door. But as he crossed the room, Ludmann caught something he hadn't noticed earlier. One thought triggered another, and he slowly removed the pipe from his mouth.

It was all there. The arrogant manner, that sudden outburst of temper, and so abruptly, the final link. Tanner was in pain, limping badly. Yet he wasn't aware of it. He simply didn't know and wouldn't believe it even if he were told. For his point of no return had come and gone as he passed through the door.

Now, within himself, the struggle began in earnest.

XXVII

The trees moaned and crackled in a stiff offshore breeze. Tanner filled his lungs with the ocean scent, thankful the weather had turned nippy. The cold and a thermos of black coffee were all that kept him awake. Leaning forward, he punched the dashboard lighter, waiting until it released. Then he lit another cigarette, cupping it with his hand to hide the glow. After a couple of quick drags, he held the tip of the cigarette over his watch and checked the time.

1:07.

A swift calculation, and then he set three o'clock as his deadline. The lights had gone off in the mansion shortly before one, which was earlier than usual but hardly suspicious in itself. If nothing happened within the next hour or so, it meant they were tucked in for the night. And still another stakeout could be chalked off to wasted effort.

His car was parked on a side road, deep in the grove of redwoods overlooking the estate. Starlight cast a milky haze over the earth, and from his vantage point on the knoll he had an unobstructed view of the front gate and the mansion. Every night for the past week—since Ruxton and his playmates had moved into the mansion—he'd kept them under almost constant surveillance. So far his vigil had produced nothing. Aside from loss of sleep and the brassy taste of too many cigarettes, there was little to distinguish one night from another. But he wasn't discouraged. He had not yet lost faith in his hunch.

Tanner never questioned the feeling. It was another of his premonitions, some dark complex of gut instinct. He couldn't explain it, but he was sustained by an almost mystical conviction that Ruxton would make a mistake.

If not tonight, then tomorrow night. Or the night after. Sooner or later, one of them would blunder. Probably not Ruxton, for he was much too clever to risk his own skin. But one of the others, more than likely Birkhead, would attempt to tie off the loose ends. There were always loose ends on any job—no matter how perfectly executed—and the slightest gaffe often blew the entire caper. Tanner was convinced someone would stumble, and he meant to be there when it happened.

Strangely enough, he also knew it would happen at night. In that sense, it was like the flashes of *déjà vu* and his dreams of Lucas Brokaw. Again, as so many times before, he'd been given a glimpse of things beyond his ken. Only in this instance, the message was clear and the warning too absolute to be misconstrued.

He was to wait and watch and simply let it happen.

A half hour later his wait suddenly ended. Headlights appeared on the driveway, and in the distance he heard the blast of a powerful engine. When the car stopped at the front gate, his pulse skipped a beat. It was the Jaguar XJS that had been delivered to the mansion earlier in the week. After a brief demonstration by the dealer, both Jill and Birkhead had taken turns road testing the car. But the odds dictated that it was Birkhead behind the wheel tonight.

Any lingering doubt was quickly dispelled. As the gates swung open, the Jaguar burned rubber and rocketed off in a burst of speed. The driver was fast and smooth, using a racer's shift, and within seconds had the car roaring flat out in fourth gear. On twisting back roads, only a maniac or a hophead drove at such speeds, and Birkhead qualified on both counts.

Tanner hit the ignition switch and barreled down out of the trees. As the taillights of the Jaguar disappeared, he jammed the accelerator to the floorboard and took off in pursuit.

Birkhead drove a car with the same indiscriminate deadliness that had kept him alive in Nam. The search-and-destroy missions, operating against an enemy skilled in guerrilla warfare, had taught him an axiom as old as man: Strike first, strike fast, and strike when least expected. Three years in the rice paddies had turned him into a killer who took emotional sustenance from his work, and while he could absorb punishment with a certain brute sensualism, he'd discovered that inflicting pain was by far the greater joy, an act of eroticism so profound that he would often come at the very instant he pulled the trigger. The memory was sharply etched, and as though the Jaguar transported him once again to the killing ground, he hurtled across Marin County with a bulge in his pants and a Colt Python stuck in his waistband.

Tonight he had an appointment with death.

Tanner skirted the parked Jaguar. A heavy stand of trees bordered the house, and he drifted quietly from tree to tree until he was opposite a side window. Avoiding the light spill, he darted forward and flattened himself against the house. Then he crouched, edging closer to the light, and slowly eased his head above the windowsill.

There were two men. Birkhead stood in the middle of the living room, an attaché case in his left hand. The other man sat on an overstuffed sofa, fully dressed but rubbing sleep from his eyes. Apparently he'd nodded off while waiting for Birkhead to arrive.

"C'mon, Chester, it's payday. Wake up and join the party!"

"Sorry. It's a bit past my bedtime. Must've dozed off."

"Well, snap out of it, for Christ's sake! I haven't got all night."

Birkhead wanted nothing to spoil the surprise, and for that he needed an attentive audience. His next remark struck directly at the sore spot, calculated to jar the man awake.

"Say, I almost forgot. Jill said to tell you she sends her love."

Wilson flinched, visibly stung. Then his features set in a petulant scowl. "How very endearing. I presume she and Curt are happily reunited?"

"Just like a couple of turtledoves."

"No doubt. But you can tell them for me that I won't soon forget their shabby treatment. All this lying and deception . . . it's inexcusable. And leaving me alone in this godforsaken house was the last straw. Tell them that, Monk. The last straw!"

"Bullshit!" Birkhead smiled. "Don't try to kid an old kidder, Chester. You could've taken off any time you wanted to. Right?"

Wilson shrugged, and a nervous flicker crossed his lips. "Well . . . yes . . . I suppose so. Except of course for the money."

"Damn right! The money. That's what this whole caper was about. Not some dippy chick."

Birkhead slapped the attaché case down on the coffee table separating them. "Go ahead, open it up. It's all yours. One million on account."

Wilson leaned forward and eagerly pressed the snap locks. His hands shook as he opened the top of the case and bent closer. Then he froze. Packets of currency were stacked in neat piles, and on top of the money was a crude, hand-lettered placard:

BANG! BANG! YOU'RE DEAD!

Wilson blinked and looked up. He found himself staring into the bore of a silencer. The chambers on either side of the pistol brimmed with pug-nosed, hollow point bullets. A moment passed. Then Birkhead grinned and pulled the trigger.

There was a sharp *phftt* and the back of Wilson's

skull exploded. A glob of brains and bone matter splattered the wall behind him. Then his body went slack, like a rag doll with its stuffing torn loose, and he collapsed sideways across the sofa. An instant later, death voided his bowels and a noxious stench filled the room.

Birkhead studied the corpse for several seconds, clearly pleased with the success of his little joke. Still grinning, he stuck the pistol inside his windbreaker and snapped the lid closed on the attaché case.

Then he turned, briskly crossing the living room, and paused to wipe his fingerprints off the doorknob. As he stepped outside, Tanner faded into the darkness, lost once more among the trees.

A few minutes after four in the morning, Tanner stood with his ear pressed to the door of a third floor walk-up. The Mission district was deathly still at that hour, and he had little trouble following the gist of the conversation. Someone inside the apartment was angry, lashing out at Birkhead, and his voice carried through the door as though it was made of tissue paper.

"I don't give a fuck what Ruxton says. You kept me waiting the whole goddamn night and I don't like it! Not even a little bit."

"Hey, take it easy, Johnny." Birkhead seemed outwardly bluff and hearty, almost apologetic. "I'm not delivering food stamps, you know. Christ, I had to make sure I wasn't followed."

"Well, you're one goddamn careful delivery boy, I'll give you that."

"C'mon, don't rub it in. I went by to pay off Wilson first. And you would've done it the same way, too. Just stop and think about it a minute. You live in a rough neighborhood, Johnny. It's bad enough coming down here with a million."

Johnny Fallon was a shrewd, icy realist. The big man was too obliging tonight, not at all himself. Fallon had a sudden urge to see him gone. To put a door between

213

them, with the bolt thrown and the chain latch in place.

"Okay, let's skip it. Lemme have the money and we'll call it a night."

"Sure thing, Johnny. If you want, I'll even wait while you count—"

Without warning, Birkhead tossed the attaché case. Fallon's reaction was one of sheer reflex. His hands flew up to catch it, then at the last instant he realized it was a sucker play. He ducked aside, deflecting the briefcase with an upraised arm, and his hand snaked inside his coat. Off balance, fumbling desperately, he jerked a snub-nosed .38 from his shoulder holster.

Birkhead shot him three times in the chest. Blown backward by the impact, Fallon slammed into the wall and his gun went skittering across the floor. He hung suspended there a moment, then his knees buckled and he slumped forward on his face. His breath came in ragged gasps and his eyes were wild and blood-gutted, bulging with pain. Yet he was dimly aware of everything about him. The footsteps. A hulking presence kneeling at his side. The cold snout of a silencer pressed behind his ear.

Then he heard a metallic click as the hammer was thumbed back. Sensed a finger tightening around the trigger. And at last, almost as though he'd waited forever, Birkhead spoke to him.

"One for the road, Johnny. Lights out."

Tanner trailed Birkhead all the way back to the estate. Hidden once more in the redwoods, he crawled from his car and stood watching until the Jaguar halted in front of the mansion. Only then was he satisfied that Birkhead had killed all the outsiders. That the men named Chester and Johnny had comprised Ruxton's entire gang.

Except for those who occupied the mansion.

Standing there, with the starlight streaming down through the trees, he looked like some avenging apparition. His face was pale and drawn, blazing with suppressed fury, and his heart thudded against his chest. A sickness swept over him, became violently physical, and mingled with it was an overwhelming sense of rage. The longer he stared at the mansion the worse his hatred became; almost convulsively, his hands clenched in a stranglehold. An instant of cold blinding torment came over him, as though some winter demon had sucked the marrow of compassion from his bones. And all around him he felt the force. Whispering to him, tugging at his sleeve. Goading him to act. To destroy.

To kill.

A long time passed while he stood there considering the word. His lips moved, mouthing it silently, until his jaw hardened around it and in his mind it became a litany. A word that brought a slow smile to his face, and at last, an easy awareness of how it would be done.

Then he turned and limped back to his car.

XXVIII

Tanner shaved with dull concentration. He hadn't slept for nearly thirty-six hours, and the bathroom was warm and steamy after his shower. But he fought off the drowsiness, watching himself intently in the mirror.

The face staring back at him was distorted, like the blurred image in a fun house mirror. Blinking, he forced the reflection into sharper focus and finished shaving with slow, deliberate strokes. Then he splashed water over his face, toweling dry, and took a closer look. What he saw startled him. Even with the bearded stubble gone, the man in the mirror appeared sallow and weary, completely drained. A man who had pushed himself to the limit and was now operating on nerve alone.

A damn fool treading a very fine line.

Still, until he'd made the phone call, there could be no thought of sleep. And afterward he had to vanish. Otherwise, he'd get bogged down with the police and perhaps the bureau. Which would never do. Not if he meant to finish the job himself. So it was simply a matter of getting lost overnight. Keeping everything he had learned to himself a little while longer. Then tomorrow morning, with his batteries recharged, he'd tackle Ruxton. He was going to nail the bastard. For once and for all.

All things considered, it shouldn't prove too difficult. Not when he told them he'd trailed Birkhead. That he was the only eyewitness. The one man who could tie them to murder.

It would end there. Precisely the way he'd laid it out in his head this morning. The only way it could end.

The phone jarred him out of his reverie. All day it

had been ringing, and all day he'd ignored it. Upon returning to his apartment that morning, he had made one call, and then he'd spent the rest of the day thinking, formulating alternatives while he waited for the last piece of puzzle. Every time the phone rang he was tempted to answer, for he knew very well it was Stacey. By now she was probably frantic with worry and growing more desperate by the hour. But until the puzzle was complete, he refused to talk to her or anyone else. Particularly Hamilton Knox.

The director would order him back to the foundation, and that wouldn't do. It was essential that he retain his mobility and the freedom to act independently—on his own timetable—without interference from anyone. Not even Stacey.

So he had let the phone ring. And as the day wore on, he'd finally come to welcome the noise. It kept him awake and functioning.

Now, freshly shaved and showered, he waited until the phone went silent. Then he checked his watch. Quarter of five. Time to place the call.

He lit a cigarette and direct-dialed the office in San Francisco. There was a pause, then three swift rings, and a crisp voice came on the line.

"Good afternoon. Federal Bureau of Investigation."

"Agent Howard, please."

"One moment."

A click. "Good afternoon. This is Agent Howard. May I help you?"

"Hello, Jack. This is Warren. Any news for me yet?"

"You dirty, low-life son of a bitch!"

"That bad, huh?"

"Worse. You conned me, Warren. Just a little favor, right? Check out a couple of routine murders. Isn't that what you said?"

"I get the impression they weren't so routine."

"Routine! Jesus Christ, Warren, you really put me on the spot. The cops weren't even aware the murders

218

had taken place. I've been on the horn the whole god-damned day trying to explain how——"

"Okay, Jack, simmer down. I'm sorry if I put you in a bind. But what I need right now are details."

"Details, the man says. All right, old friend, try this on for size. Item: Johnny Fallon. Suspected safe-cracker. Twenty-three arrests, no convictions."

"Which means he must have been a damn good box man."

"No, not good. The *best*. And would you like to know what the homicide boys found underneath the floorboard of his closet?"

"Yes, I would, Jack. Very much."

"Well, you'd have to see it to believe it, but it's an electronic gizmo straight out of Buck Rogers. It allowed Mr. Fallon to see through doors, especially steel doors. Like the kind normally found on bank vaults."

There was a prolonged silence.

"Are you still with me, Warren?"

"Go ahead. I'm listening."

"That's good. Because now I've got a question for you. The dead man in Sausalito was named Chester Wilson. Ever heard of him?"

"Not that I recall. Why? Did he have a record?"

"Oh yeah . . . a very long record! Fifteen years as one of the top cryptanalysts in the State Department. With a security classification we never even heard of. Officially, he's been on leave for the past five weeks. Unofficially, we get the word he was a week overdue, and they've been turning Washington upside down trying to locate him."

"Thanks, Jack. I owe you one."

"You owe me a whole bunch! And you can start paying off right now. First, how the hell did you know about these murders? And second, what did one of the government's top cryps have to do with a safecracker? If there's a connection, Warren, I need some answers. And I need them——"

Tanner hung up. He took a long drag on his cigarette, pondering what he'd heard. It was all so simple. So very simple when the last piece was fitted into the puzzle. After a moment's reflection, he laughed, mocking himself, and stubbed out his cigarette in an ashtray.

The phone began ringing as he went through the door.

"Warren!"

"Hi. Can I come in?"

"Of course. I've been trying to reach—"

Her look of surprise suddenly turned to shock. Tanner hobbled past her into the foyer. Lighted wall sconces clearly revealed his features, and she stifled a low gasp. His eyes were sunken with fatigue, bloodshot and rimmed by dark pouches. There was a haggard cast to his face, and he appeared to have aged overnight. Almost as though he'd been—crippled!

The thought jolted her. It was his limp! Yesterday he was merely favoring the leg, but now he was actually lame. The leg had stiffened, and he was pulling it along in a slow, crablike shuffle. She caught her breath, staring aghast as he limped across the living room and flopped down on the sofa.

Stacey slammed the door and hurried after him. Her mind was whirling, and she took scant comfort from the fact that he was safe. That he'd come to her. These past few weeks had been a hell of uncertainty. She never knew what to expect—his moods were wildly erratic—and she found herself constantly on the defensive. She had been afraid and bewildered, but since yesterday she'd been gripped by something that lay beyond simple fear. Terror. A dark premonition she wouldn't allow herself to consider.

Tonight there was a new concern. He seemed on the verge of a complete physical breakdown. Added to his emotional state, she knew it might very well push him

220

over the edge. Warily, not at all sure how to begin, she seated herself beside him on the sofa.

"Warren . . . darling, aren't you feeling well?"

"I'm all right," he replied hollowly. "Just need a little sleep."

"Of course." Her sigh was more eloquent than words. "Would you like something to eat? Perhaps a cup of soup?"

"Nothing, thanks. All I want is a good night's rest." Something flared in his eyes, and he suddenly fixed her with an intent look. "No one is to know I'm here! If anybody calls—I don't give a damn who it is—tell 'em you haven't seen me. Okay?"

Stacey was afraid to ask the obvious question, and even more frightened of the answer. She merely nodded in a small sign of acknowledgment.

"Thanks. It's just for tonight, that's all. Tomorrow it won't matter."

"Tomorrow." She had to ask, couldn't stop herself. "What about tomorrow?"

"I've got him, Stace." Tanner tried to smile. A bleak flicker, it disappeared as if the effort was too much. "I've got Ruxton and his playmates. And tomorrow's the day I put 'em on ice."

She saw it then. With the vividness of extrasensory perception, she knew he meant to trap Ruxton. But she also knew he needed rest. And it occurred to her that tomorrow was another day. Soon enough to dissuade him from whatever madness he had in mind. When he was rational and himself again. Warren Tanner and not—

Whoever he was tonight.

Gently she touched his arm. He sat perfectly still, staring at her hand as though it was a butterfly and might be scared away by a sudden movement. They were silent for a time, then she smiled.

"Shall I turn down the covers, darling? You look exhausted."

"Good idea. Tell you the truth, I am bushed."

Stacey rose, extending her hand, and Tanner heaved himself to his feet. He yawned a wide, jaw-cracking yawn. Then she took his arm, leading him toward the bedroom, and like a weary old lion, he limped along behind her.

XXIX

Birkhead's eyes fluttered open.

There was a moment of groggy consideration, then he knew it wasn't the coke. He'd been flying high when he went to bed, but he wasn't strung out now. And his mind wasn't playing tricks on him.

Someone was in the room. Very near, watching him.

Without moving, he rolled his eyes downward, squinting in the darkness. There was a figure standing at the foot of the bed. For an instant, he couldn't quite believe it. The door was locked and the windows were locked, which meant his visitor had a nifty way with locks. But the sonofabitch had bought himself one big surprise.

Birkhead grabbed his pistol off the nightstand and triggered three quick blasts into the figure. Earlier he'd removed the silencer, and the Magnum reverberated like a cannon, spitting streaks of flame. The figure moved but it didn't fall. Incredulously, Birkhead watched it come around the side of the bed, silent as a shadow, apparently unharmed. He fired again as it came closer. Then again and again, emptying the gun.

The figure laughed. A wild, demonic laughter.

Birkhead roared back at it, enraged that he'd missed at such close range. Suddenly he went berserk, bounding out of bed, and flung himself at the figure. He delivered a crushing kick, then spun and brought his fist around in a karate blow aimed at the sternum. A steel band closed around his wrist, lifting him off his feet, and hurled him across the room. He slammed broadside into the dresser, splintering it in an explosion of wood and flying glass. Dazed, he pulled himself out of the wreckage, crouched low to attack, and advanced on the figure. This time his kick connected solidly against the bedpost, and the bed collapsed with a thunderous crash. His follow-through blow whistled harmlessly past a shadow, then an electrical shock coursed up his spine. Fingers of iron dug into the carotid artery at the base of his neck; paralysis instantly numbed his entire body. Star bursts erupted before his eyes, then his vision darkened and he slumped forward.

The bands of steel caught him, slipped under his armpits and crossed over his neck, clamping down in a viselock. His brain cleared in a fleeting moment of panic, and he threw all his brute strength into one last effort to break free. But the viselock held, pressing down with inexorable force, and his neck slowly bent.

In the hallway outside, Ruxton was pounding furiously on the door. Jill stood behind him, wide-eyed with fright, clutching a kimono over her breasts. At the sound of gunfire, they had hurried from their own bedroom, all the more alarmed when it became apparent Birkhead was involved in a savage struggle. Now, as suddenly as it began, the uproar subsided. Ruxton broke off his hammering and pressed an ear to the door, listening intently. There was absolute silence, an almost ominous quiet. Then the clatter of heavy footsteps sounded on the front stairs, and two guards came running along the hall.

Ruxton stepped back, gesturing at the door. "Break it down!"

The burly guards merely nodded, and without a word, positioned themselves opposite the door. Then they charged, shoulders low, hurling themselves against the door. The wood splintered, lock and hinges sprang loose, and the door buckled inward with a grinding screech.

The bedroom was demolished, bureau and bed and chairs reduced to a tangled pile of rubble. Birkhead lay sprawled on the floor, face down, his arms splayed backward. One eye was cocked askew, blank and sightless, and his head was crooked sideways at a grotesque angle. A trickle of blood seeped out of his mouth, and a large bump protruded near the base of his skull.

His neck was broken.

Jill began to scream. A scream without beginning or end. Sheer animal terror that echoed through the mansion in a wild, ululating howl.

Tanner bolted upright in bed. His eyes were glazed and distant. His mouth flew open and a low, rending moan began deep in his throat. The sound swelled in pitch and volume until the bedroom was filled with a cry of bestial pain.

"Warren! For God's sake, Warren, wake up! *Wake up!*"

The cry lessened, broke off in a whimpering sob, and he slowly became aware that Stacey had his arms pinioned to his side. Blisters of sweat glistened on his forehead; his face was congested and hard knots pulsated at his temples. Gradually, the cloudy look faded from his eyes, but the expression on his face was manic, deranged. Then, so abruptly that Stacey jumped away, he laughed, a shrill laugh that was almost inhuman.

Stacey slapped him. Harder and harder she slapped him, until flecks of blood splattered across his mouth and the laugh abruptly stopped. A tear welled up in the corner of his eye and rolled down over his cheek. He shuddered, suddenly very cold, and a look of barren sorrow swept his features.

"He's dead, Stace. Killed . . . just now."

"Warren, it was a dream." Stacey edged closer, soothing him with her voice. "Sweetheart, no one was killed. You dreamt it."

"No. I saw it. In his bedroom. Birkhead's bedroom. He fired . . . and then . . . "

"Darling, you couldn't have. You're here—with me! You've been here all night."

"You don't understand." He raised his hands, watching them clench into balled fists, and something odd happened to his face. "I was there! I think . . . someone killed him . . . broke his neck."

Stacey was unnerved by the conviction behind his words, frightened because she knew he believed what he was saying. He clearly couldn't comprehend that it had been a dream. Another of his nightmares. She knew she had to distract him. Do something, anything, to keep him calm and give him time to collect his wits.

"Darling, I'm sure there's an explanation. There has to be. What say we fix ourselves a drink—okay? Let things settle down a bit. Then you can tell me all about it. Doesn't that sound like a good idea?"

"Yeah, it does. I could use a drink. A stiff one."

Stacey helped him into his robe, chattering on as though nothing had happened, and led the way into the living room. But even before she had the first drink mixed, he began talking compulsively, his words confused. Telling her about Birkhead and gunfire—and then the darkness.

"That's crazy!"

"Crazy or not," Jill's voice was stark, "I'm getting out of here. With or without you, Curt. I'm leaving!"

Ruxton shook his head in exasperation. "You're being ridiculous, do you know that? Stop and think about it a minute. This is stupid!"

"Maybe so, but I'm not spending another night in this house." Jill finished buttoning her blouse and stepped into a skirt. "We aren't welcome here, Curt. And if you don't believe me, then walk across the hall and have a look at Monk."

"Come off it, will you? This isn't a haunted house, and there aren't any spooks wandering around the halls. And if you seriously think Lucas Brokaw did that to Monk, then I suggest you get yourself a shrink. You're ready for the funny farm."

226

"Go ahead and laugh. But that doesn't change anything. Curt. The door was locked and the windows were locked and someone still got in there. Can't you get that through your head? Someone *killed* him! And he'll kill us too, unless we get out of here."

"Don't be absurd," Ruxton scoffed. "Monk killed himself. It's the same old story . . . drugs and liquor don't mix. He freaked out and started firing that damn gun, and then broke his neck stumbling around in the dark fighting shadows. Come on, admit it! You saw what he did to that room."

Jill was no longer intimidated by Ruxton's overbearing manner. Even now, she was still in shock, attenuated as a wire sculpture. She had lost all restraint, and terror was her single emotion—terror of what the thing had done to Birkhead and what it might do to her.

"You're wrong, Curt, and we both know it." She threw a coat over her shoulders and collected her purse from the bureau. "Monk wasn't on speed or acid, and he wasn't freaked out. He was on coke, and he didn't kill himself. Lucas Brokaw killed him!"

Ruxton grabbed her by the arms as she started past and spun her around. "Listen to me, will you? We're in no danger here. There's a guard out in the hall and the police are on the way. So why run? Even if you don't believe me, wait and hear what they have to say. They'll tell you I'm right."

"You really are a fool." Jill tossed her head defiantly. "Monk had a gun, and what good did it do him? None, that's what! And armed guards can't save you either. If you don't get out of here tonight, you'll never live to spend all your precious money. Have you thought about that, Curt?"

"That's enough! I'm staying and you're staying with me. We'll just wait and let the cops talk some sense into your head."

"No, damn you! No!" There was a harried sharpness in her words, and she suddenly wrenched herself free of his grip. "I'm leaving, and don't you dare try to stop me. Just keep away from me!"

Jill flung the door open and darted into the hall. Ruxton trailed after her, ignoring the guard's puzzled expression, and hurried down the stairs as she ran through the foyer. Before he could reach the front door, he heard the Jaguar rumble to life, followed by a screech of tires. Then there was a grinding clash of gears as she accelerated and the car roared off down the driveway. He paused, staring at the door a moment, and finally turned back toward the study.

Dizzy bitch. Dizzy stupid little bitch!

Tanner was on his third Scotch, but it hadn't helped. Slumped back against the sofa cushions, the drink forgotten, he was staring at a spot of light on the ceiling. He had talked himself out, and now his eyes were vacant, focused on some infinity in space and time. A personal limbo, where the living walked among the dead.

Beside him, Stacey sat quietly, her gaze fixed on him in a look of tragic disbelief. A cold and kindling light masked her features, like the reflection of moonlight on snow, and she found herself incapable of speech. Unwittingly, he had articulated what was deepest in her mind, the thing she couldn't bring herself to consider. The fear she had blunted with abstractions, excuses, and a dozen petty evasions. A fear not of the unknown but of Lucas Brokaw.

All her defenses had crumbled as he talked, and she now had no doubt whatever that Monk Birkhead was dead. His grisly account of the fight had convinced her. What occurred in that darkened bedroom tonight was no dream. Nor was there any question as to the manner of Birkhead's death.

And worse, she knew at last who it was that had killed him.

The glass suddenly dropped from Tanner's hand. His

228

face went chalky and the muscles along his jaw grew taut. He straightened, staring intently into a void, and his eyes burned with a look of ungodly horror. Then a seizure swept over him. His body convulsed and he was jerked off the couch, trembling violently.

"No! Go back! Don't do it! Go back!"

Stumbling forward, eyes blindly fixed on some distant vision, he tripped over the coffee table and went crashing to the floor. Before he could rise, Stacey threw herself on him, fighting to restrain his arms and hold him down. But the struggle was brief, ending as quickly as it began. A final spasm shook his body, then he collapsed beneath her, his face buried in the carpet.

He was unconscious.

Ruxton uncapped the decanter and poured himself a snifter of cognac. He was astounded by Jill's behavior and not a little annoyed that he'd lost control of the situation. Still, perhaps it was good riddance. With Monk dead, things wouldn't have been the same anyway, and a fresh start all the way round was probably best. Of course, he'd have to ensure Jill's silence, but that wouldn't present any—

The windows rattled.

A split second later he heard an explosion. Distant, muffled, yet he'd felt a tremor from the concussion.

The phone rang.

Ruxton jumped, still clutching the decanter, and whirled toward the desk. The phone jangled again, and he snatched it off the hook.

"Yes. Hello!"

"Mr. Ruxton, this is Henry . . . at the gatehouse. Are you okay?"

"Of course! What do you mean, am I okay? What was that explosion?"

"Well . . . don't you see? I thought it was you."

"Me! Make sense, Henry. What the hell are you talking about?"

"The guy in the car. The one with Miss Dvorak. That's what I'm trying to tell you—they just drove over the cliff!"

"Jill? Jill drove over the cliff?"

"No, it was him. The guy! She was fightin' him for the steering wheel and they came crashin' through the gate before I could get it open. You never saw anything like it, Mr. Ruxton. Honest to God, she was fightin' like a wildcat. But she couldn't beat him off . . . and . . . and then he drove that goddamn car straight off the cliff."

"You're mad! That's not possible."

"No, I'm not either, Mr. Ruxton. I saw it with my own eyes. Jesus Christ, I won't never forget that! I heard her screamin' all the way down."

"Not her, you fool! The man. She was alone in that car. Don't you understand—*alone!*"

"I'm only tellin' you . . . wait a minute, Mr. Ruxton. Hold on and lemme . . . yeah, it's them. It's the cops! You want me to send 'em—"

Ruxton hung up. His legs suddenly felt weak and he sat down in the chair. After a few moments, he realized he was still holding the decanter. He raised it to his lips and took a long pull, but there was no warmth in the brandy. An odd sensation, like chilled fire, crept slowly through his body.

Then his bowels went cold.

XXX

The dawn sky began to brighten.

Curt Ruxton hurried from the bathroom with his toilet kit. He was packing a single suitcase, only the bare necessities to hold him over a couple of days. The balance of his wardrobe could be forwarded to the apartment. Or simply forgotten. Speed was essential, and at the moment, his personal effects hardly seemed to matter.

Across the hall, several lab men were finishing up in Birkhead's bedroom. The body had been removed some hours earlier, and detectives had already questioned Ruxton at length. Doubtless there would be other sessions, particularly after the car and Jill's body were recovered from the bottom of the cliff. But he knew that quite shortly the police would have completed their work in the mansion itself.

And when they left he meant to leave with them. Simply clear out. For after last night he couldn't risk being caught in the house alone. Nor would he return. Never again would he set foot on the Brokaw estate.

Almost too late, Ruxton had finally been convinced. He understood at last that he was running for his life. That Lucas Brokaw was stalking him even now. Whether it was a haunt or a spirit, or some earthier manifestation, he had no idea. But he knew it meant to kill him, just as it had stalked and killed first Birkhead and then Jill. Only the arrival of the police had forestalled his own death, and as long as he remained in the house, his life was in peril. Brokaw mustn't be allowed another chance!

He had no choice but to run far and run fast.

Oddly enough, he saw in retrospect that Jill had been

right. Not only about Brokaw but, more importantly, about the money. He already had part of the fortune, and there was no need to delay further. He could just as easily collect the remainder and arrange for sale of the estate from some distant corner of the earth. All of which sounded good, yet left him with the same problem Jill had faced. He first had to escape the mansion—and Lucas Brokaw.

Suitcase in hand, Ruxton joined the detectives as they walked past his door. The lab men had turned up nothing, neither fingerprints nor physical evidence, to indicate anyone had been in the bedroom with Birkhead at the time of his death. The homicide sergeant in charge observed that it had all the earmarks of murder, but he stopped there. As for Jill, until his team had a chance to inspect the car, which was even now being winched up the cliffs, he would reserve judgment. Somewhat pointedly he directed Ruxton not to travel farther than San Francisco. Without evidence to place the "mystery man" in the car with Jill, there were several puzzling questions still to be resolved.

Ruxton knew they suspected him of some bizarre murder scheme. He also knew they would find nothing revealing in the car. But he kept his thoughts to himself. There was simply no way to explain that their "mystery man" was in truth a dead man. Nor could he very well afford to tell them *why* Lucas Brokaw had gone on a rampage. That would open a door best left closed—one that led to conspiracy, fraud, and a couple of other murders.

So he merely listened and agreed to place himself at their disposal. As they came down the stairs and trooped into the foyer, a telephone began ringing. Ruxton hesitated, on the verge of ignoring it, then excused himself and hurried into the drawing room. He caught the phone on the third ring.

"Hello."

"Mr. Ruxton? Henry here. At the gatehouse."

"Yes, Henry. What is it?"

"Sorry to bother you, but Mr. Tanner just arrived. Says he has to see you right away."

"What about?"

"Don't know for sure. All he said was to tell you it's a matter of business concerning the foundation."

Ruxton sighed inwardly. Damn the luck! He wanted nothing more than to be safely on his way. Regardless, he had no choice but to see Tanner. Better to satisfy their curiosity than to arouse further suspicion.

"All right, Henry. Send Mr. Tanner on up."

As he turned away from the phone, Ruxton wondered how the foundation had learned of the murders so quickly. Then he walked through the door of the drawing room and stopped in his tracks, visibly shaken. The foyer was empty. The detectives had gone, driven off without him.

He was alone.

Stacey came awake in a daze. She lay there a moment, numbed with sleep, yet strangely unsettled. Her hand went out, searching for him. Then her eyes flew open and she raised herself up on one elbow.

"Warren!"

No answer.

She threw aside the covers and jumped out of bed. She raced through the apartment calling his name and within moments returned to the bedroom. There she halted, and in the silty light of false dawn she suddenly saw it. The closet door was open. His clothes were gone.

She glanced at the clock. A few minutes after four.

Then it struck her, and she had a sinking feeling of dread. They hadn't returned to bed until shortly after three. Which meant he wasn't nearly as exhausted by last night's ordeal as he appeared. Obviously, he had waited for her to drift off and then he'd slipped out of the apartment.

And she knew exactly where he'd gone.

Hurriedly she began dressing, mentally calculating time and distance, trying to estimate his lead and how she might narrow the gap. Whether she could reach the estate before he was lost to her forever.

Before he became someone else. His other self.

At the last instant, she went to the phone and quickly dialed a number. There were several rings, then a gruff voice came on the line. "Mr. Knox, this is Stacey. No, don't interrupt, just listen! I haven't time to explain. Get out to the estate as fast as possible. It's an emergency!"

She slammed the phone down and rushed from the apartment.

Ruxton had a thin, fixed smile on his face. As Tanner limped across the foyer, his eyes narrowed in a cool look of appraisal. He took in the game leg and the haggard appearance, and his expression became solicitous.

"You seem a bit the worse for wear, Mr. Tanner. Hope it's nothing serious?"

"Nothing to trouble yourself about." Tanner hobbled past him into the drawing room. "I'm not here on a social call, Ruxton, so let's chuck the formalities and get down to business."

There was an abrasive quality to Tanner's voice. His square jaw was set in a scowl and his eyes were like chips of quartz. Nor was it lost on Ruxton that he hadn't offered to shake hands.

"Very well," Ruxton said with a trace of impatience. "What can I do for you? I was about to leave, so let's make it brief."

Tanner halted before the fireplace, his gaze drawn to the portrait of Stephanie Brokaw. He stared up at the painting for a long while, as if lost in thought. Then at last he turned, studying Ruxton's suitcase a moment, and looked around.

"Travelin' sorta light, aren't you?"

The inflection startled Ruxton. It was blunt and coarse, almost a peppery drawl, uncharacteristic of Tanner. A beat passed as they stared at each other, then Ruxton dismissed it with a quick gesture. "Yes, as a matter of fact, I am in a hurry. Although I hardly see how that concerns you."

"Don't, huh? Well, suppose we get down to brass tacks, and then maybe you'll see what's what. Like I said, it's business. Few irregularities we thought needed explainin'."

"Oh?" Ruxton's eyebrows rose briefly. "I presume you're talking about the murders."

"Which murders?"

"Why, last night! Isn't that why you're here?"

"Birkhead and the girl?" Tanner's smile was cold, hard. "No, what I had in mind was those other murders. You know, Fallon and that Wilson fellow."

Ruxton blinked. "I beg your pardon?"

"C'mon, don't dummy up. Johnny Fallon! The safe-cracker. It was him and his electronic gadget that got you into the vault."

"Are you accusing me of—"

"Course I am! Hell, I got the goods on you. Chester Wilson? No mystery there. You imported him all the way from Washington so he could break the code. Did a good job, too."

"You're out of your mind!"

"Not today," Tanner grunted. "I'm talkin' facts. Take your pal, Birkhead. It's all in his army record. Alpine training. Specialist in guerrilla raids. Hell, that's how he got your bunch up and down those cliffs. Real slick operation. Gotta hand it to you."

A glimmer of surprise passed over Ruxton's face, then his look became veiled. Tanner went on as though no response was necessary.

"Course, we shouldn't forget Jill Dvorak, should we? Quite a little lady. Holdin' that boat offshore while you came in here." He paused, considering. "Guess that was the tip-off. I traced the boat to your corporation, but it didn't hardly make sense. Not till I started puttin' the pieces together. Then all of a sudden the whole thing dovetailed and bingo! I had your number."

"How extraordinary." There was a moment of deliberation while Ruxton studied him. "Really remarkable, Tanner. And I must say, a very interesting theory. Of course you know you'll never be able to prove it."

"You've already done that," Tanner observed in even, brittle tones. "Murdering Fallon and Wilson was a mistake. Real dumb move. But even then I reckon it wasn't the worst mistake you made."

"Oh?" Ruxton shrugged noncommittally. "And what was my worst mistake?"

- "Birkhead's gun." Tanner's eyes bored into him. "You should've gotten rid of it. But you couldn't do that, could you? No way to explain it to the cops. Now all they've got to do is run it through ballistics and that'll tie you to both murders."

"It wasn't my gun!" Ruxton blustered. "It belonged to Birkhead. If anyone was murdered, he did it. As a matter of fact, that explains what happened last night. Whoever killed him had to be familiar with locks. So it's obvious! Some of Fallon's friends broke in here and killed him out of revenge."

"No, Ruxton. Last night was a different sort of revenge." Tanner's jawline hardened, and the words were barely audible. Yet there was a menacing undercurrent in his voice, and he suddenly started forward. "Would you like to know how Birkhead died? What really happened up in that bedroom?"

"Stay away from me! I mean it, don't come any closer!" Ruxton grabbed the phone and began dialing the gatehouse. "We'll just get the police up here and see what they think of your story. And I assure you, Tanner, they won't believe a word of it. Not a word!"

Tanner's hand closed around his neck, firmly shutting off the carotid artery. A sudden wave of dizziness staggered Ruxton. His vision blurred, swirling black mist shot through with red sparks. He dropped the phone. Then Tanner released him, and he reeled drunkenly toward the doorway.

In that single instant, Warren Tanner ceased to be himself.

His expression changed, turned immobile and dark. There was no remorse or pity in his gaze. It was a look of cold black hatred, naked and revealed. All about him emanated an evil so awesome that his face became a living mausoleum for the human spirit. A thing of life and death and the undead.

An instrument of the dead man he'd become.

"Think that hurt, do you, Ruxton? Throat a little sore?"

The voice was now raspy, the words rattled off in a staccato burst. His lips parted in a twisted grin as he limped toward Ruxton. "Hell, you haven't seen nothin' yet. Wait'll I show you what really croaked Birkhead!"

"It was you!" Ruxton lurched backward into the foyer. "You killed them!"

"They died at my hand. Deserved to die! But it was your bungling, Ruxton. That's what got 'em killed!"

"You—you're alive!" Ruxton stammered, his face wreathed in terror. *"You're him!"*

The smile became sinister. "Remember John Hughes?"

Ruxton's jaw fell open. He gasped, suddenly short of breath, and retreated across the foyer.

"I baited the trap and you took it. Remember now? Custer. The Little Big Horn. *Sergeant* John Hughes!"

Ashen-faced, completely unnerved, Ruxton wheeled away and ran to the front door. He twisted the doorknob and yanked. Nothing happened. He took it in both hands and yanked harder, tugging frantically with all his strength. The door wouldn't budge.

The voice grew louder, closer. "Get the drift, Ruxton? If you didn't know about Hughes, then how could you've known about the trick handle on the vault?" His movements were sluggish and unhurried, curiously deliberate. "There's only one way. You're a goddamn grave robber. You violated my crypt! And that's why I'm gonna kill you. Same way I killed your partners—only slower!"

Ruxton turned with his back to the door, fixed like a butterfly pinned to a board. Though he tried to speak, his voice failed, but in his mind he heard the words.

Crypt. Vault. Trick handle.

His face went slack with relief, and just for a moment he appeared to wilt. Then, as if galvanized, he charged across the foyer and went bounding down the subterranean stairway.

The tall figure scuttled after him, eyes alert and piercing, yet somehow without life. A moment later the winding corridor filled with the sound of ferocious metallic laughter. Then the echo died away, and footsteps on stone began the slow descent.

XXXI

Ruxton hurtled down the stairs. He took the last few steps in a flying leap and burst into the crypt. His throat felt dry as dust and his lungs were on fire. But inwardly he was laughing like a madman.

A slip of the tongue had saved him. That raving maniac upstairs had unintentionally spared his life. With words! Jolting him out of his panic, forcing him to think and collect himself. And at the very last instant, to use his wits.

All he had to do was activate the hidden door Fallon had discovered the night of the raid. Turn the handle on the vault and seal himself in the outer chamber. Which in turn would trigger the alarm system. Then settle back and wait for the guards to come and collect Tanner.

Tanner? Or Lucas Brokaw?

Time enough to think about that later. He heard the sound of footsteps bouncing off the walls of the corridor, and it occurred to him that he hadn't a moment to waste. There was barely enough time to put a barrier between himself and . . . that psycho. Whoever he was!

Ruxton hurried across the room and closed the vault door. One ear to the vault, the other cocked toward the stairs, he waited. It seemed an interminable wait, for the footsteps grew louder by the instant, but at last he heard the muffled thud of the lock rods. Quickly, he grasped the door handle with both hands and gave it a sharp twist to the left. There was a faint hissing noise as the hydraulic system in the ceiling was activated. For good measure, he worked the handle one final time before he turned to face the entranceway.

Shoes appeared on the staircase. Ruxton froze

against the vault door. Legs came into view, slowly descending the last few steps. Ruxton stopped breathing, numb and petrified, with no place left to run. He watched in horror as the tall figure limped across the bottom landing and paused just outside the entranceway. They stared at each other, and again the face constricted in that hideous smile.

Suddenly a series of explosive reports, almost like firecrackers, detonated within the wall over the entranceway. Ruxton's eyes flicked upward—he knew the retaining bolts had been sheared—but the figure outside remained motionless. Merely watching, the grin broader. Then the room vibrated with a deep rumble; seams appeared along the overhead section of the entranceway, and a wedge of rock emerged. The rumble intensified, became an agonized groan of rock on rock, and in the next instant, a massive stone slab dropped downward into the entranceway.

The crypt was sealed.

Ruxton's knees went rubbery with relief, and he slowly let out his breath. Then he saw it and couldn't quite believe his good fortune. A thick plexiglass window was centered in the stone slab. It was perfect! An unexpected boon and a fitting end to this madness. With the entranceway blocked, he could watch in absolute safety while the guards overpowered Tanner . . . Brokaw . . . the lunatic outside.

In a fit of laughter, almost delirious with joy, Ruxton ran to the window. The face on the other side peered back at him, eyes glittering brightly, the grotesque smile even broader. Ruxton grinned and gave him the finger. No reaction. But the opportunity was tantalizing, too tempting to resist. He put his face to the window, forming long drawn-out syllables, as though talking to a lip reader.

"Screw-w you-u-u!"

Still no reaction. If anything, the features became all the more monstrous, radiating a sort of satanic bliss.

Which was strange, and curiously disturbing. Ruxton thought by now he'd be frothing at the mouth. Or at the very least frustrated and angry that he'd been outwitted. Instead, he looked happy, almost exhilarated.

A grating sound distracted Ruxton, slowly filling the chamber again with that deep rumble. The groan of rock on rock. Surprised, he turned away from the door. Then his face went ghastly and his eyes widened in disbelief.

The entire west wall was rising ponderously into the ceiling.

Seawater rushed through the opening. A mere trickle at first, it became a surging torrent as the crack between floor and wall yawned wider. A pulsating roar, not unlike the pounding beat of the surf, was clearly audible on the other side of the wall. The water deepened, churning and boiling, sloshing across the floor in angry waves. Seaweed and flotsam skimmed along on the rising crest, and then, with a swift dreamlike suddenness, the wall simply vanished behind a thunderous mountain of ocean.

Ruxton screamed. And when the salt spray lapped at his face, he screamed louder.

Outside, the screams were merely silent howls of terror. Ruxton had his face pressed to the window, pounding desperately on the stone slab, but no sound escaped the crypt. The plexiglass offered a clear view of Ruxton's frenzied horror. He was begging, mutely imploring mercy, deliverance.

His pleas were wasted. The tall figure peering through the window chortled softly to himself. He looked on with a sense of pride and accomplishment as seawater flooded the crypt. Everything had functioned perfectly, exactly as he'd planned it so long ago. Thirty years meant nothing! Time was never a factor, not when the design was right.

And the concept! Never had he imagined how intoxicating it would be to watch it in operation. There was a sense of poetic justice here today. Brutal, even atavistic, but nonetheless man's oldest law: simple vengeance for a wrong done.

Of course he'd tricked Ruxton, lured him into the trap. But the sneaky bastard was an intruder in this house anyway. No better than a common ghoul! So what he got was little more than he deserved. Very final and damned appropriate.

"Oooh . . . God . . . *no!*"

He turned and saw her descend the last few steps. Her face was pale, one hand pressed to her mouth, but she was a vision of loveliness. The ruby pendant sparkled like dull fire against her breast, and in the dim light her russet evening gown seemed as dark as her hair. Yet that sense of vibrancy, undiminished by shadows or cold stone, radiated stronger than ever. She was exquisite.

Stacey halted at the bottom of the stairs. Her eyes were fixed on the window—on the insane face screaming soundlessly into glass—and she seemed to shrink back. Her stomach felt queasy. Something vile and brackish clogged her throat, but she knew she mustn't fall apart. She swallowed hard and clutched at the wall for support.

Then she felt his gaze, willed herself to look at him. There was an icy blue tint to his eyes, cruel and demonic, of another world. And when he spoke it was the voice of another man, a voice out of the past.

"You shouldn't have come down here, my dear. Now I don't mean to sound harsh, but I want you to wait for me upstairs. I'll join you shortly."

"No, I can't . . . I won't . . . oh, please, don't do it!" Ruxton saw her; suddenly his pounding became more frenetic. The water had risen to the bottom of the window, and he was struggling desperately not to be swept away. She kept her eyes averted, forcing herself to remain calm, and came down the last step. "Please, I'm asking you . . . let him out."

"Stephanie, I've always indulged you, but this time you're out of bounds. It's none of your affair! So be a good girl and run along upstairs."

It was unreal. Utterly, incomprehensibly unreal. Yet the name erased any vestige of doubt—he'd called her Stephanie!—and she knew it was true. His other self at last had possession. He was no longer Warren Tanner. He was now Lucas Brokaw.

Stacey took a deep breath and steadied herself. It was a desperate gamble, but she had to try. If he wouldn't do it for her, then perhaps he would do it for Stephanie. She willed herself to play the part—to become Stephanie Brokaw—and boldly crossed the line into his macabre nightmare.

"Lucas, listen to me! Surely you can stop it somehow. There must be a way. There has to be!"

"Of course there's a way. But I don't want to stop it. Damnit, Stephanie, don't you understand . . . he's got it comin'." He considered a moment, then the harsh look softened and he extended his hand. "C'mon. Long as you're here, you might as well see the finale. It's a real lulu, if I do say so myself."

His hand was cold and clammy, and she was appalled by the fierce gleam in his eye. Abruptly, it dawned on her that he really wasn't angry at all. He was exultant— enormously dazzled by himself and the wonder of what he'd done, almost giddy with delight now that he had an audience. And she had only to glance through the window to find the reason.

Ruxton gagged and spat, coughing seawater every time he screamed. But the thrashing and fighting, all his horrid shrieks for mercy, were to no avail. A surge of water washed over him and his head momentarily went under. Bubbles spouted from his mouth, then his eyes popped, and like a goldfish in a bowl, he floated to the top of the window.

Stacey clamped a hand to her mouth, felt the sting of tears. Yet she sensed there was still time, if only she could find the right words. Her eyes never left the window, but a look of repugnance came over her face and she slowly shook her head.

"This isn't the work of my husband."

"How's that?"

"You heard me, Lucas. The man I married wouldn't stoop to anything so . . . so barbaric."

"Now that's infernal nonsense and you know it. He's a swindler and a murderer . . . goddamnit, he tried to steal everything we've got!"

"Lucas, you can talk till doomsday and it won't change a thing. It's still revolting and . . . well, it's simply beneath a man of your stature."

"Awww, for chrissakes. You got no call to say that. I mean, hell's bells . . . it's no more'n he deserves!"

"I'm sorry, Lucas, but that doesn't make it right. You've degraded yourself—and our home!—and I'm thoroughly ashamed of you."

"Ashamed! Judas Priest, what would you have me do . . . pin a medal on him?"

"No, but I expect you to act like a man of decency and breeding. Let the law handle it, that's all I'm asking."

"Damnnation, it's got nothing to do with the law. It's personal!"

"Then do it for me. Won't you, Lucas . . . please . . . just for me? Before it's too late . . . ."

He frowned, muttering to himself, and finally threw up his hands in defeat. Stacey held her breath, waiting, not sure he would act in time. But he gave her a hangdog look, sighed heavily, and stepped back. Then he stretched high, raising his arm above the arched entranceway, and placed his hand on the wall. He pushed hard, straining against the rock; slowly a section of the wall separated and moved, depressed inward. Stacey's eyes widened and she stifled a gasp. In the dim light the section of rock was barely visible, but its outline was unmistakable.

It was shaped like a small tombstone.

Out of the corner of her eye, she saw him stiffen, head slightly cocked, listening intently. Then she heard it, the distant throb of machinery. He smiled, nodding to himself, and in the next instant a roaring *whoosh* shook the walls.

Everything inside the crypt blurred in a sudden vortex of turbulence. The sea wall began to close; distant pumps sucked water from the chamber through hidden floor ducts. Ruxton's mouth opened in a scream as he was whisked past the window in a swirl of water. Swiftly, within a matter of seconds, the roiling foam subsided. Then the pumps went silent and suddenly the water was gone. Several moments passed, then the floor vibrated with a faint humming noise. There was a massive groan, and as though on command, the stone slab rose back into its recess above the entranceway.

The crypt stood damp and silent, moist with the smell of brine. Ruxton lay sprawled in the corner, jammed up against the sea wall. His legs were tangled in the wreckage of the table, and the cryptography machine was wedged underneath one shoulder. He moaned, slowly regaining his senses, and rolled sideways out of the debris. Then he retched, heaving convulsively, and began spewing seawater across the floor.

"Thank you, Lucas." Stacey came up on tiptoe and kissed his cheek. "You did the right thing, and I'm very proud of you."

His eyes were fixed on Ruxton. "Maybe so, but I still say he'd have been a helluva lot less trouble dead than he is alive."

"On the contrary, if he were dead, it would be much more difficult to explain. This way, it's all very simple."

"Think so, huh?"

"Yes, I do." She gestured upward, indicating the section of stone above the entranceway. "That was the last secret, wasn't it? The one you revealed to . . . Warren Tanner."

For a moment, Stacey thought she had gone too far. He continued to stare at Ruxton, who was still coughing up his insides. Finally, he grunted and gave her a sharp glance. "Guess it was pretty obvious, wasn't it?"

"Symbolic, yes. Obvious, no."

"Yeah?" His expression brightened. "How's that?"

"Oh, really, Lucas! A grave filled with water and a blank tombstone? No one would ever have connected that with the disaster clause. I certainly didn't. Not till I saw what the disaster was and how you opened the crypt."

"Nifty as hell too!" He uttered a low gloating laugh and peered around the crypt. "Yessir, thirty years and it still worked like a Swiss clock. Better, by God!"

"And that means your fortune is safe, doesn't it?" Stacey suddenly had to know, felt compelled to ask. "But who's to claim it . . . you or Warren Tanner?"

His laugh dissolved into a slow, lopsided smile. He limped across the chamber, stooped down, and slung Ruxton over his shoulder. Then he walked back to her and nodded in the direction of the stairs.

"Let's get a move on! I've got some details to tidy up."

XXXII

The day was bright as new brass, without a cloud in the sky. An unseasonably warm breeze drifted in off the ocean as they emerged from the mansion. Ruxton was still slung over his shoulder, and he led the way down the pavilion steps. Stacey had not yet regained her composure, but daylight and fresh air were like an instant tonic after the horrors of the crypt. She was peppering him with questions, determined to hear the entire story detail by detail, however gruesome.

"So you knew all along . . . about the conspiracy?"

"Never any doubt!" His mood had changed, become faintly indulgent. "Except I couldn't prove it. Not till Birkhead killed Fallon and Wilson. Then it all fitted together."

"And you're absolutely certain Ruxton ordered the murders?"

"Naturally. He couldn't afford to be tied to a safe-cracker and a cryptanalyst. Hell, that would've blown the whole deal!"

He dumped Ruxton on the driveway, then grabbed him by the scruff of the neck and propped him up against the bottom step. Ruxton slumped forward, head in his hands, and promptly began coughing. He looked like a drowned cat, limp and wretched, plastered with a sleek coat of grit and ocean slime. Tendrils of seaweed matted his hair, and a puddle slowly formed around his feet.

Several moments passed as they stood watching him. At length, the coughing moderated and a bit of color returned to his face. Stacey appeared relieved but dubious.

"Proving conspiracy is one thing," she remarked, "but I'm not so sure about the murders. With everyone dead, it all seems very circumstantial."

"Not when he starts singin', it won't."

"Yes, but that's the whole point. Will he confess?"

"Easy enough to find out."

He bent down, one foot on the step, and spoke to Ruxton. "What about it, hotshot? Think you could oblige us with all the particulars?"

"Go to hell!" Ruxton croaked. "I want a lawyer."

He took a fistful of hair and jerked Ruxton's head back. A feral look surfaced in his eyes, and his mouth quirked again with that homicidal smile. "How would you like me to throw you back in that fish tank downstairs? Only this time it'd be the deep six and a long swim."

Ruxton froze, transfixed by the icy stare. Then his lips moved, leaking spittle. "You're crazy."

"Crazy enough, that's for damn sure. So what's it gonna be—me or the law?"

"The law." Ruxton closed his eyes. "All of it. The whole story."

"Well, that's fine! Just fine."

He turned away, dusting a speck of seaweed off his hands, and smiled at Stacey. "Looks like we're all set. Ruxton says he'll talk."

"You were serious, weren't you? About putting him back in the crypt."

"If I'd had my way, he wouldn't have got out in the first place. Only did it to please . . ."

A strange look came over his face. For an instant he appeared confused, staring at her suspiciously, then he shrugged and glanced away. "Guess the reason doesn't matter. It's done and that's that."

Stacey readily conceded the point. She sensed some inner struggle in the look he'd given her. For a moment he had wavered, torn between two women, one of them dead. But she knew he'd seen her just now—not Stephanie Brokaw—and the tempo of her pulsebeat suddenly quickened. It was a hopeful sign.

A car wheeled into the driveway, and Tanner's mouth split in a jocular grin.

"Well, now, talk about good timing. Just the fellow I wanted to see!"

Hamilton Knox stepped out of the car, trailed by one of the security guards, and hurried toward them. He had the look of a rumpled owl, bleary-eyed and testy. He still hadn't quite absorbed what he'd learned at the gatehouse.

"Poor Knox," Stacey murmured, watching him approach. "All this—and he's still lost his foundation."

"Don't kid yourself. Knox is hard as nails! Course today won't be one of his better days. He's in for a few surprises."

"You mean the money . . . your fortune."

His smile was veiled, sphinxlike. He turned, staring thoughtfully at the mansion for a moment. "You've always liked this house, haven't you?"

"Yes, always," Stacey replied doubtfully. "Why do you ask?"

"Well, in a manner of speaking, we're about to play a little poker. Knox and me, that is. Excuse the pun, but you might say I'm drawin' to a full house."

Before she could respond, the director halted in front of them, bristling with indignation. "Would someone kindly tell me what's going on here? I've just concluded a very disagreeable conversation with a police detective, who had the audacity—"

"Knox, quit bellyachin' and let's get down to cases. You owe me ten million dollars!"

The director squinted at him, astounded. "I beg your pardon?"

"Get the wax out of your ears." His tone was clipped, trenchant. "The *reward!* I've got the goods on Ruxton and his pals, and you owe me ten million." He jerked his thumb at Ruxton, who was huddled in a sodden ball, staring sightlessly into space. "He's had a rough mornin', but it did him a world of good. Fact is, he can't hardly wait to start talking. Got quite a story to tell."

"You!" His finger stabbed at the guard, who snapped to attention. "Watch over our friend here, and make damn sure he behaves himself. Any monkey business and you kick him in the rump good and hard."

Then he brusquely turned away, motioning to Knox, and walked off. "C'mon, shake a leg! Stacey will fill you in on the details."

Knox was totally nonplussed. "Where are we going?"

"Little unfinished business. Just tag along. You'll find out quick enough."

Stacey and Knox exchanged a puzzled glance, then hurried after him. He took off across the lawn at a brisk pace, angling toward the cliffs. While they walked, Stacey gave the director a brief summary of everything she'd learned. The conspiracy. The raid on the crypt. The murders. The tragic events of last night and this morning. The mass of physical evidence already gathered by the FBI and the police. All of which, linked together with Ruxton's confession and Tanner's testimony, would establish an airtight case. Curt Ruxton was *not* Lucas Brokaw reincarnated! It had been a hoax from beginning to end.

Yet she stopped short of telling him everything. She couldn't bring herself to reveal that final truth: that the figure striding along ahead of them was, to all intents and purposes, the dead man himself. It was at once frightening and wondrous, and she simply couldn't articulate it. In some inexplicable manner, the Second Coming of Lucas Brokaw was, after all, no hoax.

He was alive and well and . . .

How very strange! His limp had disappeared. He was walking tall and straight, with no visible sign of affliction. Then she realized he had led them to the small family gravesite, and when he turned, she had to suppress a cry of astonishment. The haggard look of exhaustion was gone. His features were no longer drawn and forbidding. All physical manifestations of Lucas Brokaw had simply vanished.

He was again himself. His real self. Warren Tanner.

Hamilton Knox was no less startled by the transformation. There was something odd about Tanner's behavior this morning. Quite reminiscent, in fact, of another man he'd known. An old man, long ago, and a man he'd hoped never to meet again. Nor was he satisfied with Stacey's sketchy explanation of the peculiar circumstances surrounding the previous night. It was apparent that something ghastly had occurred in the mansion. Two highly unnatural deaths within the space of a few hours. And Ruxton reduced to a vegetable, almost catatonic with terror. It was all very strange and immediately raised a chilling possibility. But he quickly shunted the thought aside. The good of the foundation was at stake here today, and he decided to play it very cagey. Better to leave certain questions unanswered and remind himself that a wise man knew when to keep his mouth shut.

Tanner walked around the graves and halted behind the tombstone of Lucas Brokaw. Then he turned, facing them. His gaze settled on the director.

"Would you like to have your foundation back?"

"Of course! I should think that goes without saying."

"You'll need my testimony to prove Ruxton was a phony."

"Yes, I'm sure we will." Knox pursed his lips solemnly. "But then, how else would you be entitled to the reward?"

"Good point. Except that convicting Ruxton won't turn the trick. Not by itself." Tanner smiled, savoring the moment. "In order to get your foundation back—and keep it—you've got to do away with that last secret. The one in the will."

Stacey's mouth popped open. She caught her breath,

on the verge of speaking, but he hushed her with a gesture. Then he grinned, eyes boring into Knox. "Otherwise, somebody will come along one of these days and spring it on you. Exactly the way it's spelled out in the will. Matter of fact, you could just about count on it."

"Yes, I daresay you're right." Knox studied his face for a time—a long look of recognition—and at last shrugged his acceptance. "Apparently you have something specific in mind. An arrangement, no doubt."

"Yeah, something like that. Only I'd say it's more on the order of a game of showdown."

"I'm afraid I don't understand."

"Simple. You call the bet and I'll show you my ace in the hole."

Tanner underscored the words with a quiet note of triumph. Then his gaze shifted to Stacey. "You're sure you want the mansion? Think on it a minute. I've got a hunch the old landlord won't move out just because we move in."

"Now that you mention it," Stacey gave him a sly, mischievous look, "I rather like the idea of a haunted castle . . . yes, I'm very sure!"

"That's it, then." Tanner turned back to the director. "We'll trade. Stacey and I get the mansion—tax free, of course—and you get your foundation. Fair enough?"

"Fair! Why it's robbery . . . blackmail! The paintings alone are worth twenty million."

"Don't be greedy. Seems to me you're getting more than half the loaf . . . about $450,000,000. And the alternative is a long string of zeros."

Knox fell silent, weighing the alternative, then nodded. "Yes, I see your point." He sighed, pondering it a moment longer, and finally threw up his hands in resignation. "Very well. You have yourself a deal."

Tanner acknowledged it with a token gesture and glanced across at Stacey. "Remember the talk we had about *déjà vu* . . . that night in the crypt?"

"Of course! How could I forget?"

"And I told you I'd seen a grave with the tombstone already in place?"

"Yes, but I thought," Stacey paused, slightly bewildered "when you opened the crypt this morning, I thought that was the last . . ."

"No. The last card is the hole card, and you never show it till the end of the game. Watch!"

Tanner knelt down and set his shoulder to the tombstone. Then he heaved, driving forward with his legs, and twisted the granite slab ninety degrees counterclockwise. A tremor shook the earth beneath their feet, followed an instant later by the dull *whump* of an underground explosion. The earth suddenly buckled around the imprint of the tombstone; chunks of dark sod erupted skyward and rained down across the gravesite. Even as the debris began to settle, a large hole became visible, exposing the shattered edges of a cement pipe. A split second later, seemingly out of nowhere, the top of a metallic cylinder appeared at the surface of the hole. Tanner bent down, pulled a long aluminum canister from the hole, and turned to face them.

The director and Stacey stood immobile, their eyes riveted on the canister. Knox's mouth hung open, his gaze wide and owlish behind the thick glasses. Stacey appeared spellbound. A moment passed as Tanner juggled the canister in his hands, staring at it with the expression of someone unexpectedly greeted by an old and cherished friend. That strange sense of elation again swept over him, and he felt some inner spark of pride that it had all functioned so perfectly. Finally, altogether reluctant to see it end, he put his shoulder to the tombstone and bulled it back into position. Then he tossed the canister to Knox.

"Inside are the original blueprints of the crypt and the underground hydraulic system. You won't have any problem getting it authenticated, but I suggest you wait and have it opened by court order."

He paused, mouth creased in an ironic smile. "That way it's foolproof. You'll have a legal ruling that eliminates any chance of a future claimant."

"Yes, it would." Knox blinked and cleared his throat. "You're aware, of course, that you could enter a claim today. After all, this is incontestable . . . the last secret."

"No, I think I'll pass. You see, if I did that, then I wouldn't be me any longer, would I?"

"Quite frankly," Knox admitted, "I'm not at all sure who you are *now*."

Tanner's smile broadened into an enigmatic grin, but he made no response. Suddenly they heard shouts in the distance. Several detectives and a couple of uniformed deputies were running toward them, alerted by the explosion. All the yelling and commotion jarred Knox out of his funk. He hugged the canister to his chest, eyes narrowed, scrutinizing Tanner for a long moment. No words were spoken, but in the exchange a silent pact was struck. At length, the director bobbed his head, the final affirmation, and then hurried off in the direction of the gatehouse.

Tanner felt a hand on his arm and turned. Stacey looked numb but curiously poised, almost serene. Her voice was warm and husky, vibrant.

"That was quite a noble gesture. The foundation . . . and Knox. You could have had it all. The entire fortune."

"Yeah, I suppose you're right. But then again, maybe I got the best end of the bargain after all. The Buddhists say that nirvana isn't to be found in wealth but rather the ability to be indifferent toward it."

"Nirvana! You mean the eightfold path? I didn't know you were a student of Buddhism."

Tanner shrugged. "It's been a long journey. Guess I must've picked it up somewhere in my . . . travels." Suddenly he smiled, watching her out of the corner of his eye. "Besides, all that money would have kept the pot boiling. And I think Lucas has earned a rest, don't you?"

"Yes, darling, I do. A richly deserved rest!" Stacey's laugh was infectious, faintly impudent. "Until the next time around anyway."

"The hell with that!" Tanner grabbed her hand and took off across the lawn. "Let's make the second time count."

A lazy forenoon breeze stirred, and with it came that old familiar presence. Its laughter whispered through the trees, and under the dome of a brassy sky, they began the long walk home.